D0483385

*Soleta face
raped*

. . . and was, because of that act, her father.

"I am no threat," he said. "Do you believe that?"

She looked away from him. "I . . . would like to believe it. I would like to think that no one is beyond redemption. But it is impossible for me simply to forget what you have done."

"No. No need, Soleta. . . . I know that apologies oftentimes cannot be nearly enough . . . but in the end, it is all I have to give."

They headed in the direction of his apartment in silence. He was walking slowly, and Soleta noticed that he was developing a slight limp. She wondered how much longer he truly had. If she were dying, she would be doing everything she could to put to rights anything that she had done wrong. What was it like for there to be things in one's past that could never, ever truly be put right?

They passed the alley where they had first really "encountered" each other. The shadows were stretching, much as they had that first time. And hands reached from the darkness, grabbed both Soleta and Rajari, and hauled them into the alley. . . .

For orders other than by individual consumers, Pocket Books grants a discount on the purchase of **10 or more** copies of single titles for special markets or premium use. For further details, please write to the Vice President of Special Markets, Pocket Books, 1230 Avenue of the Americas, 9th Floor, New York, NY 10020-1586.

For information on how individual consumers can place orders, please write to Mail Order Department, Simon & Schuster Inc., 100 Front Street, Riverside, NJ 08075.

STAR TREK®
NEW FRONTIER

EXCALIBUR

REQUIEM

PETER DAVID

POCKET BOOKS

New York   London   Toronto   Sydney   Singapore

The sale of this book without its cover is unauthorized. If you purchased this book without a cover, you should be aware that it was reported to the publisher as "unsold and destroyed." Neither the author nor the publisher has received payment for the sale of this "stripped book."

This book is a work of fiction. Names, characters, places and incidents are products of the author's imagination or are used fictitiously. Any resemblance to actual events or locales or persons, living or dead, is entirely coincidental.

An *Original* Publication of POCKET BOOKS

POCKET BOOKS, a division of Simon & Schuster, Inc.
1230 Avenue of the Americas, New York, NY 10020

Copyright © 2000 by Paramount Pictures. All Rights Reserved.

STAR TREK is a Registered Trademark of Paramount Pictures.

A VIACOM COMPANY

This book is published by Pocket Books, a division of Simon & Schuster, Inc., under exclusive license from Paramount Pictures.

All rights reserved, including the right to reproduce this book or portions thereof in any form whatsoever. For information address Pocket Books, 1230 Avenue of the Americas, New York, NY 10020

ISBN: 0-671-04238-6

First Pocket Books printing September 2000

10 9 8 7 6 5 4 3 2 1

POCKET and colophon are registered trademarks of Simon & Schuster, Inc.

Printed in the U.S.A.

PREVIOUSLY IN STAR TREK: NEW FRONTIER...

THE NORMAL LOW-LEVEL BUZZ of conversation on the bridge tapered off as Captain Calhoun stepped out from the turbolift.

He had missed an entire shift, which was unprecedented for him. Everyone understood, however, and no one knew quite what to say to him when he did reappear.

He went to his command chair, took his seat, and when he looked around at the respectfully silent crew, a smile played across his lips. It was a sad smile, but a smile just the same.

"Captain," began Shelby.

"Commander . . . it's all right," he interrupted. "All of you . . . really . . . it's all right. The important thing . . . the thing I'm not going to lose sight of . . . is that he went out like a warrior."

There were nods from all around.

"It was very . . . Xenexian of him, believe it or not. The notion of dying in one's bed is anathema to my people. To die in combat, on the other hand, is very much to be desired . . . and to die in combat while saving others is the highest, most noble passing that anyone could wish for. I will miss him . . . and regret the time that we did not spend together, and the time we will not have . . . but the bottom line is, he died heroically. All of us . . . should only be so fortunate as to have that opportunity," said Mackenzie Calhoun, five minutes before the *Excalibur* blew up. . . .

POST MORTEMS...

"I STILL CAN'T BELIEVE the ship blew up."

Mark McHenry had shown up exactly at the appointed time, which was rather surprising to Elizabeth Paula Shelby. She would have been willing to bet that if anyone had shown up late, it was going to be McHenry. The former navigator of the former *Starship Excalibur,* despite his nearly supernatural ability to know precisely where he was in the galaxy at any given moment (with or without instrumentation), still seemed like a rather unstable individual to Shelby. She had grown accustomed to him, at best, but never truly comfortable. If there was any member of her crew that she suspected would "flake out" at some point, it was McHenry.

Her crew.

Mentally she corrected herself. No, it wasn't her crew anymore, was it. They were just . . . people. People getting together at a San Francisco bar that was a popular hangout for Starfleet personnel. Puckishly named for the Starfleet oath, the bar—Strange New Worlds (its motto: "Explore Us!")—had been around for as long as anyone could remember. The only bar with a longer-standing reputation than Strange New Worlds was the Captain's Table, and that was considered more of a popular myth than anything else. "Worlds," as it was known for short, was copiously decorated with assorted Starfleet paraphernalia. There were dedication plaques salvaged from ships that had been decommissioned or destroyed, ornaments acquired from worlds throughout the Federation. There was a fascinating wall which had nothing but bladed weapons from dozens of primitive worlds, each of them gleaming behind glass, time having done nothing to diminish their capacity for destruction. There were pictures of various Starfleet captains and notables, many of them signed by the subjects. In short, Strange New Worlds radiated years, decades of tradition.

Shelby was paying no attention to any of it.

The command crew (former crew, dammit!) had agreed that there would be a get-together, a post mortem. Robin Lefler had been the organizer, which was certainly consistent for her. No one was more of a go-getter than Ensign Lefler. Shelby had been the last one to agree to come, and even when she had agreed she had done so reluctantly. In retrospect, as she sat across the table from McHenry, waiting for the others, she decided that she had behaved poorly. She should have been spearheading the assembling of the crew, not trying to avoid it. She should have presented a cheerful face, she should have been more supportive, she should have been . . . been something other than what she was.

"Commander?"

McHenry was looking at her curiously, snapping his fingers in her face. She blinked in surprise and focused on him. "Commander?" he said again.

"What's the problem, McHenry?"

"Well," he said reasonably, "it's just that I've been talking for a while now, and I noticed you weren't contributing much to the conversation. And then it occurred to me that maybe I was just hogging it, so I shut up so that you could jump in. Except there was a staggering lack of it. Jumping in, I mean. You just sort of sat there and stared off into . . ."

"Space?" she asked, her lips spreading into a mirthless smile. "Well . . . space is my business, isn't it."

"Is it?" inquired McHenry.

It seemed an odd thing for him to say, and she wanted to pursue it, but then someone else approached the table. It was Robin Lefler—without her mother, Morgan, in tow. Shelby was a bit grateful for that, because Morgan made her nervous. She hated to admit that, even to herself (certainly she had not said it to anyone else). But the simple truth was that Morgan Primus was still a woman whom Shelby couldn't get a feeling for. She had exotic features and an air about her that made her seem as if she were partly removed from the time in which she lived.

As for Robin, she could not have been more of a contrast to her mother. She had a perpetually open face that seemed incapable of any sort of guile. Small wonder that she was the most abysmal poker player on the ship . . .

Not was, dammit. Had been *the most abysmal poker player on the ship.*

The unexpected, automatic scolding caused Shelby

to pause in her musings before continuing on the path down which they were taking her. Yes, Robin had indeed been atrocious at cards, unable to conceal glee when holding a good hand, equally unable to hide her disappointment when the cards did not fall in her favor. Morgan was a walking question; Robin was a walking punch line.

"Hello, Ensign," she said. "Where's your mother? I thought you two were virtually joined at the hip these days."

But Robin was smiling as if Shelby hadn't spoken. "I'm afraid I don't answer to that anymore."

"Answer to what . . . ?" said Shelby in confusion, and then she noticed the additional pip on her collar. "Lieutenant! Now, are we sure this time?"

"I had it confirmed three ways from Sunday," Lefler told her. There was an empty chair between McHenry and Shelby, and Lefler was leaning on it. "I wasn't subjecting myself to that kind of embarrassment again."

Lefler had had good reason to be embarrassed. A computer glitch had misreported Lefler as having received a promotion to lieutenant, and she'd been quite enamored of the promotion until the error had been turned up and the rank correction made. Lefler had not been pleased about being "busted" back to ensign, and so she was justifiably proud that this time it was one hundred percent legitimate. "They told me that you were partly responsible for getting me the bump up, Commander."

Shelby shrugged but couldn't quite erase the smile. "You deserved it, Lieutenant."

"I love it," Lefler told her. "No more having to put up with the old low-rank crap duties. As a lieutenant, I'll have—"

"Brand new, higher-ranked crap duties," McHenry informed her, sounding somewhat more amused than he would have wanted to let on.

"Shove off, McHenry," Lefler said without heat. "You're just worried I'm going to be breathing down your neck."

"Your breathing down my neck would be the most excitement I've had since Burgy and I broke up," McHenry sighed regretfully.

Lefler swung the chair out and was about to sit when suddenly Shelby put a hand on the seat and said softly, "No. That's Mac's chair."

McHenry and Lefler exchanged glances, and then Lefler said quietly, "Of course. I'm sorry." She stepped around the table and sat at another, unclaimed seat.

"So . . . as I was saying . . . where's your mother?" asked Shelby. There had been a brief flash of anxiety when she'd warned Lefler away from the chair reserved for Captain Mackenzie Calhoun, but now that the moment was past, so was Shelby's concern.

"She's researching vacation sites. There'll be some time before we're reassigned, and she suggested it might be nice if we could get away together somewhere, just mother and daughter. Work on the relationship without the pressure of day-to-day starship life on us."

"Well, good thing the ship blew up then. There's a pressure reliever for you."

If McHenry had been fishing for a laugh, his hook came back spectacularly bereft of results. The women just stared at him, and Shelby's face was darkening as if a cloud were draping itself over her. "It was just a joke," he said.

"Oh. Was that what it was? It was certainly wearing

a cunning disguise," Shelby said with no trace of amusement.

McHenry mumbled something that very vaguely sounded like "Sorry." Shelby hesitated and then decided that it would be wisest not to pursue it.

Other crew members were now strolling in. There was Soleta, the erstwhile science officer, poised and elegant as her Vulcan heritage dictated. And here came Burgoyne 172, the Hermat who had helped conceive the child being cradled in the arms of Chief Medical Officer Selar. It was almost amusing to watch her. The Vulcan doctor was trying to hold her newborn offspring in such a way that it seemed as if the infant was only of passing interest to her. But the looks she would give the child, the sudden and swift reactions to the smallest instance of the baby's discomfort, were more than enough to convince any onlooker of just who was in charge of the relationship: Mother or child? Yes, definitely no contest. The child . . .

The child . . .

Just what *was* it again.

When Shelby had first inquired, it had been the common, offhand inquiry one always makes. Boy or girl? The problem was, when one was dealing with an offspring whose mother was a Vulcan, and whose father was a dual-sexed "Hermat" named Burgoyne, the usually harmless question suddenly became a loaded one. Selar had said, "Boy," and they'd gone on to state that they'd named the boy "Xyon," after Mackenzie Calhoun's late son. Nevertheless, there'd been something about the way that Selar had said it. It seemed to Shelby that she wasn't answering in a matter-of-fact way, as she did with pretty much every other question. Instead she had spoken quickly, as if wanting to terminate the conversation as quickly as possible. As if . . .

. . . as if the entire discussion was uncomfortable for her.

Burgoyne started to sit in the empty seat next to Shelby, but she put a hand quickly down. "Mac's chair," she said.

Selar cast a slightly puzzled look at Burgoyne, but then little Xyon whimpered slightly for attention and Selar looked to him instead. "Of course. Foolish of me" was all Burgoyne said before s/he moved to another chair on the far side of the table.

A waitress began taking drink orders, and the officers started making small talk with one another. It seemed so odd to Shelby, so labored. On the *Excalibur,* there was always something to discuss. There was some circumstance involving the ship, some situation that they were mired in . . . any of a hundred distractions, big and small, that formed the basis for conversation, relationships, and social intercourse of all types. It all seemed to build up from the commonality forced by the late, lamented starship.

There was a slight, repetitious vibration from the floor beneath her feet, which was enough to signal Shelby that Zak Kebron was coming. The others felt it, too, but it didn't slow down their conversation. Soleta seemed most interested in little Xyon. Outwardly she was treating the child almost as a matter of scientific curiosity, but Shelby suspected that Soleta was wondering how and when the Vulcan mating urge, *Pon farr,* would affect her. Burgoyne was engaged in an animated conversation with McHenry. Now, that was certainly an odd thing to see. McHenry and Burgoyne had been involved before circumstances had brought Burgy and Selar together. Shelby liked to believe that she had seen much of what the galaxy had to offer and that nothing fazed her, but still . . . a relationship that jumped both species and gender was a new one even for her experience.

"Commander? You okay?" It was Lefler, leaning forward and speaking to Shelby. Her tone was soft, but nevertheless there was something in it that promptly caught the attention of the others at the table. Suddenly all eyes were focused on Shelby, and she shifted uncomfortably in her chair, disliking being subjected to sudden scrutiny.

"I'm fine," she said with the irritable tone of someone whose attitude didn't match her words.

"Good." It was the deep, basso voice of Kebron. The massive security officer was standing directly behind Shelby, taking in the assemblage with his level gaze. He glanced at the empty chair next to Shelby. "Reserved for the captain?" he inquired.

"Yes."

"Of course" was all he said. He moved to another section of the table and looked disapprovingly at the narrowness of the chairs. He pulled two together and sat, looking less than comfortable but obviously resolving to deal with it with his customary stoicism. The waitress came back over upon seeing the new customer, which was understandable; Kebron was somewhat hard to miss. "You're a Brikar, right?" she said. "I've heard Brikars are sort of like rock people. Is that true?"

"No."

When he said nothing further, the waitress shrugged slightly and held up her order padd. "What can I get you?"

"Magma."

McHenry covered his mouth to hide a snicker. Shelby rolled her eyes.

"You want magma." The waitress did not appear amused. "We don't serve magma."

"I had it here last time."

"When was the last time you were here?"

"The Mesozoic era."

Now Burgoyne was laughing as well. Selar and Soleta simply looked at each other with the air of those who did not suffer fools gladly.

The waitress blew air impatiently between her lips and, tilting her head slightly, asked, "Can we just, you know . . . forget I ever said anything about 'rock people'?"

"Gladly. Scotch."

"On the rocks," McHenry put in.

Kebron fired him a sidelong glance. "Don't push it."

As the waitress, shaking her head, walked away, Lefler looked back to Shelby. "Commander . . . maybe you should really talk about it. Maybe," and she glanced at the others, "maybe we all should. About the destruction of the *Excalibur*. About how it happened. About . . ."

"You've missed your calling," Burgoyne said wryly. "You should be a ship's counselor."

"My mother's said that, too," Lefler admitted with a laugh. "She told me she'd be so proud to have a ship's counselor for a daughter."

"Lieutenant . . . Robin," Shelby said, placing a friendly hand on Lefler's, "I know you're just trying to help. And maybe there's something to be said for what you're suggesting. But the simple truth is this: We've been reliving it, all of us, for the past few weeks. Board of inquiries up one side and down the other, poring over every detail again and again. Every minute of the ship's last five minutes of life, everything that all of us did, and endlessly being asked—and asking ourselves—whether there was anything else we could have done, any other way we could have handled it. I don't know about you, but I am . . ." She drummed her fingers on the table. "I am tired. I am so tired of second-guessing myself. That's what these inquiries do to you. They don't just try to answer the questions that the board has. They start raising all sorts of questions in your own head, to the point where you don't know which end is up, what's right and what's wrong."

"You did nothing wrong."

It was a new arrival who had spoken. They looked up and saw that Ambassador Si Cwan had come up behind them. His advent was quite the contrary of Kebron's. Whereas Kebron had telegraphed his coming with every step, the erstwhile crew of the *Excalibur* hadn't noticed the Thallonian until he was right up behind them. Whether it was because they were so engrossed in discussion, or because Si Cwan just had a preternatural knack for entering a room unseen, Shelby couldn't be sure. Standing next to him was his younger sister, Kalinda. The change that she had undergone had been quite something to see as far as Shelby was concerned. She had first come aboard the *Excalibur* confused, out of place, unsure of something as fundamental as her own identity. Now, however, she had a regal and confident bearing that was nearly on par with that of her brother. However, there was still a slight twinkle of mischievousness in her eye that Shelby found amusingly appealing.

"Thank you for the vote of confidence, Ambassador," she said. "Please, take a seat."

He glanced at the one next to Shelby but said nothing, as if he intuited its purpose. Instead he and Kalinda took up chairs at the far end of the table.

"What I was saying," continued Shelby, "is that we've all gone over those last, depressing minutes so many times . . . that, frankly, I'm sick to death of post mortems. I suspect we all are." There were concurring nods from around the table from everyone except Kebron, who didn't really have a neck that permitted nodding, so he tilted his upper torso slightly.

"Therefore, I suggest we make an agreement. For our mutual sanity, none of us ever discusses the destruction of the *Excalibur* again. We all know what happened. There's no need to belabor it ad infinitum, ad nauseam. So let's just not talk about it. No recriminations, no second-guessing, no finger pointing . . . because that's what any talks about it would invariably devolve into. And I know this group. We won't all be blaming each other."

"No. We'll be blaming ourselves," said Lefler. Again there were nods.

"So we're agreed?"

There were choruses of affirmation from around the table, and Shelby let out a relieved sigh. "Good. Good, I'm glad. And I think that's a decision that Mac would approve . . . of . . ."

"Would have approved of," Selar corrected.

Everyone looked at her, and she looked at the scowls focused upon her. "It is simply proper grammar," she said coolly. "It is proper, after all, to speak of someone in the past tense when they are . . ."

"Selar," Burgoyne stopped her softly. "Not now."

At that moment, someone from an adjoining table came over and rested a hand on the empty chair next to Shelby. "Excuse me, we could use another chair . . . is someone using this—"

"No," said Shelby.

"Oh, good," and he started to pull away the chair.

And it was Kebron who rumbled, "Move that chair, lose the arm."

The officer froze where he was and looked around at the stony faces at the table. He released the chair and said with obvious annoyance, "Boy, you people are touchy." He went in search of another chair as Shelby gently slid the chair back into place.

"You didn't have to do that, Zak," said Shelby.

"I know."

"I'm glad you did."

"I know."

They stared at the empty chair for a time longer, and then Shelby raised her glass. "To Mackenzie Calhoun . . . the best damned captain in the fleet."

"Short. To the point. Indisputable. I approve," said Si Cwan, lifting his glass, and the others joined as well. They clinked glasses and drank in silence.

"So . . . what now?"

It had been Lefler who had asked, but it was really on the minds of all the people at the table. Finally it was Shelby who spoke as she said, "Well, Lieutenant . . . *Lieutenant*, I say again, just in case you can't get enough of hearing that," she added with a faint smile, "you know the regs on that as well as anyone."

"I know that part," Lefler said.

"I don't," said Kalinda, looking around in confusion. "Would somebody mind explaining it to me?"

"When a ship has been lost—although exceptions are sometimes made in times of war—there's a pre-scribed 'cooldown' period for the senior staff," explained Soleta. "The thinking is that the loss of a vessel is a traumatic event, and officers need time to cope and come to terms."

"What nonsense," said Si Cwan with a snort. "If one has experienced a setback, the best thing to do is throw yourself right back into the same situation. That way you can—"

"Die faster?" asked Kebron.

Si Cwan ignored him. "If one has time to dwell on the circumstances that have brought one to an unfortunate pass, such thoughts can hamper one's effectiveness. The more time you have to think about it, the more you're liable to second-guess yourself."

"There's something to be said for that," admitted Shelby.

"Which is why," Selar spoke up, "you have requested immediate reassignment and a waiver of the waiting period."

Shelby looked up at her in obvious surprise. "How did you know that?"

"I did not know it," Selar replied. "Until you confirmed it just now, that is."

"Vulcans," growled Shelby.

The others looked at her with interest. "You asked for a waiver? Really, Commander?" asked Lefler.

"Well, there's special circumstances . . ."

"A ship," McHenry said immediately. "You're angling for command. That's it, isn't it."

"Well . . ."

"Come on," Lefler prompted. "You're among friends, Commander."

The word, for some reason, thudded in Shelby's head. *Friends.* Was that what she was among, truly? She wanted to open up to them, tell them what was on her mind. And yet . . .

And yet . . .

"The truth is," she said, pushing her doubts aside,

"I've gotten word through the grapevine that Captain Hodgkiss of the *Exeter* is being bumped upstairs in Starfleet, and his command is coming open. I'm putting my bid in now, and as near as I can tell, I'm the front-runner."

"That's great!" Lefler said. "You really think you have a good shot?"

Shelby nodded.

"If you'd like," offered McHenry, "I can put in a good word for you."

"As can I," Si Cwan added.

Kebron made a rude noise. "Recommendations from you two? She'll be busted in rank within the week."

"You know," Si Cwan said, "I like you better when you're saying almost nothing."

McHenry leaned forward and said, "What about us?"

Shelby felt a stirring of dread in the pit of her stomach. "You?"

"Are you bringing us along? As your new command crew? Keep us together?"

It was the question that Shelby had been dreading, and she had absolutely no answer at the ready because she still hadn't managed to sort out her feelings on the matter. When she spoke, her mouth was open and talking and she had no idea what words were going to come out until she heard them. "As much as I can see Si Cwan's point regarding getting right back into the saddle . . . there's something to be said for the cooldown period. Particularly considering the circumstances that we were in. Exploring a territory with virtually no Federation backup, a single ship trying to lend aid to, and pull together, an entire sector of space? It was one hell of an assignment and, frankly, I'm amazed that we . . ." She paused, looked at the empty chair, and then amended quietly, ". . . that as many of us . . . survived it as we did . . . and for as long. Since Starfleet is extending you the time off, I'd suggest you take it. Don't be like me; I'm angling for the assignment against Starfleet counselors' orders. Besides, I . . ."

"Besides . . . you what?" said Burgoyne. S/he had one elegantly tapered eyebrow raised. "There's something else you want to say, isn't there."

"Maybe she hates us," suggested McHenry.

"No! No, Mark, that's absurd," she said defensively. "You don't think that. I hope none of you thinks that. But the problem is that there are already some extremely capable command people in place on the *Exeter.* It's not exactly fair to shunt them aside, no matter what my personal preferences are. Would any of you be comfortable with my just walking in and dismissing the command crew there out of hand? Well? Would you?"

There was a thoughtful silence around the table.

"I have no problem with that," McHenry said.

"Me neither," said Lefler.

"Seems logical," said Soleta.

"I would if I were you," Si Cwan told her.

"Let's just kill them," rumbled Kebron, which drew laughter from the others.

Shelby felt her heart sink. It was going to be tougher than she'd anticipated. "It's just that . . . well . . . what's the best way to put this?" She scratched her chin thoughtfully. "The crew that we had—the sensibilities, the style, the mix of personalities—was unique. I've served aboard a variety of starships and I've never seen one quite like it. And I can't help but think that this particular mix of personalities worked as well as it did because of Mac." She was relieved to see that there was slow nodding from around her. "Mac created something very special aboard the *Excalibur.* Something that wasn't exactly regulation, but not exactly anarchic, either. And it worked because of him. And I'm . . . not sure that it would work without him. You see what I'm saying?"

"You're saying it'd be like trying to make an award-winning cake batter without eggs," said Lefler.

"Yes!" Shelby slapped the table in affirmation. "Yes, that's exactly it. One of the key ingredients would be missing, and because of that, the cake wouldn't rise."

"Actually, eggs do not cause the cake to rise," Soleta said immediately. "That happens because of—"

"We're getting off track here," Shelby said quickly. "The point is, Mackenzie Calhoun was what made it work. I'm . . . not him. And that's not an easy admission to make because, to be perfectly honest, for a time there I felt as if I was infinitely superior to him. More qualified, a better leader. But in the time I was with him, I came to appreciate him for the truly great captain that he was. If I tried to be just like him . . . I'd fall short. And you people would suffer because of it. It's not fair to me, and it's not fair to you."

Once again there was a considered silence at the table. Shelby was sure she could hear her heart thudding against her ribs.

It was Selar who broke the silence. "She is correct."

"You agree with the commander, Selar?" asked Burgoyne.

"That would be implicit in 'She is correct,' yes," Selar said with lacerating sarcasm. "To maintain the previous crew would be to maintain the ghost of Mackenzie Calhoun at all times. We would be trying to re-create that which can not be re-created. Furthermore, consciously or unconsciously, we would be holding Commander

Shelby up against Captain Calhoun in all matters. Even if we did not intend to do so . . . even if we said nothing to give her cause to think that we are . . . the commander would very likely wonder if we were consistently measuring her against Captain Calhoun."

"But didn't she run that risk as second-in-command of the *Excalibur?*" inquired Soleta. Shelby was amused to watch the exchange; they were acting as if she were no longer seated at the table. "She was stylistically different during those periods, but there were no difficulties."

"She was always seen as a temporary replacement," Selar replied briskly. "Even if any of us did disagree with anything she did, there was always the knowledge that Captain Calhoun would be returning shortly. But now . . ."

"We'd be stuck with her," said McHenry, and suddenly he turned to Shelby, looking a bit chagrined. "Sorry. No offense meant."

"None taken," Shelby said, although she wasn't entirely sure about that.

"I'd miss you all terribly, though," said Lefler.

"People come and go," Burgoyne said with a small shrug. "It is the nature of the life that we have chosen. You can't really avoid it."

"I suppose," sighed Lefler.

"I, myself, do not mind at all the notion of time off. It will allow me to return to Vulcan," Selar said. She glanced down at Xyon with that air of faint, distant fascination, as if she could not believe it possible that the infant was in her arms. "There are certain . . . avenues to be pursued to prepare Xyon for his future, and I must—"

"We must."

Burgoyne's correction was quiet but firm, and Shelby felt an immediate edginess entering the proceedings. She had a very strong suspicion that they were all seeing a definite hint of a discussion that had already been held between Burgoyne and Selar.

Sure enough, Selar leaned forward and said in a low voice, which was still easily heard by everyone else at the table, "We have discussed this already."

"No, we have not. Because a real discussion doesn't consist of you telling me what will be, period, end of conversation."

"Is there a problem?" asked Shelby delicately.

"No," Selar and Burgoyne both said immediately.

And I thought Vulcans didn't lie, thought Shelby, but naturally she said nothing. "Oh, good. And I'm sure if there were a problem, the two of you would be able to work it out since, of course, there is the child to consider."

"I assure you, *Commander,*" said Selar with as testy a tone as she ever adopted, "that my child's—"

"Our child's."

"—welfare," she continued, ignoring Burgoyne's interruption, "is of the greatest importance."

"And what about you, Si Cwan?" asked Shelby, suddenly feeling that it would be best if she steered the conversation in a different direction. "You and Kalinda. You're not part of Starfleet. Will you return to Sector 221-G?"

Kalinda looked in confusion at her brother. "Return to what . . . ?"

He glanced at Kalinda and smiled. It was something that the imperious Thallonian, as red-hued as most of his race, didn't do all that often. Shelby realized that he had a rather attractive smile, and she also noticed that

Robin Lefler seemed just a bit entranced by it. "Sector 221-G is how they refer to Thallonian space. You studied star charts, little sister; I'd have thought you'd have noticed that."

"Forgive my lapses, Cwan," she said with amused sarcasm. "I was trying to assimilate a lot at one time."

"Could you use a word other than 'assimilate'?" requested Shelby.

"Oh. Uhm . . . okay," said Kalinda uncertainly, not at all understanding Shelby's reaction but obviously not wanting to give offense. "I was trying to . . . absorb . . . a lot at one time?"

Shelby nodded in approval.

Si Cwan, making no effort to explain Shelby's reaction to his sister, instead said to Shelby, "To be honest, I am not certain. Without the backing of a starship or similar impressive vessel, my endeavors to pull together the fractured worlds of our former empire would be doomed. My other great incentive for returning to my home space would have been to find Kally . . . except she is right here," and he indicated her. "So I am left wondering what the purpose would be. I find that I am left somewhat at loose ends. There is not much call for a former ruler whose entire empire fell apart and whose homeworld was shattered from within by a gigantic flaming legendary bird."

"On the upside," said McHenry cheerfully, "if there is call for a former ruler whose entire empire fell apart and whose homeworld was shattered from within by a gigantic flaming legendary bird, then you're probably the front-runner for the job."

"I will take great comfort in that, McHenry. The thought will keep me warm on many a cold night."

"You do have a knack for defusing a situation,"

Shelby said. "People tend to listen to you. You have a great deal of . . ."

"Charisma?" suggested Lefler, not taking her eyes off Si Cwan.

"I was going to say 'presence,' but that's certainly another acceptable word," said Shelby. "The point is, the title of 'Ambassador' was given you purely as a courtesy. A means of describing just what the hell it was you were doing on the ship. But if you were actually to join the Federation diplomatic corps, you could be tremendously effective."

Kalinda laughed at that in a tone that immediately caught Shelby's attention, and not in a positive way. "You seem to think that's funny, Kalinda."

She leaned forward and said, "What you are suggesting—if I'm understanding you correctly—is that Si Cwan go around to different worlds and represent the viewpoints and agendas of the Federation."

"Well, essentially, that's what it would entail."

And she laughed again. "Si Cwan represents only Si Cwan. I fear very little good would come from what you're suggesting."

"Is that the case, Cwan?" asked Lefler.

Si Cwan smiled. "I fear my sister knows me all too well. I had no difficulty representing the Thallonian point of view because it was my own. If I were to take up a post with the Federation, however, it will inevitably require me to fight the good fight on behalf of something that I do not truly believe in. Not only would I be a hindrance, but also in that sort of situation I might even prove something of a danger. No . . . no, I am afraid that I will have to search elsewhere for finding a new purpose in the galaxy."

Kebron looked around with faint impatience, having

finished his drink some minutes ago and not having seen the waitress since. "Perhaps you could work here. They're apparently short on help."

"Thank you for your suggestion, Kebron," said Si Cwan, controlling his mirth with relative ease. "And what will you do during your 'downtime.' A shame paper is a thing of the past in your society; you could serve as a weight for stacks of it."

"I have my plans," he said vaguely.

"And they would be—?"

"Mine."

They all knew better than to try and pursue that line of conversation. "Well, the truth is, my mother will be thrilled," said Lefler. "She said she wouldn't mind having some nice time off. And she also said that she thought it would be a good chance to reestablish mother/daughter bonds. For us to get to really, truly get to understand each other."

"Do you think she's right?" asked Shelby.

Lefler shrugged. "Who ever knows what's going through that woman's head?" She turned to McHenry. "What about you, Mark?"

"I don't know what's going through her head."

"No, I mean what are you going to do? In the off time?"

"Oh." He spread his hands wide and said, "I'm just going to be a bum. Not do anything of consequence. Not think about anything."

"Is that possible for you?" asked Soleta. "Your mind always seems to be moving, whether you want it to or not. I've known you for nearly two decades and I don't believe you're capable of not thinking about anything."

"Thanks, I'm flattered . . . I guess. Perhaps," he said thoughtfully, "I'll catch up on cartoons."

"On what?" Soleta looked at him blankly. There were puzzled expressions on the part of just about everyone else.

"Cartoons. Ensign Janos showed some to me. He managed to find some ancient holovids, some transfers that were done. Drawings that are given a semblance of life via slight variance of drawings in—"

"I know technically what they are, McHenry," said Shelby. "I'm just not sure how and why they'd be of interest."

"I like to think about the universe, Commander," McHenry said with a wry grin. "Think about how it all fits together. But a cartoon universe opens up a whole new world of possibilities. The laws of physics don't seem to be terribly involved. Is it because they exist in a world of chaos . . . or is it that there are indeed laws, but they're different ones? And if one believes in those laws, can they be applied to the real world? Are laws and rules physical absolutes . . . or are they all in the mind? It's an intriguing notion to pursue, don't you think?" When Shelby stared at him blankly, he turned to Soleta. "Don't you think so, Soleta?"

"No," she said.

He looked at her with pity. "And you call yourself a scientist. So what are you going to do that's so wonderful, then?"

"I will be going home," said Soleta. "It is the fifth anniversary of my mother's passing. I think it would be best if I were with my father at this time."

There were murmurs of sympathy from around the table. Soleta inclined her head slightly. "Your condolences are appreciated, although not particularly essential. I have long since come to terms with her death. My being with my father will simply be a matter of courtesy."

"Vulcans are very fortunate," said Shelby. "That you can compartmentalize that way. Just . . . decide to move on and do so. Humans aren't quite that tidy. We can't control how long we mourn."

"Yes, you can. You simply choose not to," said Soleta.

Shelby looked at her curiously. "You're telling me that you can just . . . decide when to stop missing someone? You're saying that you can simply decide that you won't miss . . . him," and she indicated the empty chair with a tilt of her head. "Just take that initiative, make that call. Decide that today you will mourn, tomorrow you won't? You can really do that?"

"You sound surprised, Commander," Selar stepped in. "You must comprehend relative perceptions of such matters. To us, our ability to do just as you describe is not at all difficult to understand. What is difficult to understand is why you cannot do the same. Mourning is not like a disease that must be treated and has a life of its own. You do it until you decide not to, and then you move on."

"It's not quite as easy as that," Shelby said quietly.

"Yes. Actually, it is."

And suddenly Shelby felt a hot flash of temper as she looked at the Vulcan doctor's complacent expression. Her infant had fallen asleep in her arms and looked serene and peaceful, and for some reason the sight in its entirety angered Shelby tremendously.

"Tell me, then, Doctor, precisely how long you chose to mourn your husband? Was that a conscious, carefully prescribed period of mourning? Or did you just forget him seconds after he died, or minutes, or what—?"

"Ooookay, this is getting out of hand," Burgoyne said immediately, and it was clear that the others were starting to look uncomfortable.

"No," Selar said to Burgoyne and the others. "No . . . it is a fair question. The answer, Commander, is precisely eight months, two weeks, and one day."

Shelby stared at her. Selar's Vulcan demeanor was utterly inscrutable.

And Shelby, in spite of herself, laughed. The others weren't quite sure how to react, and then Selar shook her head but there seemed to be—just ever so slightly—the barest hint of upturned amusement at the edges of her mouth. Immediately there was a collective sigh of relief from around the table as Shelby said, "I'm sorry. That was uncalled for."

"You felt it was necessary to say. Therefore it was called for." She didn't seem especially perturbed. Then again, being a Vulcan, that should not have been a surprise.

"I guess I should envy you."

"Envy is illogical. But I can see the reasoning for it," Selar told her.

From then on, things proceeded more calmly. There were no more flare-ups, no outbursts, no exhibitions of temper. Instead there was simply a group of people, talking about this and that, occasionally laughing or kidding one another. It was a good feeling, a relaxed feeling. For a time, Shelby even felt as if she was with family. It was a sensation that she found most disconcerting, and she shoved it away because it represented to her something with which she simply did not want to deal.

After a time, conversation turned once more to Captain Calhoun. They began to trade stories and recollections, sometimes correcting each other, other times embellishing. On several occasions "improvements" were made upon tales that they already knew very well, and they were all perfectly aware that the add-ons had been made. But no one said anything at those times. Instead they would just look with reverence at the empty chair.

Finally Selar announced that it was time for her to leave, claiming fatigue. Burgoyne naturally departed with her, although Shelby could have sworn that Selar looked vaguely uncomfortable. And once they had left, it was as if a plug had been pulled from a drain. One by one, or occasionally in pairs, they departed. No one said anything about the likelihood that this was the last time they would all see each other. It was as if no one wanted to deal with it. So instead there were murmurs of "Later," or "See you around," or "Stay in touch."

Shelby knew the routine all too well. There had always been other crews, other departures, and other promises that this time—this time—they would stay in touch. And they always meant it, really, truly, absolutely. There would even be efforts initially before—invariably—time passed and the communiqués from the old crew members stopped coming. Why? Out of sight, out of mind, that was why. There was a reason that old Earth sayings became old; it was because they were true.

There was no question in Shelby's mind that she was going to be the last one out. What surprised her was that it came down to her and Soleta. For a time the young science officer sat in contemplative silence opposite her, and then she said, "Those were interesting stories. About Captain Calhoun."

"Yes. They were."

"Many of them were not as I recalled them. There seemed to be a tendency to exaggeration."

"I know," Shelby said, smiling. "That's how you build legends. You make them bigger and bigger, because people don't like to believe in real life. They're surrounded by real life; they don't need regurgitation of what's already around them. Legends are to give you something to aspire to. So you have to make them bigger than life."

"I see. So that is to be the legacy of Captain Calhoun? Impossible exploits?"

"Well," said Shelby thoughtfully, "the interesting thing is that, in Mac's case, some of the things he did for real were so much bigger than life, that it doesn't need all that much building up. His reality was . . . well . . ." She shrugged. "Surreal. Or maybe superreal. I don't know. I've probably had too much to drink." She swirled some liquid around in the bottom of her glass and came to the startled realization that she had forgotten what it was that she had poured for herself.

"Probably," agreed Soleta. She gave it some more thought. "So do you approve of the truth or don't you?"

"It's not that simple, Soleta."

"Sometimes it is, yes." Her eyes narrowed. "You weren't truthful with us."

"I already explained. Talking about Mac, it—"

"Not about that. About why you do not wish to keep the command crew together . . . or at least, not together with you. The fact is that you do not like us."

At first Shelby couldn't say a word. Her mouth was moving, but nothing was coming out. Finally she relocated her voice and, mustering as much hurt as she could manage, said, "Soleta! How can you say that?"

"It is not difficult."

"After all we've been through, how can you say that . . . I mean, it's absurd."

Soleta finished out the last of her own drink. "Commonality of experience, even purpose, does not dictate commonality of personalities. I do not think the less of you; you could not help it. The situation virtually dictated your frame of mind."

"I'm not following . . ."

"You were brought aboard in order to make certain that the more maverick Captain Calhoun would act in a manner consistent with Starfleet protocol. His command style was different. His command choices were different. 'Eccentric,' to put it delicately. They were not the crew that you would have chosen. Therefore, by definition, you had a natural antipathy for them."

"I think you're way overstating it, Soleta."

"Am I?"

She started to speak, then looked down, unable to meet Soleta's gaze. "Well . . . maybe not too way overstating it. But somewhat. Besides, it became moot. I learned to accept the crew for all its strengths as well as any perceived weaknesses on my part."

"Nevertheless, your antipathy did not simply disappear. Rather, it was something that you had to work to overcome. If you climb a mountain, that does not cause the mountain to disappear. It simply means that you are able to get over the obstacle if you truly dedicate yourself to it. The obstacle, however, remains, and it was something with which you had to struggle constantly. Face it, Commander . . . the crew of the *Excalibur* was not exactly your dream crew. You held yourself separate from us. Your hesitancy and lack of comfort were quite evident, even though your ability to hide it became so polished that you succeeded in fooling those who desired to be fooled."

"Really," said Shelby, unamused. "And who would that be? Those who desired to be fooled, I mean."

"Everyone but me. Well . . . and perhaps Selar. But Selar does not seem to like anyone, so perhaps that's not a fair comparison."

"So you and you alone decided that I didn't like the crew."

"No, you decided that, Commander. I simply observed it. That's my job, you see. To observe the natural world and draw conclusions about it. People are part of that natural world, so of course I observe them and draw conclusions."

"And your conclusion was this antipathy you say I have."

"You are a lover of regulations, Commander. A lover of order. You embrace the more arcane military aspects of Starfleet with more zeal than any officer under which I've served," Soleta told her. "The *Excalibur* did not have a spit-and-polish crew. That is what you are hoping to assemble on the *Exeter*. Believe it or not, I certainly wish you the best of luck. I hope that you are able to put together a crew that Admiral Jellico would be proud of."

"I'll put together a crew that I'll be proud of, and I couldn't give a damn what other people think." Feeling the drink swirling about in her head, Shelby stabbed a finger at Soleta and demanded, "What are you saying? That I care more about regs than I do about people?"

"I had not been saying that, but I wouldn't disagree with that assessment."

"Then you couldn't be more wrong. Then you haven't been paying the least bit of attention to the person I am and the person I've become. What I care about most, though, is the interaction between the people and the regulations. Rules were created for specific reasons, and most of the time, those reasons involve the protection of others. When you toss aside the rules, you risk the safety of all concerned. That's something I never entirely got Mac to understand." She shook her head, looking discouraged. "He was so used to being self-reliant . . ."

"He led armies, Commander, in his youth," Soleta pointed out. "Someone who has legions of men backing him up is very much aware that no one person can carry the day by himself. You may be underestimating his capabilities."

"Well, that's certainly a mistake I won't have the opportunity to make again, will I," shot back Shelby.

"You sound upset, Commander."

"You're damned right I'm upset! Dammit, Soleta, I haven't slept in weeks. Every time I start to drift off, I can see Mac in my head. I haven't strung more than an hour or two of sleep together since we lost the ship. I'm coming off the loss of one ship and I have to overcome all my apprehension as I vie to be commander of another. And you sit here now and tell me that, hell, I never really liked the *Excalibur* crew to begin with. Maybe this is just some weird trick of logic so that you don't have to admit to missing me when I'm gone, or to try and vilify me in your own mind so that you won't have to wonder why I'm not bringing you along as science officer. Hmmm?" Shelby laughed in what sounded remarkably like triumph. "No, you didn't think of that at all."

"You, Commander, have had a bit to drink."

"I, Lieutenant, am perfectly fit, thank you very much. And I don't appreciate being insulted by—"

"Insult?" An eyebrow arched. "Did you perceive insult? My apologies. I simply thought I was stating fact."

"No. It was opinion; opinion that I don't happen to agree with."

"You are saying that you do not value regulations and procedure over people."

"That is exactly and precisely what I am saying."

"I am half-Romulan."

Shelby felt as if she had just been whapped with a mental two-by-four. All of the pleasant buzzing she'd been feeling from the alcohol was dispelled in an instant. "Wh-what?"

"I am half-Romulan," Soleta said again. "My mother was Vulcan, but my father, Romulan. I did not inform Starfleet of this."

She felt as if all the color was draining from her face. "But . . . but you have to. Regulations clearly state—"

"That anyone with blood ties to a race considered actively and aggressively hostile to the Federation must offer full disclosure of those ties or face being discharged from Starfleet." Soleta was amazingly calm. "I did not know of the ties at the time that I enlisted in Starfleet. I since discovered the truth, but have chosen not to apprise Starfleet of it. I am concerned that the delayed revelation could have a negative impact on my career. That I would be relegated to minor duties and be subject to such intense monitoring and scrutiny that I would find it intolerable and be forced to depart Starfleet anyway."

"Soleta, this . . . this is crazy . . ."

"Furthermore," continued Soleta as if Shelby had not spoken, "any officer who learns of any undisclosed blood ties to an actively and aggressively hostile race is obligated to report those ties immediately to Starfleet." She tilted her chin toward Shelby's comm badge. "You can use that, I imagine. Someone must be on duty somewhere. You can call it in."

"Soleta, I . . . I don't understand why you're telling me this. Is this supposed to be some sort of test or something . . . ?"

"The *Excalibur* blew up. We all know the cause. But what if that cause was not what we thought it to be? What if I was a saboteur? What if I was in fact responsible for the loss of the ship? Should that not be investigated? Doesn't Starfleet have a right to know?"

"What are you saying, Soleta? That you were partly responsible? That you were part of some . . . some Romulan plot?"

"I'm not saying that," Soleta told her. "In fact, I'm saying I'm not. But are you going to inform Starfleet and have them investigate?"

"Soleta, I don't know why you're playing this ridiculous game . . ."

"This is not a game. This is a scientific inquiry. It's a test, no different than any other test I conduct upon an unknown."

"I'm not an unknown, dammit. It's me. Commander Shelby. We served together."

"We served on the same vessel, yes. Was there anyone on the ship with whom you ever really felt together? Or did you keep us all at arm's length for all the reasons that seemed right at the time?"

For a moment, Shelby thought briefly of Kat Mueller, the night-shift executive officer with whom she'd felt at least a measure of comfort . . . up until she'd discovered that Mueller and Calhoun had had an affair, at which point all she could envision was Mac in Kat's arms. Mueller providing Calhoun with something that she, Shelby, was unable to.

But what was it? Was it the same comfort level that she was apparently unable to provide others in her former crew? Was that the element that had been holding her back in her own quest for promotion? Was—

Questions, unbidden, were tumbling about in her head, and there was Soleta just sitting there, watching her, scrutinizing her. Soleta, who had just taken a horrific chance, putting forward something as personal and potentially damaging to her career as what she had just told Shelby, in hopes of discovering . . .

. . . what? Something about Shelby? Something about herself?

Did the questions never stop?

When she was very young, she had once said to her mother, "Mommy . . . I can't wait to grow up so that I know everything for sure."

And her mother had smiled down at her and she had said, "When you grow up, the only thing you'll know for sure is how much you don't know." It was not a comment that she had really understood. Of course, now she did understand it. She just didn't like to acknowledge it.

Shelby met Soleta's gaze and then looked down. "Soleta," she said finally, "I don't believe for a moment that you had anything to do with the destruction of *Excalibur.* I also don't believe that the circumstances of your birth are anyone's business but yours. You're a fine officer, and a fine—if slightly eccentric—woman. That, to me, is all that matters. I don't see any need for pulling Starfleet into any of this. If you insist on pushing the matter, and it comes out that you've told me this 'aspect' of your background, naturally I will admit as much to Starfleet."

"You would likely face disciplinary hearings for being less than candid with Starfleet."

"It's a risk I'm prepared to take. Is there anything else you want to tell me? You know . . . maybe you have an uncle who's a Tholian. Or maybe your third cousin on your grandfather's side had carnal knowledge of the Grand Nagus. Something like that?"

Soleta actually smiled. Shelby realized, belatedly, that she'd seen such broader signs of obvious amusement on Soleta's face before. Soleta had usually covered them quickly, as if embarrassed by the slip. Mentally Shelby had always chalked it up to poor training as a Vulcan. She now realized that it was Soleta's Romulan influence, for Romulans were far more open to displays of emotion, by breeding and temperament, than Vulcans were. Well, perhaps that wasn't such a terrible thing. Rather than her Romulan heritage prompting her to betray the Federation or some similar sinister activity, it was just causing her to crack a smile every now and then. Certainly that tendency wouldn't cause an end to life as it was known.

"Commander Shelby . . . there may be hope for you yet," said Soleta.

"I shall take that as a compliment."

"It was intended as such." She rose at that point, and Shelby did so with her. Reflexively, Shelby stuck out a hand to shake Soleta's, but instead the science officer held up her hand in a familiar V-fingered salute. "Peace and long life."

Automatically, Shelby returned the gesture. "Live long and prosper."

Soleta inclined her head slightly in acknowledgment of the correct response. There seemed nothing more to be said, and Soleta—characteristically—didn't say it. Instead she strode to the door of the pub. Just before she exited, though, she turned and said to Shelby, "Captain Calhoun would have been proud of you."

And then Shelby was alone.

She stared for a long time at the empty chairs around the table . . . at the empty glass in front of her. At the emptiness of a life which she had once thought so full.

A hand rested on the back of the chair next to her. She glanced up. It was some young officer who had just arrived with several friends. "You seem to have a few empty chairs here. Mind if I take this one? Or is someone going to be sitting here?" he asked.

He was cute. Once upon a time, when she was another woman in another life, she might actively have made a pass at him. Now all she could do was admire his "cuteness" in an abstract way, but be aware that somehow it was from a distance and not really relevant to her life.

She glanced at the chair that she had aggressively kept vacant the entire evening, and then said, "Sure. Take it. It's just an empty chair."

He slid the chair away from the table and Shelby stared at her reflection in the polished surface of the table until long after last call, and long after a weary bartender had ushered the last of the other customers out. Finally, she drew her coat around herself and walked off, alone, into the darkness, dwelling on the irony that—with all the people she knew who were alive—the only one she really felt comfortable having with her at that moment was the ghost of Mackenzie Calhoun.

SOLETA

SOLETA HAD BEEN BORN and raised on a colony world.
The colony had been rather small, with no more than a
few hundred settlers. Growing up, she had known the
names of every single resident, and had not had the
slightest difficulty in learning them all. And they, naturally, knew her. Soleta, the daughter of T'Pas and
Volak, two of the finest scientific minds on the planet.

But the Vulcan government had eventually decided
that the talents of her parents could be put to better use
back on the homeworld, and so they had been relocated
there and had dutifully served the needs of their people
at the science academy. Deep down—way deep down,
since of course it would not have been appropriate to
let such anger bubble to the surface—she had resented
the call of duty that had returned them to their native
world. For it had been during that time of experimenta-
tion and research that T'Pas had come into contact with

a little-known and quite virulent virus. It had smashed through her immune system as if it didn't exist, and she had died in a matter of weeks. That was the last time Soleta had been on Vulcan. She had gone to her mother's deathbed and promised her, then and there, that she would resume her Starfleet career.

She pushed the thoughts from her as the shuttle angled down toward the shimmering Vulcan surface. She fancied that she could feel the heat even from orbit. The shuttle was populated entirely by Vulcans, nineteen passengers along with Soleta descending to the arid world below. Soleta realized that she was the only one looking out her window. Everyone else was staring resolutely ahead, or reading something with the quiet focus that was so typical of the way Vulcans did everything. It was as if exhibiting enthusiasm or interest in the impending arrival might be considered gauche somehow.

"Typical," she murmured. Then she realized that she had spoken out loud, and felt momentarily foolish. But once again, no one paid her any mind. She might as well have been invisible. *Typical,* she thought again, but this time made sure to keep her mouth shut.

The shuttle landed in the main Vulcan spaceport and Soleta was among the last to disembark. The moment she stepped out of the shuttle the thinner atmosphere, the heat, hit her like a hammer blow. She reeled slightly from it. Then she mentally balanced herself, determined not to let it get to her.

There seemed to be something missing all around her, and it took her a few moments to realize what it was. It was noise. She had been to any number of spaceports in her life, particularly during the years when she had wandered after taking a leave of absence from Starfleet. And whenever she had passed through one of them, there had always been a sheet of noise draped over them. People calling to one another in greeting, or others shouting for people to step aside because flight connections had to be made. Plus, of course, there were occasionally the religious nuts who were trying to convert those who were newly arrived to whatever the dominant faith was. Soleta had once been sentenced to two days in lockup after arriving on Plexus IV, since she had been unaware that refusing to stand and listen to the sales pitch for the local gods had just been made into a crime. A crime, naturally, punishable by two days of imprisonment. During those two days a reformer stood outside her cell and told her about the Plexian deities. What had made the experience truly memorable was that a day/night rotation on Plexus was the equivalent of forty-seven Standard Earth Hours.

Soleta had managed to shorten her sentence by the simple expedient of placing herself in a contemplative trance so deep that they thought she was dead. They'd carted her body out to the morgue and, once in the clear, she had risen off the slab, scaring an attendant completely out of his wits. When she quietly made her departure from the planet some two weeks later, she was mildly amused to see that she had been added to the list of gods as a minor deity. The prospect of someone being jailed because they didn't want to listen about her divinity was not something she chose to dwell upon.

In any event, the Vulcan spaceport was a stark contrast not only to Plexus, but all other spaceports as well. The Vulcans went about their business with a minimum of discussion. There was no idle chatter, no loud explosions of sentiment or enthused greetings, and certainly no reformers, government sponsored or otherwise. Those people who were there to greet others did so with a Vulcan salute, a few softly spoken words, a nod of the head. That was all.

She saw a few humans arriving on another flight. They started barreling through the spaceport in typical human fashion, laughing and yammering about the flight. Then they noticed that virtually everyone around them was staring at them with silent, mild reproof. Their words died in their throats as, very quickly and very uncomfortably and very, very quietly, they made their way out of the spaceport.

"Soleta."

Just her name, spoken quickly and efficiently. Her hearing was, of course, sharp enough to catch it. He had called her with precisely the amount of calculated volume required to get her attention: no more and no less than that.

She turned in the direction of the voice, and sure enough, there was her father. There was Volak. He was exactly as she had remembered him: tall, distinguished, eyes glittering with quiet intelligence. She noticed that there was a hint of gray developing at his temples.

"Peace and long life," he said, raising his hand in the common greeting.

Soleta faced him and then, purely impulsively, she threw her arms around him and hugged him quickly.

If she had screamed out a string of incoherent profanities, she could not have gotten a more stunned reaction from the others around her. The quiet of the spaceport actually got quieter, all ambient sounds being sucked away, as absolutely everyone stared at them. The Vulcans were too controlled to express shock, disgust, or any other disagreeable emotion, but there were ways of making disapproval known.

Unlike the unfortunate humans, however, who had felt shame or embarrassment over their behavior, Soleta could not have cared less about public disapproval. She did not wish to shame her father, though, so she quickly released him and searched his face for some indication that he was upset with her.

Instead there was something akin to quiet amusement in his eyes. At least, that's what she hoped it was. "You have not changed," he said.

"Is that a good thing or a bad thing?" she asked.

"It is neither good nor bad. It simply is," he said.

Soleta had a bag slung over her shoulder. It was no problem for her to carry; nevertheless, Volak slid the weight off her and took it upon herself. She did not bother to tell him that she could handle the weight. He must have known that. He simply chose to assume the burden himself. She found the decision charming, if a bit antiquated in its thinking.

Having no desire to subject him to further silent mortification through inappropriate behavior, she followed him out of the spaceport without offering another word. They used public transport to return to the small, austere apartment where Volak had resided ever since the death of T'Pas. Soleta had asked him once why he was relocating, considering that the previous residence was much nicer.

"That was our place," he said simply, and that was all he had needed to say.

He had invited her to stay with him, but she had demurred. The apartment wasn't really large enough to accommodate guests, even though Soleta's needs would be minimal and she was capable of sleeping on the floor as easily as anywhere else. It wasn't going to be necessary, however, since Starfleet maintained a facility for Starfleet officers who were staying short-term on Vulcan, just as they did on a number of major worlds. So that was where Soleta was intending to settle in during her stay.

"You must be hungry after your trip," he said.

She wasn't. "Yes, I am," she said.

He nodded, appreciating the obvious bending of the truth, since it gave him the opportunity to prepare food for them. All the time that Soleta was growing up, her father had handled most of the food preparation in the house, since he truly enjoyed it and her mother couldn't cook worth a damn anyway. Making food just for one-self wasn't nearly as fulfilling as for two or more.

Minutes later, a bowl of *plomeek* soup was in front of her, and a large pot of *vrass* was simmering. Volak sat opposite her, holding his own bowl of soup carefully in his large hands. They nodded to each other slightly, the traditional greeting at a dining table, and then dipped in their spoons and started eating.

"Excellent as always, Father. Time hasn't diminished your culinary mastery."

"Thank you."

"I like the gray in your hair. It makes you look distinguished."

He looked at her quizzically. "It reflects the passage of time and the wear and tear of existence on one's person. Anything beyond that is purely subjective and—if I may say—illogical."

Soleta did not allow the edges of her mouth to turn up. But she did sigh heavily and say, in a voice tinged with tragedy, "It is an illogical world, Father, no matter how much we may wish it otherwise."

"You speak blasphemy," he told her.

She nodded. "Yes. Along with eighteen other major languages. How is work?"

"It is work," he said. He had gone from research into teaching. "The students appear to listen and learn."

"This year's crop of students is on par with the last?"

"Yes, and the year before. There is a consistency."

"Interesting," said Soleta. "Human teachers always seem to feel that each class is of lesser quality than the year before, no matter what the subject may be."

"That, I would think, is more of a measure of the teachers' growing disaffection than any true decline in the student body itself."

"You're very likely right. So . . ." She paused, not sure she wanted to bring up the subject, but feeling that it should be broached. "Are you seeing anyone?"

Volak blinked owlishly. "I do not understand the question. I see you."

"You understand it perfectly, Father. It has been five years. . . ."

"To the day," Volak said quietly, "as you well know, since that is why you are here. Do you think it appropriate to discuss my social life considering that this is the anniversary of your mother's passing?"

"As a matter of fact, yes, I do." She took another sip of the soup. She noted that it was not up to his usual standard. In fact, it was somewhat bitter. He had misjudged the ingredients, and she could not recall that happening before. She did not comment on it immediately, however. Instead she continued, "I think discussing what Mother would have wanted or not wanted is entirely appropriate. You are still young, Father, with many years left ahead of you. That is a long time to spend on your own."

"If I have many years ahead of me, then that is

certainly plenty of time to explore the concept of remarriage."

"Except that the longer you're on your own, the easier it's going to be for you to settle into a life of loneliness. The humans have a saying, you know."

"Do they."

"Yes. They say that if you fall out of a tree, you should climb right back up."

He looked at her askance. "Why?"

"Why should you climb back up?"

"No, why did you fall out of the tree?"

Soleta shook her head. "That is not actually the point I was trying to make, Father . . ."

"It is pertinent, however. If you have fallen out of the tree because a branch snapped beneath you, then the tree may very well be rotting or dead. Climbing into the tree once more would prove foolhardy since another fall would be the likely result."

"All right," Soleta said patiently, "you should climb back into the tree unless it is dead or dying. However, if you—"

"Furthermore," Volak continued as if she hadn't spoken, "you, the climber, might suffer from vertigo or some other psychological impediment. Or perhaps an inner-ear infection has upset your sense of balance. In such an instance, it would be as inadvisable to climb the tree again as it would be to go swimming within half an hour of consuming a meal."

Soleta stared at him for what seemed a very long time, and then she said, "If you are thrown off a horse, you should get back on the horse."

"Why? The horse clearly does not wish to have you as a rider. Certainly the horse's desires in the matter should receive some consideration in the—"

"Father!"

"I believe the *vrass* is done." He rose from the table and went to get the pot while Soleta sat there, shaking her head in slow disbelief.

The *vrass* was worse than the *plomeek* soup. Undercooked, excessively chewy . . . it was not remotely up to Volak's standards. Worse yet, he didn't seem to notice, eating it without comment.

"I take it this has been your way of saying that you do not wish to discuss the prospect of engaging in a renewed social life," she said.

"Searching for a new mate is simply not a priority at this time," Volak told her. "In point of fact, it may not be a priority at any time. That is, however, my decision to make. I should like to think that you would respect it."

"Of course I respect it, Father. However, it saddens me."

"Saddens?" He cocked an eyebrow.

"Yes, Father. Saddens. In the privacy of this, your very small apartment, I think that I, your daughter, should be allowed to admit that something about the way you are presently living your very sheltered life saddens me."

"Of course you may admit it. But it is illogical."

"I know. But sometimes you do things because they are illogical, and you just do not care about it."

"That is—"

"—also illogical, yes, I know." She shook her head. "Are you upset with me that I hugged you in the spaceport?"

"Being upset would be futile. You did what you felt was appropriate. I, and everyone else there, did not feel it was appropriate. But you have always felt it necessary to do what you thought was right. I must respect that, for it is what makes you unique. And I would not exchange that, no matter how much 'embarrassment' is inflicted upon me."

"Thank you. I think."

"You are welcome. I think." He indicated the *vrass*. "You have not consumed much of your meal. Is it inadequate in some way?"

She wanted to bend the truth again, to spare his feelings. Then she remembered who and what she was talking to. Taking a breath, she slid the bowl aside and said, "Yes, as a matter of fact, it is inadequate. To be specific, it tastes terrible."

"Does it?" He appeared amazed . . . which, for him, meant the raising of both eyebrows. He took a large bit of it, rolled it around in his mouth as if truly tasting it for the first time. His face remained impassive, but he nodded slowly after a moment and said, "You raise a valid point. This is substandard. My apologies."

"I am now officially concerned, Father. Producing a meal that is borderline inedible is unprecedented."

"It is nothing."

His dismissive tone of voice didn't fool her for a moment. "Father . . . you know me as well as I know you. Something is indeed bothering you, and I am going to continue to inquire of you what it might be until you tell me. It would be highly illogical, and a waste of both our times, to prolong the process."

Volak seemed to consider the point a moment, and then he inclined his head slightly. "I bow to your flawless reasoning. It is of comfort to know that the time that was spent teaching you Vulcan disciplines was not entirely wasted, even if you choose to ignore them at your whim."

He was silent for a short time longer, as if trying to determine the best way to bring it up. Soleta waited patiently. Finally he slid the inedible food aside and leaned forward, his elbows on the table, his level gaze fixed on Soleta. Something about his demeanor had changed. Soleta had been on high-density worlds that had less gravity than the look in her father's eyes.

"He has been in contact with me," said Volak.

She stared at him blankly. "He. What 'he' would that be?"

"Rajari. He is out of prison."

Soleta felt the blood draining from her face. She stood up so quickly that she banged her knee on the underside of the table.

"Are you all right?" Volak asked.

"Am I all right?" Soleta backed up, coming to rest in a corner of the room. "Why would I not be all right? I return to Vulcan on the fifth anniversary of my mother's death, to be here for you and support you as a good daughter should. And I find out that the Romulan bastard who raped my mother and put me into this world, instead of rotting in a camp where he belongs, is apparently walking around free and harassing the only real father I've ever known." She shook her head as if she could somehow dispel the horror of it through sheer disbelief. "Did he escape? Is that what you're telling me? Have the authorities been alerted to—"

He shook his head. "No. He was released."

"Released?" She could scarcely believe it. "How was he released? Why? Whose idiotic decision was that? When did you hear from him? Has he come here? Did he threaten you? If he threatened you, perhaps we can have him put back away to—"

Volak was on his feet and coming around to his

daughter. He placed his hands on her shoulders to steady her. "Soleta . . . calmly. Your reaction is not aiding in the orderly dissemination of information."

"I don't care!" she said heatedly. "I don't care about orderly dissemination! I care about that monster doing more damage than he's already done! I—"

"Soleta," and there was iron in his tone, "there will be no further discussion of this until you have remembered enough of what I taught you to be able to handle this matter in the manner of a true Vulcan."

"You mean as opposed to the Romulan half-breed that I am?"

There was such sting in her tone that she instantly regretted the words as soon as they were out. Volak, however, was far too disciplined to let them have any impact upon him. Or, at the very least, to allow that impact to show. Nevertheless, Soleta was instantly contrite. "I'm . . . sorry, Father. I know that is not what you meant."

She took a deep breath, found the stable center after some effort, and then walked slowly to the chair and eased herself into it. She folded her hands and placed them primly in her lap. "All right, Father. Tell me what happened."

Instead of replying immediately, he walked over to the comm screen that was situated on the wall. "I received a communiqué from Rajari. Except, in point of fact, it was not addressed to me. Instead it was directed to your mother. Obviously Rajari was unaware of the fact that she was dead."

"When did you get the communiqué?"

"Five weeks, three days, eighteen minutes ago."

Soleta shook her head in quiet amusement. But then her mind returned to the seriousness of the situation at hand. "Did you store it?"

"Of course." Volak was already accessing it, and a moment later, the image of Rajari appeared on the screen.

Soleta was quite annoyed with herself that her first impulse was to cut and run. She felt a trembling in her leg and fought it off angrily. A flagging of her spirit was not going to do her a bit of good.

Nevertheless, looking at him forced that hideous moment, years ago, to come spiraling back to her. That time when, back on the *Aldrin,* Soleta had been a young officer who had decided to talk to a captured Romulan spy and saboteur. She had never seen a Romulan in person, and considered it a matter of scientific curiosity.

She had come there to perhaps learn something. Instead she had learned far more than she could ever possibly have expected.

She pushed the thought away from her, scrambled the image in her mind so that the sneer of the captive Romulan would be wiped away. The Romulan that she was looking at now bore a resemblance to that one from years gone, certainly. It was, after all, the same one. But none of the arrogance was there. Then again, it wasn't as if he appeared merciful or pleasant or was anyone that she would want to spend five minutes with, unless it was five minutes spent throttling him. His hair was a bit thinner, his complexion somewhat paler. There was hardness in his eyes, though, a hint of the mercilessness that he had possessed when he had assaulted Soleta's mother. T'Pas, who had thought that the crashed spy might actually be a defector from the Romulan Empire. She aided him, and had paid a terrible price for her naiveté, to be brutalized by the depraved, bullying bastard. To this day, Soleta could not believe that her mother and father had gone through with actually having her. Certainly their repeated, failed attempts to have a child of their own had hampered their judgment. Soleta knew that that could be the only reason, for the only logical choice would have been to abort the pregnancy. Had Soleta been in her position, she knew that was what she would have done.

So there he was, Rajari, after all these years. He stared out from the comm screen, but his image was frozen. Soleta looked to her father, her face a question. Volak was watching her with mild uncertainty. "Are you prepared, Soleta?"

Soleta realized that the tension in her body was quite visible. Her entire body was curved forward, like a gargoyle or some sort of large cat ready to strike. She forced herself to calm once more, and said, "I am a Starfleet officer, Father. I believe I am capable of watching a simple transmission, no matter who sent it."

"Very well" was all he said, and activated the message.

"Greetings, T'Pas," Rajari began. The sound of his voice was like a deep wound to Soleta's heart, but she pulled even the vaguest hints of emotion out of the mix and watched him with utter dispassion. Rajari continued, "I hope that this transmission finds you well. I am . . . quite certain you remember me. In case you were unaware, I was in a Federation prison camp for some time. I would still be there, most likely, were it not for the Dominion War."

"The Dominion War?" said a confused Soleta, looking to Volak. He put a finger to his lips, indicating that she should be quiet.

As if answering her puzzled exclamation, Rajari said, "I knew some information that was of strategic use to the Federation in their battles against the Cardassians. It is impressive what one can pick up when one is pursuing a career of illegal weapons transport and smuggling. Believe it or not, I was able to provide the Federation with some inside information that not only saved lives, but also enabled them to make some serious headway in their conflict. In a way . . . I am a war hero." He laughed very softly at his vague attempt at humor, and Soleta felt a slight thudding in her temple. "That, plus . . . certain extenuating circumstances . . . prompted the Federation to arrange my early release. That was most kind of them, was it not? Granted, it was the price for what I told them. Then again, they could have gone back on the arrangement, and what recourse would I have had, eh? So . . . I am free."

"Free." Soleta echoed the word in disbelief.

"You may wonder why I am communicating with you now," Rajari went on. His expression was unreadable. "Think of it as taking care of . . . unfinished business. You see . . . you deserved more than what I gave you. Much . . . much more. I regret that I was unable to attend to you as I truly should have. Given another opportunity, I would have handled you very differently. Then again, life is not in the habit of giving second chances. I have one now, though, and I am going to endeavor to make the best of it. So . . . I wanted you to know that . . . and I hope . . . if my luck holds out," and he smiled thinly, "I will see you in the afterlife. Farewell."

There was silence in the room for long minutes after the image vanished.

"Have you shown this to anyone else, Father?" she asked finally.

"What is there to show? I checked with the local

Starfleet representatives and they affirmed that he had indeed been released. There is nothing else to be done."

"Nothing else to be done?" Her training went right out the window as she made no effort to keep the incredulity from her voice. "Father, he threatened you! We heard him!"

"The message was to your mother, not me. Obviously he is unaware that she is dead."

"And if he finds her gone and you here, do you think that you are safe?"

"What reason would he have to do me harm."

"He's a mad-dog sadist, Father. He doesn't need motive, merely opportunity." She was pacing furiously now. "I don't have to tell you this; you know it yourself. That's why you're so distracted."

"I was merely preoccupied with my internal dispute as to whether I should show the transmission to you or not."

"Don't lie to me!"

"Vulcans do not lie," he said mildly.

"Yes, we do, Father. We lie to ourselves, just like any sentient being. We're just as capable of self-delusion as the lowliest human."

"Perhaps not the *lowliest* . . ." said Volak thoughtfully.

Soleta growled in frustration and ran her fingers through her thick, dark hair. Her fingers bumped up against the IDIC hairpin that she customarily wore . . . the pin that her mother had given her as an heirloom. The one that Rajari had recognized while he was imprisoned on the *Aldrin*, which had prompted him to start boasting about the poor, helpless Vulcan colonist who had sported a similar hairpin. A colonist whom he had raped, and had a great time while he was doing it.

And all the time that he had been chortling about his "accomplishment," he was unaware that the young Vulcan Starfleet officer he was addressing was the issue of that ungodly union, wearing not a similar hair clasp, but the exact same one. She had realized, though, and it had taken all her training not to scream, or to shut down the force shield and blast him to pieces right then and there.

Feeling that pin now reminded her even more starkly of the encounter, and she pulled her fingers out of her hair as if, like the legendary Gorgon, she had sprouted snakes in her head and one of them had bitten her hand. "Tell you what, Father," she said. "Why do we not go out to dinner? Whatever the reason for your distraction, this is somewhat inedible. Allow me to treat you to dinner. After all, you are certainly entitled, considering all the meals you prepared for me. It is equitable."

"If you were interested in equity," Volak pointed out, "you would prepare a meal for me with your own hands rather than suggest we go out."

"I had assumed you were interested in a meal that was more edible than this, not less."

Volak naturally caught himself before he could laugh, but Soleta knew her father well enough to be aware that he had found the comment amusing. "I defer to your judgment. Shall we . . . ?" and he gestured toward the door.

"Before we go, Father," she said, "I would like you to give me a copy of that message, if it would not be too much trouble."

"Trouble? Not at all. But why would you desire such a thing?"

"I want to have a brief chat with the local Starfleet representatives, and I thought it would help to have a copy of it in hand."

He duplicated the message onto a file chip. But when he handed it to her, he kept her hand in his a moment longer than he needed to. "Was I in error showing this to you, Soleta?"

"No, Father. And you are very likely correct. Even if Rajari's intentions are hostile, once he learns that Mother is gone, then he has no further business in your life. I am sure you are quite safe."

"My father is in mortal danger. How obvious does this need to be in order for Starfleet to do something about it!"

Commander Holly Beth Williams spoke with a slow drawl as she turned away from Rajari's message, which had just finished playing on her desktop viewer. She had a round face, seen-it-all eyes, and short brown hair. "I'm sorry, darlin', I'm not seein' it."

"Not seeing it! He spoke about unfinished business. About handling her differently. About seeing her in the afterlife. The meaning is obvious: He's planning to kill her."

"Why?" asked Williams. "Even were your mother still with us, she'd pose no threat to him."

Soleta felt nothing but frustration. She had come to the Starfleet offices on Vulcan in hopes of alerting them to the situation so that Rajari could be found and thrown back in prison once more. Instead all she was encountering was a series of officers who weren't willing to see it her way. When she'd finally been brought to Williams, the woman's friendly demeanor ("Call me H.B.," she'd said cheerily) had given her reason to believe that she'd found the right woman. But Williams' mild reaction to the message was dashing Soleta's hopes. "Monsters do not require reasons, Commander. That is part of what makes them monsters."

"It's 'H.B.,' darlin', remember? Or 'Holly Beth.' Don't answer to 'Holly.' "

"Your sobriquet is of less interest right now to me than it should be, I admit," Soleta said evenly. "This message—"

"Is simply not clear cut enough for me to request any action be taken. Which I believe is what everyone else here is telling you, except you don't seem willing to listen."

"I am not the one who is unwilling to listen," Soleta shot back. "I admit, the contents of the message are somewhat veiled. Naturally Rajari would phrase it in that way. He would be aware that others might view the message, and would not be so foolish as to provide overt evidence of threats for all to see. But I have met him. I know him. I know what he is capable of."

"And what would that be, exactly?" asked Williams. She leaned forward, her fingers interlaced, obviously curious.

"Anything."

Williams sighed and shook her head. "Computer," she said after a moment, "pull up file on former Romulan prisoner, Rajari."

"Working," the computer informed her.

The screen shifted, and Rajari's picture appeared on it. This time, however, it was accompanied by text. Williams tilted the screen away from Soleta and said, "It's marked 'Confidential,' Lieutenant. Sorry." Then she scanned the contents, nodding slowly and even muttering to herself slightly.

"Well?" prompted Soleta after a time.

"He was released, just as the message says. Beyond that, I'm afraid it's confidential."

"Confidential? Information about a convicted spy, smuggler, and saboteur is confidential? What about my father's life, Commander? Where does that fit into the parameters of Starfleet concerns."

"I told you, you can call me . . ."

" 'H.B.,' yes, I know!" said Soleta, her exasperation showing ever so slightly. "But what I should or should not call you does not concern me. What concerns me is my father's safety! I would spend the rest of my life guarding him if possible, but it is not possible, nor would he permit that. Assigning Starfleet officers to guard him is also impossible, obviously. Something must be done about Rajari before he comes to Vulcan and kills my father! At least alert the spaceports!"

"I don't see where that would do any good. If he has a private conveyance, he could wind up landing anywhere on Vulcan. Besides, alert them to what? He's done nothing illegal. There's nothing he could be held for."

"This is insane! What has to happen here, Commander? Does my father have to wind up with a knife in his back for Starfleet to say, 'Oh dear. It appears that we allowed a madman to go around at his whim and destroy people's lives! Our fault.' This is my father's life we're talking about, Commander. Perhaps that is an abstract concern to Starfleet, but it is not to me."

Williams was studying her with open curiosity. "No offense, but I can't say's I recall ever seein' a Vulcan get worked up about anything."

"My apologies," Soleta said evenly. "Were I a better Vulcan, perhaps I would be able to discuss my father's impending murder with sufficient dispassion."

Commander Williams leaned back in her chair,

studying Soleta with such a piercing gaze that Soleta felt as if it were boring into the back of her head. Finally she said, "I regret, Soleta, that I am not at liberty to provide you with any information about Rajari. His known whereabouts are confidential. Computer, time please."

"Thirteen fifty hours," the computer replied promptly.

"My apologies, Lieutenant," Williams said as she rose. "I have a meeting I must attend. You can see yourself out, I'm sure." And without another word, she strode briskly around the desk and out the door.

Soleta, confused at the abrupt departure, watched her go. Then she looked back at the computer screen . . . and realized that it was still activated. The "strictly confidential" information was sitting there, hers for the taking.

Which was, she realized, exactly what the commander's intention had been.

Wasting no time, Soleta was around the desk in a flash. She read over the contents of the file as quickly as she could, committing the facts to memory with her customary ease.

There was no great detail in the file as to precisely why Rajari had been freed beyond that which she already knew. It even made specific mention of "extenuating circumstances," just as he had, but did not go into detail. It did, however, tell her where he was . . . or at least where Starfleet had its last record of him being.

"Thank you, H.B.," she said softly.

Less than a day later, she was with her father at the spaceport. She was cutting her stay short. He did not ask why, nor did she feel the need to volunteer the information. In truth, both of them had a fairly clear idea of what was going on, but neither of them chose to say it out loud. She started to head for her shuttle, and then Volak said, "You made no endeavor to embrace me."

"I would not want to provide any further painful embarrassment," said Soleta, turning back to him.

"Ah. That is considerate."

"Thank you." She started to leave once more.

And then Volak said, "Your mother once said that she thought me capable of enduring any amount of pain."

This stopped Soleta in her tracks. She turned to face him again. "Indeed."

"Yes."

"It might be," she said thoughtfully, "of scientific interest to see whether or not she was right in her assessment."

"You may very well be correct," said Volak.

This time when she hugged him, she did not care who was watching.

ADULUX

"HELLO. WOULD YOU LIKE to tell us why you're about to jump off the roof?"

Adulux froze where he was, the stiff wind whipping his dying robes around him. They were the dying robes that had been passed down from father to son, as was the custom on Liten, for several centuries. They were, in fact, nothing particularly impressive to look upon. The sleeves were tattered and the garment was badly in need of patching, which was an odd state of affairs for a garment that was worn only during a brief time in one's existence. The truly sad matter was that Adulux had no one to pass the robes on to, for all his hopes for the future had vanished along with his beautiful wife, Zanka.

He had not yet looked down. He had stepped to the roof's edge while looking resolutely forward. He was concerned that if he actually looked at the plunge that awaited him, he might lose his nerve.

As were all Litens, Adulux was not especially tall, with fairly slender build and skin that was tinted a soft green. His brow was slightly distended, his thick black hair brushed back and down. When he listened carefully to someone, he tended to tilt his head slightly, giving him a perpetually quizzical look. He was looking somewhat quizzical at that particular moment, trying to figure out who the two individuals were on the roof, why they had come there at this particular point in time, and why they looked vaguely . . . wrong.

The one who had spoken was the shorter of the two. He was a Liten, to be sure, as was his companion. But he had an air about him, a seen-it-all attitude that Adulux had never discerned in any Liten before. He was also clad rather unusually, wearing a long tan coat and a strange hat that was tilted rakishly to one side. He had an air of amused detachment about him, as if he were curious about what Adulux was about to do, but not so interested in the outcome that he was going to do anything to try and avert it.

The taller one was . . . well . . . much taller. Wider, too. He was likewise a Liten, but the most powerfully built Liten that Adulux had ever seen. Indeed, he might possibly have been the most powerfully built Liten that anyone had ever seen. His head seemed so close-set to his body that it appeared he had no neck at all. He was dressed in a similar manner to the smaller one, but without the hat.

"Well?" asked the shorter one. "I asked you a question. Are you going to want to take all night to answer it?"

"Wh-who are you?"

"No one interesting. Not as interesting as you, in any event."

"How am I interesting?" demanded Adulux. He thought that he had never heard anything as absurd in his life. Everyone knew just how incredibly dull he was. Even his beloved Zanka had become exasperated with him and his plodding, predictable, routine ways. "How am I more interesting than you? Than anybody?"

"Anyone who is about to leap to his death is automatically interesting."

It seemed a reasonable enough statement, and Adulux had to agree, albeit reluctantly, that there was some merit to it. But he wasn't about to step away from the edge of the roof just because of one passing meritorious comment. "Don't come any closer," he ordered.

"I actually haven't moved since we started talking," the shorter one pointed out. The taller one had said absolutely nothing up to that point. He seemed content merely to watch and let matters unfold. Adulux suspected that if he did indeed jump, the big one wouldn't shed a tear or care one way or the other. The shorter one continued, "I was just curious as to why you are doing this, and thought you could enlighten me."

Adulux thought long and hard about it, and realized that he had nothing to lose. He was, after all, going to be dead in a minute. So what he said here was of no real consequence. "It's the aliens," he told them. "They've ruined my life."

"What aliens?" inquired the shorter one.

There was something in his tone, some vague, momentary hesitation, which prompted Adulux to think that the newcomer knew more than he was telling. The big one might know more, too, but he wasn't saying anything at all, so there was no way to judge. "You know the ones."

"I do?"

"Yes."

"If I know them, why am I asking?"

"Everyone knows them," Adulux said scornfully. "What sort of Liten are you, anyway? The elders have been covering this up for years. It's common knowledge. Alien visitors come to this world to torment us and aggravate us, and so far the government has done nothing to put an end to it."

The newcomer took a step or two toward Adulux, but it seemed more a thoughtful movement rather than an attempt to snatch Adulux back from the brink of disaster. Ten stories below Adulux, sweet oblivion and a freedom from this hellish existence awaited him, but the newcomer didn't seem to be conscious or caring of that. "What sort of alien visitors?" inquired the newcomer.

"I don't know!" said Adulux in clear aggravation. "The tormenting and aggravating kind. What does it matter what sort of alien visitors. I know of them, and they know where they are and what they are. And they know that I know they . . ." His voice trailed off and his tapering fingers rubbed his temples. "I lost track of what I was saying."

The big one finally spoke. He rumbled, "Not a problem. I lost interest five minutes ago."

"You're not helping," said the shorter one, and he turned back to Adulux. "I believe that we can help you, if you'll tell us everything that happened."

"Help me? How can anyone help me?"

"We can. It's our job."

He looked up at the two newcomers. "You are . . . what are you?"

"Let's just say we're specialists in this kind of situation."

For the first time in what seemed ages, Adulux felt the slightest bit of hope beginning to blossom within him. "You . . . you've dealt with this type of thing before?"

"Oh, yes. Many times."

"And you've found aliens?"

"We can't say. Confidentiality and all that. We couldn't really answer your question without betraying any of our clients' privacy." He looked slightly apologetic. "You know how it is."

"Of course I do," said Adulux, who didn't. "I . . . don't have a good deal of money to hire you."

"Don't worry about it. We have easy payment plans, and don't charge for anything until after the job is done. Fair?"

"More than. So . . . so what happens now?"

"Well, that depends. If you step off the roof toward us, we go someplace, have something to eat, and you tell us what happened to bring you to this state. If you step off the roof in the other direction, then our job is pretty much done. It's up to you."

Adulux considered the offer. There really seemed to be no serious downside. If this business with the two specialists didn't work out, well, the roof wasn't going anywhere. The Sentries had him under suspicion in the disappearance of his beloved Zanka, but they weren't going to make a move yet to apprehend him. Not until they were sure. He could always return and complete the terminal business that awaited him.

Convinced that he was doing the right thing in the short term, he glanced down before turning to step back toward the roof and safety.

The plunge awaiting him was dizzying. Looking down ten stories was far more formidable than looking up the same ten stories from street level.

The world swirled around him. Adulux's arms pinwheeled, trying to grab the air itself for support, but naturally there was none. He toppled forward, twisted in midair even as he fell. His upper torso slammed against the roof edge, slowing him for a split instant, and then he was hanging by his fingers.

The shorter of the two was there, shouting his name, grabbing him by the wrists. But he lacked the strength to pull Adulux up.

The roof trembled, and for a moment Adulux in his panic thought that there was some sort of quake, as if the planet's gods themselves were determined to tear him from his precarious perch and send him plummeting to his doom. Then the massive being was standing over him, reaching down and gripping him by the wrist. Adulux was stunned by how cold his grip felt. It was as if he were being enveloped by rock, even though the flesh certainly felt like Liten flesh. Then his mind seized up as someone who was displaying absolutely no effort in doing so hauled him to the roof. His feet kicked the air and suddenly they were on the hard surface. He looked up at his savior. "How strong are you?" he gasped in wonderment.

"Strongest one there is," intoned the big one.

He looked from one to the other. "Who are you two?"

"Name's McHenry," said the shorter one. He chucked a thumb at his companion. "His is Kebron."

"Kebron? Mk . . . kennery? Those are unusual names . . ."

"We're unusual people," said McHenry. "Now . . . why don't we go somewhere with less altitude and you can tell us exactly how you got to this point."

Adulux surveyed them with a flicker of residual suspicion. "How did you know I was up here? How did you know I needed help? Your help?"

"It's our business," said McHenry. "Right, Kebron?"

Kebron grunted noncommittally.

The eatery was sparsely populated, owing to the lateness of the hour. Aside from occasional glances sent Kebron's way, mostly by females who seemed appreciative and men who appeared jealous, the three of them attracted no attention. Nevertheless, Adulux kept looking around nervously.

"You appear a bit on edge . . . no pun intended," said McHenry.

"I'm worried that Sentries are watching me."

"Sentries. Oh, yes. The local constabulary."

He nodded vigorously. "They suspect me because of Zanka's disappearance."

"Why don't you tell us the entire thing from the beginning," McHenry suggested.

Adulux nodded, although it was clear that he was not particularly looking forward to it. "Zanka and I . . . we were not getting on particularly well. She wanted to dissolve our bonds. I did not."

"Bonds? You were tied up?" McHenry said, looking somewhat uncomprehending.

The response did not exactly bolster Adulux's confidence. How were these two going to be of any help in finding his Zanka or putting his life back together if he had to explain every simple thing. "Bonds. Life bonds," he said, as if speaking to a child.

"Oh. Of course," said McHenry, and he thumped his head with the base of his hand as if chiding himself. "Forgive me. I'm new to this . . ."

Kebron cleared his throat loudly.

". . . line of work," McHenry finished. "So I was thinking of bonding in its offensive sense of, well . . ."

"Keep talking," Kebron said to Adulux, endeavoring to ignore McHenry.

"Zanka wanted to dissolve our bonds," continued Adulux, casting one more suspicious glance at McHenry. "We had been discussing it for many months. She said she wanted more than I was able to provide her. She said I was boring, uninteresting. She told her friends how dull I was, how unwilling I was to take risks. She . . . demeaned me. Humiliated me."

"I am sorry," said McHenry, and he sounded sincere.

It made Adulux feel slightly better, and he continued, "So one night, a week ago, we went out together, to someplace relatively remote. It was an endeavor on my part to recapture some of the romance of our youth. I thought it would help." He shook his head, disconsolate. "Who knew it would backfire so badly?"

"How did it backfire?"

He gave them a haunted look. "Are you sure you will believe me? I've told this story so many times, and the Sentries just give me these . . . these contemptuous stares. As if I am not only lying, but they think I'm stupid for thinking they'll believe the lie."

"I assure you, we'll believe you," said McHenry. "Won't we, Kebron?"

Kebron said nothing. He was staring with distinct lack of interest at the food they'd ordered which was sitting in front of them. McHenry and Adulux had already finished theirs.

Adulux wasn't enthused by the lack of support from Kebron, but he pressed on. "She told her friends that I was taking her somewhere with solitude. She thought it a great joke, I assume."

"But she went with you anyway."

"To laugh at me, most likely. Nothing more. But I

was desperate. I would have done anything to recapture her love. Do you have any idea what that is like?"

"Yes," said McHenry without hesitation. This drew a sharp look from Kebron, but no comment.

"So there we were, in a secluded, romantic area with a wonderful view of the city in the distance. The moons were overhead. The breeze was sublime. And she . . . she . . ."

"Showed no interest?"

"Very little. But it became moot very quickly. When . . . when they showed up."

"They."

"We were in our vehicle, and suddenly there was this . . ." He gestured helplessly. "This light overhead . . . blinding . . . and this whining, so deafening that it rings in my head to this day. The vehicle wouldn't move. We leaped out the doors, started to run. The huge light was following us, and I could barely make out the shape of the vessel . . ."

"A vessel. A flying vessel?" asked McHenry. "A spaceship, you'd guess?"

"Yes, exactly!" Adulux felt a flare of hope. He could tell from McHenry's demeanor, from his tone, that he wasn't dismissing the claims out of hand as the authorities had (or at least as they had pretended to do, since the Elders' official posture on extraterrestrials was well known). He was simply taking down, mentally, the details without making any sort of judgment. He was actually listening to Adulux. "The light was too bright for me to make out any details, but it was definitely of offworld origin. As we ran, Zanka, she . . ." He choked a moment from the memory. "She reached out, grabbed at my hand. And suddenly there was another flash of light, brighter than anything until that point, and I hit the ground. Everything faded into a haze and I lost consciousness. When I came to . . . she was gone. No sign of Zanka. No sign of the vessel."

"And you went to the authorities . . . ?"

"They came to me, actually. I made my way home, still in shock. I could scarcely believe what had happened. It was like my mind was shutting down. I awoke the next morning, convinced that the previous night's events had been a dream . . . and then there was a pounding on my door."

"The Sentries," McHenry guessed.

Adulux nodded. "Yes. The Sentries. Zanka's friends had become concerned when she did not return the previous night to regale them with tales of my foolishness. The Sentries began to question me. I told them what had happened. Of course, they did not believe me, or at least they said they did not, as per instructions of the Elders. Thanks to a governmental policy of disbelief, I am being made to suffer even more than I already am." His voice became low and desperate. "They think I did something with her. They believe I killed her and hid her body away or destroyed it somehow, out of a fit of anger over her refusal to rebond with me. But I did not do that thing, McHenry. I could not have. But no one will believe me."

"I believe you. As does Kebron. Correct, Kebron?"

Kebron grunted.

Adulux took a deep breath and asked the question that he'd been most fearing. "Can you help me?"

"Yes," said McHenry firmly. "We can . . . and we will. So why don't you take us to where she disappeared . . . and then, with any luck, we'll have a little chat with the aliens."

SOLETA

THE TITAN COLONY was one of the first to be established by the then-fledgling space program of Earth. At the time of its founding, it had been considered absolutely state-of-the-art, an exciting and breathtaking advancement for Earth, the Saturnian colony being the farthest point that humanity had ever established as a place to develop.

That was centuries ago, and it had gone to seed somewhat since then.

The main entry port to Titan colony was Catalina City, named—so it was said—after the wife of one of the colony's founders. Rajari was supposed to be there, at least according to Starfleet records. He had been set up in an apartment there, given a "fresh start" by the Federation, according to what she'd read. So it was there that Soleta had gone, in order to . . .

Well . . . that was the sticking point.

Soleta's righteous indignation over the freeing of Rajari had gotten her all the way to Titan, but now that she was there, she wasn't entirely sure just what she was going to do. She couldn't simply walk up to him and shoot him. Was she to warn him off, perhaps? Tell him to stay away from her father? That might work . . . right up until the point where Rajari laughed in her face, as he most likely would. Why should he care about her threats, or what she wanted? She was nothing to him. Nothing except the daughter of the woman whose life he had forever damaged.

So Soleta was in something of a quandary as she made her way through Catalina City. As she tried to figure out exactly how to handle Rajari, she also couldn't help but register disappointment with the state of the city itself. What had once been a rough-and-tumble, hard-bitten frontier establishment had metamorphosed, over the centuries, into little more than a tourist trap. Tourism was Catalina City's primary stock-in-trade, and even that was a dying one after all these decades. People who were new to space travel would come to Catalina City to see what was once the showcase, the jewel, of Federation exploration. But the years had long since passed it by, and the city was merely a shadow of its former glory days. She felt as if she could smell the decay in the air. Buildings were badly in need of repair, garish lights flickered on buildings throughout. There was a general seediness to the place that saddened her, for certainly the pioneer spirit which had created the city would never have wanted it to end up like this.

There was nothing, however, that she could do about that. Instead she needed to focus her attention on the problem at hand, and that problem was Rajari.

She headed for his apartment, having gotten the address off the records. It seemed to her that, as she drew closer to the area where Rajari resided, her surroundings became even more depressed-looking.

Then Rajari walked past her.

It was a fortunate thing that he was paying no attention to her whatsoever, because Soleta did a very obvious double-take. She stared after him, not quite believing that she had seen what she had seen. Not believing that the man who had just disappeared into a bar was the man she was seeking.

She blinked several times as if that might somehow correct the vision that was now embedded in her mind. Then she turned on her heel and backtracked, heading toward the bar into which Rajari had gone.

She stood at the door and peered in. Rajari was not only seated at the bar, but he already had a drink in his hand. She stepped gingerly into the bar, allowing her eyes to grow accustomed to the much dimmer lighting.

No one gave Soleta a second glance. That was largely because she was not wearing her Starfleet uniform. She had opted for less obvious civilian garb, believing that not attracting attention might be preferable (although she had taken the precaution of keeping her comm badge with her; it would provide a quick and convenient means of identification should she find herself in a sticky situation). Her relative anonymity would certainly enable her to get closer to Rajari in order to accomplish . . . well, whatever it was she thought she was going to accomplish, although she still didn't really have an idea of what that was.

Yes. Yes, it was definitely Rajari, although she still had trouble believing it. It was nothing short of miraculous that she had recognized him at all. He looked nothing as he did in the transmission, and it made her wonder whether he was wearing some sort of disguise, or whether he had simply let himself go quite that quickly. Five weeks was not all that much time, but apparently he had used it well . . . or not well, depending upon one's point of view.

His hair was quite long now on both sides and down the back. Whereas it had been black and gray when short, now that it was grown out it was almost entirely gray. His eyebrows had been trimmed. Thick beard stubble decorated his face. He still had the distinctive protruding forehead of a Romulan, but that was somewhat downplayed by the overgrown hair. More important—some might even say shocking—his ears were bobbed. What she could see of them through the overlong hair was as neatly rounded as any human's had ever been. Indeed, as she stared at him, she started to wonder if she wasn't totally imagining it.

But no. No, she was absolutely positive. Despite the hair, the stubble, despite the ears . . . it was definitely Rajari. She knew it in her bones.

Why had he done this, though? There was a fairly diverse ethnic mix in Catalina City. Did he think people would notice? Or if they did notice, did he think they'd care? She found it hard to believe that he was so determined to blend in that he had gone to such extremes. What other reason then?

Her mind still whirling, Soleta took a seat at a table in a far corner, where she could keep an eye on him without being particularly noticeable. A waitress came over and Soleta ordered a drink from her, which she then proceeded to nurse for several hours. Every so often the waitress would drift by the table, see that Soleta's glass had not appreciably lessened in its contents, roll her eyes, and walk away. Soleta suspected that, had the bar been more crowded, they might well have chased her away. As it was, she was left alone to observe her target.

Rajari, paying her no mind at all, drank steadily and heavily. He spoke to no one. He looked at no one. Most of the time he stared into his glass, as if trying to divine the secrets of the universe that might be hidden within. Occasionally he would look up and look into a large mirror that was mounted on the wall opposite. It was as if he was trying to see some aspect of himself in that largely unrecognizable reflection. Soleta wouldn't have been at all surprised if he hadn't been able to see any. She knew who she was looking at, and she could barely see anything of the man he had been, either.

As she observed him, it gave her time to try and determine just what it was she was hoping to accomplish. She was rather annoyed to realize that, given all the time in the world, no plan was any more forthcoming than it had been before. This was most unlike her. Soleta was meticulous with planning the parameters of anything in which she was involving herself. One did not embark on an experiment if one did not know precisely how one was going to proceed. She started to wonder if perhaps the destruction of the *Excalibur* was factoring into her present course of action. Because the fact was that if she had waited until she had developed a specific plan of attack, she might never have come up with anything reasonable and, as a result, never embarked on this lunacy in the first place. But the loss of her ship had instilled within her—at least for the time being—something of a "live for the moment" philosophy. She was acting on impulse. She was going where the mood struck her. She wasn't sure that she liked it, but she likewise wasn't entirely sure she didn't like it.

Perhaps those were the parameters of the experiment in which she was engaged. She had become her own test subject.

Lost in her reverie, she suddenly noticed that Rajari was gone.

She jumped up quickly, looking around, and caught a glimpse of him in the street, walking away from the bar with such a brisk step that it was hard to believe he had consumed as much alcohol as he had. Soleta quickly paid her bill and headed out the door. For a panicked moment (at least, as panicked as Soleta ever allowed herself to be) she thought she had lost him. But then she saw him just disappearing around the corner. She wasn't entirely sure why she had been at all disconcerted. He simply seemed to be heading back to his apartment. It wasn't as if she didn't know where that was.

Nevertheless, she started after him, moving briskly. Considering that he wasn't observing her, she wasn't at all worried about him spotting her following him.

Still, there was no telling whether Rajari would head off in some other direction. Who knew? Perhaps he was preparing to leave Catalina City, and the bar was his way of passing the time until his shuttle left. If he never returned to the apartment, if he left the city at this point . . .

Her one fear had been that Rajari would leave Titan before she could get there. That they would cross in the night, as it were. She had checked beforehand, and there had been no record of anyone by his name leaving the colony, but naturally that was hardly conclusive. She could not take the chance that, after having arrived on Titan while he was still in residence, she would then accidentally let Rajari slip through her fingers simply because she wasn't moving quickly enough.

So Soleta picked up speed until she was practically sprinting down the street. She rounded the corner of a building and didn't see Rajari on the street. She slowed, trying to figure out which way he had gone, and as she did so she passed an alleyway.

Before she knew what had happened, a dark figure stepped out of the alley and grabbed her by the throat.

The hand clasped around her, cutting off her air. Her eyes widened as she saw Rajari's implacable stare, even in the alley made even darker by the darkness that was already descending upon the city. Soleta croaked helplessly, brought her hand up to try and apply the Vulcan nerve pinch. Her right hand clamped down . . . on a collar made of some sort of metal, hidden beneath the shabby cloth of his loose-fitting shirt. She couldn't get into any sort of contact with the nerves of the skin beneath.

"A very convenient bit of armament," Rajari told her, his voice low and even. She could smell the alcohol on his breath, but it had done nothing to weaken him as near as she could tell. His hand closed even more tightly on her throat. "Vulcans make excellent assassins, you know. There aren't many of them . . . but the ones that exist are lethal. One has to be prepared. Now . . . there'll be one less."

He shoved his full weight against her, pinning her. She was crushed against the wall, his free hand holding her right arm stationary, her left arm immobilized by the positioning of her own body. She had a phaser shoulder-holstered inside her jacket, but she couldn't get at it. She tried to push him away. No luck. He was too strong. The alley stank of decay and garbage, and she envisioned her body lying there for days without anyone noticing. Rajari adjusted his grip ever so slightly, probably to begin the final chore of crushing her breathing apparatus completely so that she would suffocate right there in the alley. When he did so, however, he inadvertently allowed one bit of air into her lungs, giving her the opportunity to blurt out just one word.

"*T'Pas*," she managed to get out before speech was one again not an option.

But it was a name that snagged Rajari's attention. He tilted his head. "What do you know of T'Pas," he inquired sharply.

Soleta rasped at him, unable to say anything.

He glanced around as if checking to make sure that there was no one else around. When he saw that they were alone, he eased up slightly. "I said what do you know—"

"I heard you," she rasped out. "She was my . . ."

Shut up!

The warning came unbidden in her head, but the moment she heard it she knew that it was good advice. Under no circumstance should she tell Rajari that she was T'Pas's daughter. He would probably kill her right then and there as part of his campaign of vengeance. Of course, he would very likely kill her anyway. It wasn't as if there was going to be a guaranteed answer in this circumstance. She was just going to have to play it instinctively. This, of course, might very well be a seriously foolish move, because thus far her instincts had gotten her into an alleyway with the hand of a killer Romulan on her throat.

All of this went through her mind in a split instant and then she said, "—my good friend. You . . . you sent her that communiqué . . . you—"

But he didn't seem to register anything she had said

beyond the first sentence. "Was your good friend? You're not anymore?"

"She's dead."

He released her instantly.

Her hand went to her throat, rubbing it reflexively. She sagged against the wall, sucking air gratefully into her lungs. She was now free to go for her phaser, but she held off on doing so since he was making no aggressive move toward her. As a matter of fact, Rajari seemed about as far from threatening as he could possibly be. He looked as if she had smacked him with a hammer. He was gazing in her general direction, but she might as well not have been there for all that he was focusing on her. "Dead?" he said tonelessly. "How? She was . . . so young . . . ?"

"A virus. Unexpected." Her voice was still raspy, and she suspected it would remain that way for some hours.

"When?"

"Five years ago."

He shook his head and then laughed softly. "Five years. It's not as if I just missed her. Still . . ." He looked up at her. "Her friend, you say? You are . . . were . . . her friend?"

"Yes," she rasped.

"And you came all this way just to tell me that she was dead."

"No. I came here because of the communiqué . . . the message you sent."

"Oh yes. So you said." He sounded quite distracted. "How foolish that must have sounded. Endeavoring to make amends and apologies to a woman long dead."

"Amends and apologies?" Despite her raspiness, there was fire in Soleta's voice. "You threatened her."

"Threatened her? Are you insane?"

There was no hint of duplicity in his voice. His face was open and, amazingly, sincere-looking. Mere moments ago he had worn the dead-eyed expression of one who not only was capable of killing, but would do so with no second thought, no doubt, no regrets. Now he seemed . . . vulnerable somehow. It was hard for Soleta to figure out which one was the real Rajari . . . or if either of them was. "The message you sent . . . you spoke of unfinished business . . . of seeing her in the afterlife."

"You cannot be serious. You thought that a threat?"

"What else could it have been?"

"Child, you know nothing." Now there was a bit of the sharpness in his voice. "The contents of the message were not for you. You know nothing of—"

"I know you raped her," she blurted out.

He seemed taken aback, and his face clouded. "So . . . you do know that. She told you that, did she?"

No, you told me that, she wanted to shout at him. It was painfully obvious that he did not recognize her, did not remember her from years back on the *Aldrin.* It wasn't surprising. The circumstances were very different. She herself was different. How innocent she must have looked back then, how clueless. She was also wearing her hair quite differently from the way she had been then, and she had taken the precaution of removing the IDIC hairpin. If he'd seen that, he would have been far more likely to make a connection.

"Yes. She did."

He backed away from her, bumped up against the other side of the alley, and simply stood there. She said nothing. She wasn't sure what there was to say.

"I was trying to apologize to her," he said.

She blinked in confusion. "What?"

"Apologize to her . . . for what I had done to her."

"I . . . do not understand," said Soleta. "If that was your desire, why didn't you come right out and say it."

"Because I didn't know who might see the message," he said. "What if her mate saw it before she did. I have no idea whether she ever told him or not. What would you have had me say? 'My dear T'Pas, I very much regret I raped you.' How could I do such a thing to her, particularly if she had managed to conceal it from her husband all these years? So I endeavored to be vague."

"You were so vague that you convinced me you wanted to hurt her."

"That is unfortunate. I would never hurt her . . ."

Soleta's temper flared, and she reined it in. Nevertheless the edge to her voice was still very evident as she said, "You would say that? You, of all individuals?" Unfortunately it came out with more of a croak to her voice than she would have liked.

Rajari looked chagrined. "Yes. Yes, of course, I can see why you would react in that fashion. I, who hurt her so badly, now speak of consideration and feelings. My apologies. I . . ." He shrugged helplessly. "I do not know what else to say."

Nor did Soleta, who had to admit to herself that she was feeling a bit flummoxed at the moment. She had built up this encounter, or one similar to it, in her mind in any variety of ways, but she had never envisioned it going anything like this. She had to remind herself that this person she was facing was a lifelong liar, a vile creature. "You spoke of unfinished business, and of seeing her in the next life. How else was any reasonable person supposed to interpret those comments other than that you were intending to come after her and, very likely, terminate her."

He frowned, and it seemed to Soleta as if he were running the words through his head, reviewing the comments, breaking down the sentences and seeing them through her eyes. "Yes. Yes, I can see where you might think that. Language is such an imprecise business, isn't it. I told her that she deserved more than I gave her. That I was unable to attend to her as I should have, and that I should have handled her differently. I intended it to mean that I should never have treated her so badly in the first place, but I see now that an offensive, even attacking posture could be interpreted from those words. In attempting to leave a situation better than the way I found it, I instead made it worse. What a botched attempt at reparations." He looked closely at Soleta, as if truly seeing her for the first time. "You know . . . you remind me of someone."

"Do I?" Soleta kept her cool. "And who might that be."

"Let me think . . . yes. My sister. You look quite a bit like her, around the eyes and mouth."

"I am not your sister," she said tersely.

"No, of course you are not. She is dead. As dead as T'Pas, I fear."

She had no idea why she said it, but she said "I am sorry for your loss" nevertheless.

"Considering I was trying to strangle you a few minutes ago, that is very generous of you," he said with no hint of irony. "Hopefully my apology to you now will not be as botched as my similar endeavor to T'Pas, but I am sorry that I tried to hurt you. I thought you were, well . . ."

"An assassin." She looked at him curiously. "Why would you be concerned about assassins?"

"One who has been in my profession for so long need always worry about such things."

"And the unfinished business? And the comments about the afterlife?"

He actually seemed amused by her. "You ask a good number of questions. You should be a scientist. My 'unfinished business' will remain my concern alone, if you do not mind . . . or, for that matter, even if you do mind. As for seeing her in the afterlife, well . . . that was not a threat intended to indicate that I was going to send her into it. So you need not have been concerned in that regard." He laughed softly to himself. "You must have been quite a good friend to her, to go to all this effort on behalf of her memory and her still-living mate. That must be why you're here, of course. It is the only possible explanation. If she is dead, as you say, then you must have been concerned that my unquenchable desire for vengeance was going to extend to her mate. You are truly here on his behalf rather than hers. Rest assured, child, he faces no danger from me. It is over. I am over. All of it . . . all of it . . . is over."

He walked away from her, shaking his head slowly, seemingly having forgotten that she was there at all. *Let him go!* the voice in her head said again, but this time she ignored the advice. There was something in his manner, his attitude, that prompted her to call, "What are you talking about? What's over? What did you mean about the afterlife?"

He stopped walking, but did not answer immediately. Instead he simply stood there for a time, then squared his shoulders and turned back to face her. "When I spoke of the afterlife, child, I did not do so meaning that I was going to send her there. I meant that I was going there and was simply going to await her . . . although I suppose now she is awaiting me. She'll very likely be setting up a warm welcome for me. Yet another disincentive for proceeding in that direction, but unfortunately I have not been given much choice in the matter."

"What do you mean?"

"What do I mean? Must I spell it out for you, child?" He grimaced. "Very well. I will simplify it. The reason I said I would see her in the afterlife was because I thought I was going to predecease her. I am dying, child. The incurable, degenerative bone disorder called Hammons syndrome. Do not let my little display of strength just now fool you; the rigors of even the mildest space travel right now would send me into oblivion even faster than I am already going. I am a prisoner of this dying body, and it in turn is a prisoner of this world. I am not going anywhere except into the grave. And I will have no one to mourn for me, no relative to care in the least about my passing. I will look back upon my life, see only the acts of brutality and torment that I have performed, with nothing of consequence to show for my time on this sphere. At the end of my life, I have accomplished nothing of which I can be proud. That is what I have come to realize, that is what motivated me to send a message to T'Pas. Your journey here from wherever it is you came from has been as great a waste as the entirety of my life. You, however, are still relatively young. You will have more chances to accomplish things of worth. I will not. There, young woman. Does that answer your question?"

With that he turned on his heel and strode away from her.

And Soleta knew at that point that everything he had

told her was true. She had no reason to believe it . . . but she did. Which meant that her task here was done, the job settled. She could depart Titan, never look back, and never concern herself one bit with the monstrous brute that had sired her. He was dying? Fine. Her mother would have been happy to hear that. Her father would be happier still. And Soleta was happy. Yes. She was. It didn't matter that he seemed more scared and pathetic than anything else. Whatever was happening to him now was well deserved. She should feel no bit of remorse, no dreg of pity. Under no circumstance should she feel sorry for him, for he had led a foul life. If he was paying for that now, it was certainly no concern of hers.

He stopped.

He turned.

He walked back toward her, and she braced herself. Her hand strayed in the general direction of her phaser, although she made no move to pull it from concealment. Rajari stopped several feet away.

"Would you care for a drink?" he asked. "I noticed you sitting in the bar, staring at me, for a small eternity. In that time, you had exactly one drink. I thought you might like another. It might ease your throat."

"Considering you did the damage, it is hardly generous of you to make the offer."

"Very well." He shrugged, turned and walked away.

Let him go! If you have an ounce of brains in your head, let him go! Have nothing more to do with him! Depart Titan immediately and do not look back.

She headed after him.

He presented an interesting subject. If she could detach herself from the emotional turmoil of the situation—which she should certainly be able to do, as a

Vulcan—then she had to admit that he presented a potential for an interesting psychological study. Which was, admittedly, a bit far afield for her. Then again, one does not learn and grow if one isn't willing to take chances.

She caught up with him within a block. He seemed surprised to see her . . . but perhaps not too surprised. "You have reconsidered my offer?"

"You remain a vile and contemptible brute. I will accompany you for a brief time only to get a greater peace of mind in ascertaining whether you pose a threat to the mate of T'Pas."

"Very wise," said the dying Romulan. And they headed back to the tavern.

McHENRY & KEBRON

ZAK KEBRON WAS NOT particularly happy. He was not especially inclined to verbalize about it, for it was not Kebron's way to articulate that which annoyed him. However, it was very clear to McHenry that Kebron was getting somewhat impatient.

No less so, obviously, was Adulux, and as the moons shone down upon them, he was far less reticent than Kebron when it came to making his feelings known.

"This is getting us nowhere!" Adulux said in exasperation. In truth, McHenry couldn't entirely blame him. Every night, for a week, the odd trio of McHenry, Kebron, and Adulux had come out to the spot where Adulux's wife had last been seen. Initially, they had simply remained right where they were. Over time, however, they had expanded the parameters of their search area, although "search" might have been too strong a word. McHenry wasn't actually searching. He was simply waiting. McHenry's nature was such that he could have gone on doing the same thing for months, but Adulux was not quite as sanguine. "Nowhere!" he repeated. "How is this going to get Zanka back?"

"Patience," McHenry said calmly. He was seated on a rock, gazing serenely at the sky. "These things require patience."

"You can afford patience!" Adulux told him. "You do not have the Sentries coming around your home, questioning you over and over! They still believe that I inflicted some sort of evil against Zanka!" He put his hands to his head and shook it in frustration. "I should simply have jumped off the roof when I wanted to!"

"You still can," Kebron pointed out.

"Kebron, that's not helping," said McHenry.

Adulux let out a grunt of frustration and stomped off to a far side of the clearing. Kebron now moved over toward McHenry and said in a low voice, "He's right. This is getting us nowhere."

"This is a stakeout, Zak," McHenry replied, equally softly. "You're a security head. I'm surprised you know nothing of old-style police procedures."

"I do know of it. I know of projectile vomiting as well. That does not mean I'd care to experience it," Kebron replied.

"Look, you asked me to come along on this. I wasn't looking for this assignment. I was ready to be a bum, remember? You're the one who came to me. You said you wanted backup on this. That you wanted someone who would be the 'brains' to your 'brawn.' "

"And this is using your brains?"

"Yes!"

"Tragic," Kebron said with a shrug. Then he looked

at his shoulders in mild surprise, still unaccustomed to having a body that did such things as shrug in a noticeable manner. It was the little things that he was still having trouble adjusting to. For instance, although he did not have much of a neck, it was still there nevertheless. But he still wasn't in the habit of turning his head; instead he angled his entire torso when he wanted to look around.

"Perhaps you're right," McHenry said finally. "Perhaps we've been too complacent. There might be patterns that we can detect. If nothing happens tonight, we'll speak to more of the locals during the day, and see what else we can find."

"Joy," said Kebron.

"If it really bothers you, Zak, we can just go back to Nechayev and tell her that some idiotic students from a university noted for its arrogant student body got the best of two Starfleet representatives." He squared himself off against Kebron and said challengingly, "Do you want to make the call . . . or should I?"

Kebron stared at him for a long moment. Then he grunted.

The rest of the evening passed without incident, and when the sun came up the next morning, Kebron and McHenry set to work.

KALINDA

S<small>I</small> C<small>WAN</small> <small>HAD ALMOST DRIFTED</small> to sleep when he heard
her scream.

He had been up rather late this night, pacing the quar-
ters that had been so generously provided by the United
Federation of Planets. No one had forgotten that he had
wound up as ambassador on the *Excalibur* through a
rather dubious series of events, including stowing away.
But he had more than proven his worth since that time,
and the spacious suites that the UFP had given him as a
place to reside on Earth had been more than kind. Gods
knew it was not remotely as luxurious as what he had
been accustomed to on Thallon. On the other hand,
Thallon was now little more than floating bits of space
dust, and his suites were a substantial cut above his accommodations on the *Excalibur.*

Nevertheless, he'd felt a bit at loose ends, still trying
to determine these past weeks just how he might serve

in some useful capacity. This night he had been up rather late, staring restlessly out at the stars, dwelling on the fact that he had roamed them practically at will. He sorely wanted to get back out there, continue in his endeavors to pull back together the scattered worlds of the fallen Thallonian Empire. Until such time that a ship was assigned there, however, he quite simply lacked the backing to do so. So he was left to ponder his future role in life.

He had drifted to sleep while doing so, sitting upright in a fairly comfortable chair as the starlight danced in the night sky. His last thought before falling asleep was how, when one was out in space, the stars didn't twinkle at all. It was a totally different experience out there, one that seemed purer somehow. To those who continually resided on a planet's surface, a star's twinkling was inviting. To those such as Si Cwan who had strode among them at all, twinkling was an abomination, a corruption of the purity of a star's light.

Then the scream had ricocheted, like a thing alive, down the short hallway that led to Kalinda's room.

Si Cwan had snapped to full wakefulness in a little under five seconds. Interestingly, before those five seconds had passed he had already leaped to his feet, charging down the hallway while his brain worked frantically to catch up with his body. "I'm coming, Kally!" he shouted, absolutely positive that someone had broken into their home. His mind started ticking off lists of enemies who might be making some sort of strike against them. Kalinda had been missing in the wilds of Thallonian space for so long, and they had only recently been reunited. There was no way that Si Cwan was going to allow his little sister to be snatched from his bosom once more. There was absolutely no question in his mind: Whomever he found in her room, he would put the intruder down like a wild animal if any harm were done to Kalinda.

He thundered into her room, poised and battle-ready . . .

. . . and found a frightened young woman, and nothing else.

Kalinda had remembered the visions she'd suffered when the Quiet Place had called to her, in the way that one might remember something that happened to someone else. She had literally been another person at that time, brainwashed into believing that she had another name, another identity.

They had not come to her while she was awake . . . at least, not at first. Instead they had haunted her dreams, first occasionally and then every single night. Her days slowly developed into long, tortured witnessing of the sun as it passed inexorably through the sky, bringing her to the inevitable night of more writhing about, knotting of sheets, profuse sweating and torturous sessions of dreams. As time had passed, even her daylight hours began to lose their safety. The visions would dance just below her subconscious, and she knew they were there if she chanced to turn her mind's eye in that general direction.

Finally, unable to resist the siren call, she had gone to the Quiet Place. She had been confronted with the secrets and curiosities of that most mysterious of worlds, a place that some felt was haunted by the tortured souls of the dead. She had never quite been sure of the truth of that, or even the truth of what she had fully experienced. What she had known, though, was that once she had come through that place, she thought she would never have to deal with it again.

She had been right . . . to a certain degree.

But every so often, she would wake up in that sort of cold sweat that told her she had seen True Things in the night. True Things that were happening, or were going to happen.

Tonight . . . tonight she awoke with a True Thing dream that was more violent, more frightening than anything she could recall.

The blood pumped so violently through her that not only could she feel her heart, but also she sensed the synchronized thudding of the veins against her forehead.

A hand rested on her shoulder and it startled her so that she let out a yelp of alarm. She swung a small fist and tried to knock the hand away, but the hand was joined by a second on her other shoulder, and now she twisted violently against it. "Let me go!" she cried out, "let me—!"

"Kally!" It took a few moments for Si Cwan's voice to penetrate a mind numbed with terror. "Kally, it's me! Calm down! Kalinda!"

"Cwan . . . ?" She managed to find her voice.

"Yes."

"Oh, gods," she said, clearing her throat since it was so choked with emotion. She threw her arms around him tightly, trying to steady the shuddering in her chest. "Oh, gods, I'm so glad . . ."

"What's wrong? What happened?"

She looked him in the eye and said, "A dream."

Clarification might well have been required for someone else. After all, to awaken in a state of near panic simply because one has had a bad dream is generally considered to be within the province of a small child, not an adult young woman. But Si Cwan knew immediately, from the great significance she had attached to that simple word, that there was more at stake here than just a simple nightmare that a slumbering id might have conjured.

"A dream," he said. "One of those kinds?"

She nodded, looking a bit forlorn.

"I was unaware that you continued to have any along those lines." He sat on the edge of the bed, her immediate intense anxiety clearly having passed. "You had said nothing to me of them."

"I did not wish to worry you," she told him. "No harm was resulting from them. They were minor, affording me no true fear. It wasn't as if the Quiet Place was summoning me back . . ."

She had had to say it, of course, because that was naturally going to be his first concern. She knew she'd been right when she saw him, ever so slightly, let out a sigh of relief. Even so, he said, "You're certain about that?"

She nodded.

He ran a sympathetic finger along the underside of her chin. "Do you wish to tell me about it?"

She said slowly, "I am not convinced enough that I fully understand it myself to be able to explain it properly."

"You can only try."

"I know. What I saw was the vision of . . . of a man. There were many Thallonians around . . . but he himself was not. He was . . . I do not know what he was, truthfully. He was quite short, and yet seemed taller, for reasons that I do not understand. He had the oddest hair, it was . . ."

96

"A ring."

She blinked in surprise. "Yes! Almost like a crest that circled his head perfectly. It was white. And he had a mustache that was as white as his hair, with long ends. He looked a bit human, but he had sort of . . ."

"Fins. At the sides of his head. And red eyes."

"Yes!" She couldn't quite believe it. "Very red. I could see from the way they were staring." She had been sitting in bed, but now she was on her feet, too amazed to remain in bed like a child. "Who was he, Si Cwan? Obviously, you know him . . ."

"He was not a Thallonian, you were correct in that," Si Cwan said. "His name is Jereme, he was from the race known as the Kotati, and he was our teacher."

"Teacher?" Then her face cleared. "Yes! Yes, I remember now!"

It was not unusual for Kalinda to have difficulty recalling things that happened far in her past. Those who had brainwashed her had done a superb job, and there were some things that were simply a massive effort for her to recall. Original memories had been damaged, unfortunately, and Kalinda was working a sort of catch-up effort to pull them together. "He was our self-defense teacher. Well . . . yours," she amended. "I was so young . . . I was allowed to sit in on some of your classes, though."

"Jereme was the only non-Thallonian individual who ever acted in any sort of teaching capacity for the royal family." Si Cwan smiled. Clearly the memories alone were enough to fill him with a warm, nostalgic glow.

"You look so happy," Kalinda told him. "You always look happy when you're thinking or talking about the past."

"I am. Sometimes I think that's the only time I am happy."

"That's so sad," said Kalinda. "You should be able to draw happiness from looking toward the future. If you don't, and if you can't, then what's the point of living it?"

He looked at her with dark suspicion. "You are supposed to be my little, know-nothing sister. How dare you bandy about sentiments which indicate wisdom beyond your years."

It took her a moment to realize that he had his tongue planted firmly in his cheek when he had spoken, but when she did, she bowed slightly and said, "At least one of us has wisdom."

Then Si Cwan frowned, drawing together the rest of his recollections about his old teacher. "Despite the fact that he was not Thallonian, Jereme was considered one of the greatest self-defense experts alive. He taught self-defense not only in the capacity of the body, but of the mind. Since he was non-Thallonian, he came and went as he wished. He had teaching facilities in several different locations. Schooling with Jereme was unlike anything I experienced with any other teachers. There were no regular, formal, scheduled lessons. Whenever he would show up, that was when the lessons would be. In a way, particularly when I was growing up, it made every day a little more exciting. Because when I would wake up, I would always wonder, Is today a day that Jereme will show up?"

"He meant that much to you?"

"Oh yes. He taught me how to think, how to move. Look at me, Kalinda. I'm not exactly an easy-to-miss individual. But thanks to Jereme, I can move across a room without being seen, given the right circumstances."

"The right circumstances being all the lights shut off."

"You, young woman, are going to get yourself into

trouble someday with that acid wit of yours. But you have not told me; what was Jereme doing in this dream of yours."

She looked down. "I . . . was trying to put off saying it."

"Saying what?" His face clouded. "Kalinda . . . if there is something I should know, delaying it will not make it easier to hear. What did you see?"

"There was . . ." She licked her lips, which had suddenly gone dry. "There was . . . blood . . ."

Si Cwan steadied himself. It was important for him to remember that this was not a trained clairvoyant or prognosticator. This was his young sister, still haunted by recent experiences, still trying to adapt to whatever abilities she might or might not possess. It was vital that he say and do nothing to upset her, no matter what it was she said or thought. "Where was there blood?" he said with impressive calm.

"On him . . . on . . . everything. Everywhere." Her breath caught in her chest and she worked to calm herself as she continued, "He was lying on the floor, and he was just staring at me. It was as if there was some message in his eyes that he was trying to convey to me . . . except there was no life in there to do it, so all I was seeing was . . . was the lost hope. The blood was thickest on his chest, and there was a spreading pool of it under him, and on the walls, as if it had just . . . just sprayed and . . ."

She stopped. She couldn't say any more. "Kalinda," Si Cwan started to say, putting a hand out to her.

She batted it away with surprising ferocity. "Are you going to make me say more? Do I have to keep describing it! Gods, Cwan, it's worse than if I'd just seen it with my own eyes! I felt it, too! You have no idea what it's like . . . you can't ever know, just feeling something like that, like acid splashed on your soul, it's . . . the . . . it burns away, it . . ."

He reached for her then, saying nothing, but pulling her toward him. For a moment she resisted, and then she allowed herself to almost collapse against him, sobbing. She sobbed violently, clutching at him. "I'm sorry . . . I'm sorry . . . I should be strong . . . I should be . . . and . . . and you . . . he was your favorite teacher, he . . . I'm sorry . . ."

He said nothing, merely rocked her back and forth, waiting for the hysteria to play itself out. Finally, when she was showing signs of calming, he said, "Now listen to me, Kally . . . listen carefully . . . you don't know for sure that what you saw was true, do you."

"What are you saying? That I'm lying? That—"

"No, no. Not at all." He smiled. "I'm not saying that. Not at all. But what you saw, what you 'know' from your dream . . . do you know it as surely as that you know you're sitting here with me, for instance?"

"I . . . I suppose not," she said uncertainly.

"There, you see?" He smiled gently. "There are true dreams . . . but there are also false ones. You are young yet, and unschooled in these matters. So before we do any wringing of hands, tearing of shirts, and tragic songs of times past, the best thing to do is to get in touch with Jereme and see how he is."

"How will we do that?" The notion that Jereme might actually be alive, that her dream might be the product of simply an overactive imagination, was somewhat heartening to her. "Will it require a quest? Will we have to roam the systems until we find where Jereme currently is? Perhaps we'll face overwhelming odds, and have to fight our way through in—"

"I was actually thinking more along the lines of sending a communiqué to him at his school on Pulva, where he lives in semiretirement."

"Oh." She was significantly crestfallen upon hearing that. "That's where he is? You're sure?"

"I cannot anticipate everything. If he's gone off to visit friends, he would not be in residence. But to the best of my knowledge, he shut down all his teaching facilities save for his first, the one on the world of Pulva. There he maintains a small school, filled with dedicated students. He still teaches, of course. Nothing could stop him from teaching."

"Except for being dead."

Si Cwan's face darkened, and instantly Kalinda regretted the words. He obviously sensed her chagrin, however, and waved it off. "Do not concern yourself, Kally. I am quite sure he will be fine. You'll see." He sighed deeply. "Come . . . I doubt either of us will get much sleep the rest of the evening. I'll send the message immediately and then perhaps we'll play a few rounds of Pente. I have not beaten you at that for some time."

"Aren't we insufferably sure of ourselves."

"Yes. We are." Except that it was obvious to anyone who looked close enough that, when it came to his opinion as to the current status of his old teacher, Si Cwan was anything but sure of himself, insufferably or otherwise.

Despite her determination to await a response, Kalinda wound up falling asleep around midmorning. It was not particularly surprising; she had, after all, had far less than a good night's sleep. Much to her relief, her slumber was uninterrupted. It was as if, having had the awful vision in her sleep and then having told Si

Cwan about it, she had essentially gotten it "out of her system." Her dreams were harmless, even happy things, including a pleasant one in which her beloved Xyon was still hale and hearty and alive, traipsing around the galaxy somewhere and having all manner of adventure. Even as she slept, she wished with all her heart that that one was true, and part of her mind even told her it was. But she knew better, even though in the dream Xyon leaned toward her to kiss her. The moment their lips came together, the dream dissolved around her, tissue in water, and she wished that she could recapture the soggy shreds and reweave them into a pleasant sleeping fantasy once more. Unfortunately for her, such was not possible.

She had fallen asleep reclined on the couch, in the midst of the fourteenth game of Pente against her brother. She was almost certain that she'd actually been in the process of winning, but she couldn't be absolutely sure since she was falling asleep in the course of that particular match and might have just been dreaming that she was on the verge of triumph. When she awoke, it was still daytime, but the sun had moved further along its path and the long shadows of midafternoon were stretching across the parlor.

Si Cwan was seated opposite her. He didn't appear to notice that she was waking up. Instead he was simply sitting there, holding an almost empty glass in his right hand, idly tapping his index finger against it and making a rhythmic "plink" sound. He had not changed out of his nightclothes. He was just sitting and staring.

Si Cwan didn't seem to hear her at first, and then finally took notice of her and shifted his gaze to her.

He said nothing.

He didn't have to. She knew just by looking at him.

"It's true. Isn't it," she whispered.

Very slowly, as if the weight of the world was on the back of his skull, Si Cwan nodded his head.

She was off the couch, on her knees before him, clutching his hand tenderly. "Gods . . . Si Cwan, I'm so sorry . . ."

"It was just as you described it," he said distantly. "Actually, they found him that way two days ago. But they have not yet made the information public. Searching to see if he has any relatives whom they can inform first." He shook his head, still looking stunned. "They're wasting their time. He had no one in the universe except his students. They were his family. They were somewhat dumbfounded that I knew about it."

"What happened? I mean, I doubt it was an accident . . ."

"You doubt? You *doubt?*" He made no effort to keep the utter incredulity from his voice. "Chest carved, blood everywhere, and you 'doubt' it was an accident? Unless, what . . . ? You're holding out a possibility that somehow he managed to . . . I don't know . . . kill himself in the most gory, disgusting way possible. Or perhaps it was an accident; he stumbled and fell onto a knife forty-seven times."

Her eyes glistening, partly from anguish and partly from anger, "I—"

But she got no further, because he put up a hand and on his face was a genuine look of utter contrition. "I'm sorry," he said, his voice barely above a whisper. "I'm sorry, Kally, I'm . . . not dealing with this very well, I'm afraid. That's no excuse, though. I am . . . very, very sorry."

She shook her head in a dismissive way, telling him with her body language alone that he shouldn't be concerned over his outburst. Then she took a deep breath and said, "Do they have any idea who . . . did it? Will they get back to us when they have a better idea?"

"No, they're not getting back to us. They won't have to, because I'm going to Pulva. I've already booked passage. I think you should stay here."

"Like hell."

"I had a feeling that would be your response, but I had to try. I booked passage for two."

"And what will we do once we get there?"

"Do?" There was an edge in his voice that chilled her. "We find out who did this thing. We find out who killed our teacher. And once we do, then I guarantee you: He will be the one whose life becomes one long, horrible waking dream . . . for as long as I leave him alive to dream it. Which, I guarantee, will not be for very long at all."

SOLETA

"YOU SAW . . . GOD? You aided the Federation because you saw God?"

Soleta was making no effort whatsoever to hide her incredulity. Rajari downed the contents of his glass while she stared at him. "You saw God?"

"Are you going to be saying that many more times? Because you're becoming a bit repetitive."

"How do you expect me to react when you tell me this, Rajari?" Soleta had no idea what to make of this. Sitting in a tavern on Titan, being informed by a creature whom she hated more than any other in the entirety of the galaxy that some sort of Supreme Being had revealed Himself to him. "You say to me that a Romulan deity appeared to you, and that was the reason that you chose to provide information and aid to the Federation during the Dominion War. That it had nothing whatsoever to do with a desire to shorten your sentence."

"Correct."

"May I ask why you said nothing of this to the Federation?"

"How do you know I didn't?"

"Because," she said with conviction, "there would likely have been some mention of it in Federation rec . . . ords . . ." Her voice trailed off as she realized her error.

Too late. Rajari's eyes narrowed and he said, "And how did you get access to Starfleet records? Are you Starfleet yourself? You very likely are. You have that air of command arrogance about you."

"There are any number of ways that such records can be accessed," she said, sidestepping the question.

She was going to continue beyond that, but to her surprise and relief, Rajari nodded and shrugged. "That is true enough. Any means of information that one person can build, another can crack. I had been wondering how it was that you were able to find me. You see, though, my reason for paranoia. If you found me, others can."

"What others?"

"Any number of others. The Cardassians would very likely have little love for me, were they to learn of my involvement—however humble—in the war. Then there are my own people, the Romulans."

"The Romulans? Why would they—?"

"Old enmities."

"I think your choice of the word 'paranoia' is apt," Soleta said, clearly skeptical. "What you did is not especially different from what the Romulans, as a race, did during the Dominion War. You helped the Federation. How can they condemn you while condoning their own activities? As for the Cardassians, their homeworld is in a shambles. Certainly they have other things to worry about besides the activities of one man."

"There is more to it than that, young one. Some grudges go far deeper than mere political alliances. I have had . . . disagreements, shall we say . . . with certain powerful individuals for whom I performed smuggling chores. There are always disagreements, young one. Smuggling is a high-risk profession with plenty of opportunities to upset customers. Unfortunately I have offended my share. As problematic as a voyage through space would be for me, I might risk it if it meant returning to my homeworld. I would rather end up dead there than living here. But it would be pointless; my government made it quite clear to the Federation that I am considered an undesirable there. If nothing else, they know that I turned over information on the Cardassians, and they fear what I might have told the Federation about the Romulans as well. They believe that I would have said or done anything to gain my freedom."

"When in fact your actions were motivated by devotion to a higher power," Soleta said dryly.

"That is right. That is exactly right." If he heard the faint sarcasm in her tone, he gave no indication of it. "Oh, make no mistake, I was not totally friendless. I have some allies back on Romulus, people who fought the good fight to try and aid in my return. But there are others, an assortment of senators and proconsuls, who have been in power for so long that they have an iron grip on what happens and does not happen. They have no love for me, and they blocked all attempts by my allies to permit my return. Indeed, my allies garnered some trouble for themselves. One or two of them were even declared traitors and executed, simply because they tried to arrange for a dying man to return home. A great price to pay for friendship, do you not think so?"

"It must anger you greatly. Make you want to avenge them . . ."

"Avenge them?" He smiled sadly. "What good would that do? It would not bring them back. If there is one thing I understand, it is that. Oh, once I would have had exactly the attitude that you suggest. I would have sought vengeance. But one cannot find a higher power and still believe that vengeance is anything except an empty pastime that accomplishes nothing."

She considered it a moment. "What God appeared to you, if I may ask?"

"No one God. It was . . ." His eyes shone with the memory of it. "It was all of them. All the gods in the Romulan pantheon. They did not appear to me, exactly. It was more that they . . . entered me. Entered my heart, my soul. I was lying there on my rather shabby bunk in the Federation prison camp where I was interred. I was depressed, despondent. And suddenly . . ." He smiled beatifically. "I wasn't."

Soleta couldn't help but think that, if he was sincere, then what she was seeing was very moving. If he was lying, then it was a stunning acting job. "And yet, as I mentioned, you said nothing of this to your captors."

"Why would I want to? They most very likely would not have believed me. Indeed, I have spoken to no one of this . . . until you. You seem to be someone I can trust."

"You still no longer think I am an assassin."

"No. I turned my back on you and walked away, twice. Either time, you could have shot me with that phaser you have hidden in your jacket."

Her jaw twitched slightly in irritation. "You're very observant."

"I have been known to be so."

"May I ask, if you are dying, why are you so concerned about assassins? Why should a dead man be concerned about dying?"

He scratched his chin thoughtfully and said, "I suppose it is the principle of the thing. To lose my life is one thing. To have it forcibly taken from me . . . I do not like that notion. If nothing else, I have no desire to give my enemies that sort of satisfaction."

They were silent for a time. Then Rajari said, "You do not believe me, do you. That I have found the gods . . . or they found me, depending upon how you wish to look at it."

"It is a bit outside my general field of endeavor," Soleta said. "As you surmised, I am a scientist by trade. Science and personal theological revelations do not generally mesh very well."

"Delicately put. But it is the truth that I am telling you."

"The truth as you perceive it."

"What more does any of us possess than that?" he asked with a shrug. "When the gods came into me, I knew then and there that I had to change. That once that knowledge had been revealed to me, I could no longer go on as I had been. I had to make every effort possible to make amends for what I had done. In aiding the Federation against the Cardassians, I hoped to bring about an end to the war—and, as a consequence, peace—that much sooner. It was only then that I was diagnosed with my disease. The gods can be fiercely ironic at times. They place into me a realization of the life I have led, and a desire to atone for it . . . but at the same time, they foist upon me this illness. Repentance is mine . . . but only for the limited period that they provide it for me. One almost has to wonder what the point is."

"Perhaps the gods . . . if such they be . . . feel that it is better late than never," suggested Soleta.

"Perhaps. It is futile to speculate, I suppose. We are not to question the ways of the gods."

"How eminently convenient for the gods" was Soleta's wry observation.

"Spoken like a true skeptic."

"I am someone who learns through observation. The existence of God, or gods, hinges not upon observation or quantifiable study, but upon faith. My faith is in science."

"The universe, child, is too varied and multifaceted a thing to place the entirety of one's faith in anything," Rajari said. "If I have learned any one thing, it is that. You must leave yourself open to all experiences, for you never know what is going to present itself. A universe where anything is possible is a far more interesting place, don't you think?"

He smiled at her.

He is a monster. A beast. He raped your mother. Do not trust him. Do not see something of your own smile, which you always hide, in his face. Perhaps his gods

Your gods. You are half Romulan.

. . . his gods choose to provide guidance and direction, but you are under no obligation to provide him anything. Get off Titan. Now. Before it's too late.

"I do not even know your name," Rajari said abruptly. "You have the advantage of me. What is your name?"

DON'T TELL HIM THAT!

"Soleta."

You are a fool and an imbecile, and I'm not going to waste time talking to you anymore. And with that, Soleta's inner voice stalked away.

"What will you do now, Soleta? Now that you have ascertained that I present no threat, will you depart? Or will you remain for a time?"

"What reason have I to stay?"

Rajari looked down for a moment, then back at her. "I do not have much longer," he said. "A month. Two at most. The end, when it comes, will come quickly. My body will virtually collapse upon itself. Having someone to talk to . . . from time to time . . . might be nice."

"You cannot be serious. You cannot possibly think that I am, in any way, your friend." She shook her head. "Whatever you think you have become now, Rajari, I am still more than aware of what you were. That cannot be overlooked or forgiven, no matter how hard I try."

"Spoken as someone who hasn't tried at all, of course."

"That is not the point."

"Why do we not make it the point? Think of it another way, then. You wish to ascertain the safety of the mate of T'Pas. For all you know, I still pose a threat. After all, when one is dying, one does not have to be concerned about long-term consequences. But if you remain here until I am dead, you will then know first-hand, beyond any doubt, that whatever threat I may have posed is over."

"That is true enough," she admitted.

"Furthermore, you will have the chance to see me suffer. You will be able to see that the one who brought such strife upon T'Pas has come to his own horrible, fitting end. That will bring you some measure of satisfaction, will it not?"

She tried to decide if, in fact, it would. She was somewhat relieved to find that the answer was no, and she said as much.

He shrugged once more. "Have it your way, then. I will tell you what: I am going to leave now. I will return to my home, such as it is. I will return to this very table at precisely this time tomorrow. If you are here, fine. If you are not here, fine. I leave it in your hands. Yours . . . and the gods'."

He rose from the table then, bowed slightly with his fingers interlaced, and left the bar.

It was at that point that Soleta knew it was time for her to leave. Rationalizations were already running rampant through her head. Here was a chance to make a fascinating scientific study of the nature of evil. Was anyone truly beyond redemption? Was it possible for the most despicable of creatures to change his nature?

And what of Soleta herself? The knowledge that she was half-Romulan had almost destroyed her. It had certainly forever corrupted her abilities to properly use the Vulcan disciplines that had been drilled into her. This would be an opportunity for her to fully study and understand the lineage that flowed within her blood, that she had tried to push away all this time. In getting a better grasp of the Romulan mind-set—particularly the mind-set of her biological father—it might serve to make her a better officer, a better person. It might—

Her internal voice, despite its earlier resolution to the contrary, came roaring back with a vengeance.

Are you insane? He RAPED YOUR MOTHER! Get the HELL OUT OF THERE! He's not a matter of scientific curiosity! He's not a means of self-exploration!

He's a BEAST, and all the rationalizations to excuse this morbid curiosity with your origins are not going to change that! Leave! Leave immediately! Leave right now! Leave yesterday if it is a temporal option! Leave, Soleta, right now. In the name of your mother's memory, in the name of everything you hold dear, SET ASIDE YOUR INSATIABLE CURIOSITY, JUST THIS ONCE, AND GET THE HELL OUT OF HERE!

When he showed up the next evening at the appointed time, she was not there.

He took his place at the table where they had once been, ordered a drink, and sat there contemplating it. And when Soleta sat down opposite him, he could not have been more surprised.

"You're late," he said.

"Actually," she replied, "you were early."

And so it began.

McHENRY & KEBRON

ALTHOUGH THERE HAD BEEN little indication in the city of a planet that was under any sort of alien siege, in the rural areas that Kebron and McHenry were investigating, they found a very different story.

The central government, i.e. "the Elders," had very little to do with the area that was primarily farming territory. The farmers of Liten were hardy, rugged individualists who were accustomed to following their own ways and being left to their own devices. They sought no help, and got precisely what they sought.

However, now that the situation had arisen where they were living in constant mortal terror of alien visitation, they would not have minded some sort of government intervention.

"But it's not going to happen," said the Widow Splean, a feisty old Liten woman whom McHenry and Kebron were in the process of interviewing. She was the fifth Liten farmer they were speaking to that day. McHenry had had some initial concern that the Litens would feel some trepidation about talking to strangers. Naturally they would have felt even more trepidation had they known that the strangers they were speaking with were offworld alien beings, but the genetic surgery that had been practiced upon both McHenry and Kebron more than did the job of blending them in with the local populace (although there had been only so much that the Federation scientists could do with Kebron's mass; then again, Kebron *was* supposed to be the muscle for this little expedition, so removing his greatest asset would have been folly).

"You mean the government is never going to take a hand in solving your problem?" McHenry inquired. He had identified himself and Kebron as special investigators aiding a Liten victimized by aliens, and that had been more than enough to prompt the locals to open their doors and hearts to him. He was sitting in the old woman's living room. Kebron, as sociable as a virus, remained outside.

"Never. Because if the Elders decide to investigate, then that automatically means that they're acknowledging a problem exists. That is the last thing they'd want to do." The widow shook her head in annoyance. "We've no one to blame it on except ourselves, really. We're independent stock, we farmers. We were arrogant enough to believe that we could handle whatever nature threw at us. But this . . . this business," and she pointed heavenward apprehensively as if someone or something might descend from the sky at any moment. "This is unnatural. But will the Elders help us now that we really need them? Of course not," she snorted disdainfully. "Why should they stick their necks out when it's not their own lives on the line. People hereabouts are talking about selling their property, moving away. There are 'For sale' signs up all over."

McHenry knew this himself, having seen some of them posted. He leaned forward, concerned. "Has anyone died as a result of all this? Have the aliens killed anyone?"

"Not to my knowledge," she said, shaking her head, which seemed to be teetering uncertainly on her neck. "They just terrorize us. They cause property damage. They make hideous noises. They wave weapons around. It's no way for people to live. No way at all."

"Is there any one place that they tend to appear more than any other?"

"Not really. Because, naturally, if they did, then people would know simply to stay away from that one area, right?" Her light green hands fluttered aimlessly. "They can be anywhere, at any time . . . but the aliens mostly come at night. Mostly."

"Have you ever seen them yourself?"

"No, thank God. But I've heard enough about them."

"How do they arrive? In a burst of light? Or with a sort of . . . whistling sound?" He made a fair imitation of a transporter.

"No." This time she shook her head so vigorously that McHenry thought it was going to fall off entirely. "No, they usually come, so I've heard, in a sort of . . . of spaceship. Blows the grass about something awful, and it moves so quickly. One minute it's there, the next, vroooom! Gone!"

"That's very interesting."

She leaned forward and took his hands in hers. "Can you help us?" she said with an air of desperation. "Can you find a way?"

"I'm sure we can," he said.

Moments later he was outside with Kebron. "Well?" said the disguised Brikar. He was scratching at the back of his neck. The genetic surgery was continuing to sit poorly with him.

"Same story as the others, with minor variations, including those who actually claim to have witnessed the 'aliens.' " He scratched his chin thoughtfully. "The only one whose story doesn't match up, interestingly, is our 'client.' No one else has talked about blinding lights or disappearances."

"Meaning . . ."

"Meaning that there are two possibilities. Either there are two entirely different sets of alien beings visiting this world . . . or else Adulux has been lying. Maybe he really did do something fatal with his wife, and he's been using this entire alien-visitation thing to cover it. To produce some sort of credible cover story. That's how he hoped to get away with it."

"He was going to get away with it by jumping off a roof?" Kebron did not sound entirely convinced.

"Well, maybe by that point he thought he *wasn't* going to get away with it. I don't know."

"No. You don't."

"And you do?" McHenry asked with a flash of impatience.

"No. But you're the one talking."

They had been walking down a dirt road, but now McHenry stopped and turned to face Kebron. "Then feel free to talk," McHenry challenged him. "Tell me what you think. Put forward your own theories. If you think there's any chance of tracking down these idiots who are terrorizing these people, or figure out what's going on, then why don't you come up with it right now instead of just being reticent or sarcastic? Well? Go ahead." He folded his arms.

Kebron reached into his pocket and pulled out a tricorder. It seemed tiny in the palm of his hand.

"Incoming vessels have detectable ion signatures," he said.

McHenry stood there feeling a bit foolish. "Oh. Right. And if they're coming in vessels, like runabouts or something, we can use a tricorder to guide us to wherever they are."

"Yes."

"Instead of just having lengthy stakeouts and being somewhere other than where they are."

"Yes."

"That's, uhm . . ." He rubbed his toe into the ground. "That's actually a very good idea, Zak."

"Yes."

"Wish I'd thought of it."

"You would have."

Feeling slightly mollified by that, McHenry looked up and said, "Do you really think so?"

"No."

When they met up with Adulux that night at the prearranged spot, their client had never looked more shaken. He did not hesitate to tell them why.

"They're going to arrest me," he said, sweat pouring from him like a geyser. "I know it. They questioned me again today, for hours. They're asking all sorts of personal things about my life with Zanka. They're building a case against me, piece by piece, and it doesn't matter to them whether it's true or not. They just want to make an arrest. The last thing they need is for some sort of connection to alien activities

that the Elders want hushed up. I'm going to be arrested. Arrested, tried, condemned, all in the name of
politics. Is there anything in the world worse than
that?"

"Listening to you," said Kebron.

Adulux was so flustered and flummoxed that Kebron's comment didn't even register. McHenry was
grateful for that, and he took the agitated Liten firmly
by the shoulders and said, "You're getting yourself
worked up over nothing. We'll find them. We have a
device that's going to help us." He held up the tricorder.
"This will tell us when the aliens are coming, and
where they're coming to."

"That?" Adulux stared at it. "What is it?"

"It's a gizmo," McHenry told him.

"A gizmo," Adulux said reverently, as if he'd just
been presented with the Holy Grail in a nicely gift-
wrapped box. "Can I hold the gizmo?"

"No," said Kebron, but McHenry had already handed
it to him. Kebron grunted in annoyance. Adulux, for his
part, was turning the tricorder over and over, looking at
it in wonderment. "It's very impressive, the gizmo.
What does this flashing light mean?"

"Flashing light? There shouldn't be a flashing light
unless . . ."

He took the tricorder back immediately and stared at
it. He checked the readings with mounting enthusiasm,
and then said to Kebron, "Company."

"About time."

"Company?" Adulux looked from one to the other,
and then heavenward. "You mean they're . . . it's . . .
they're . . . ?"

"That's right. Coming in fast. I read them at half a
mile, north-northwest. Come on."

Seconds later, they were in Adulux's vehicle and tearing across the road toward the alien touchdown site.

There were three aliens, and as happenstance would have it, they had landed at the farm of the Widow Splean.

The old woman was on the porch of her house, screaming in protest, as the aliens marched about, howling and chattering and laughing uproariously. Two of them had thick, shaggy manes and piglike snouts, and were making hideous snorting noises. The third was blue-skinned with antennae and a look of utter contempt, not only for the world around him, but even to a degree for his companions.

Their ship having landed on the front lawn, they were in the process of demolishing the fence that the Widow Splean had erected with her husband several years previously. It had been the last thing they'd done together before he'd perished in that unfortunate threshing accident. The Widow Splean cried out in frustration, but the aliens paid her no mind.

"I'm getting my blaster!" she shouted at them, and turned to head back into her home to do that very thing. But the blue-skinned alien was cat-quick, and before she had gotten two steps toward her door, he was right there on the porch with her. He grabbed her by the arm and swung her around, and his remarkably white teeth were a stark contrast to the deep blue of his face. "I would not do that if I were you," he said, and he pushed her off the porch. The widow went down with a strangled cry of protest, and he circled her while laughing contemptuously.

His associates, having demolished the fence, were now looking for other sport. Watching them nearby was a benign-looking farm animal, called a Furn, which customarily provided liquid sustenance on a daily basis. It was large and bulky and not really capable of running, even if it had had enough brains to do so in the face of imminent danger. The two piglike aliens headed toward the Furn for the amusement value of tipping the creature over. Once on its side, it would be utterly unable to right itself, and would likely die if someone did not get it back on its feet. The Widow Splean lacked the muscle power to accomplish this feat, and by the time she managed to get any neighbors over to help, the poor beast would likely have been done for. Not that the aliens cared.

"Please, just go! Go away! Don't hurt my Furn! I've never done anything to you!"

The aliens laughed, the two piglike ones placing their hands firmly against the beast and preparing to shove.

And then a firm, clear voice said, "All right. That's enough."

The blue-skinned one, who had the best night vision, saw them first. It was three Litens, including one very large one, emerging from the darkness. The foremost one had spoken. "Leave her alone. Leave them all alone. It's over."

"It's over?" The blue-skinned alien laughed at that. "Nyx, Quiv . . . look at this. We're being told it's over."

"You're not going to bother any of these people—"

"Us," the larger one seemed to correct him.

"—bother any of us ever again," said the Liten who was approaching him with an amazing lack of fear.

"He's coming for you, Krave," said the one named Nyx, calling an amused warning to the blue-skinned alien.

Krave was utterly unintimidated. He knew that the Litens were not only a fearful race, but also physically quite weak. They presented no threat whatsoever to a young Andorian in good shape. Whatever threat this new arrival might be presenting, it was bluster at most. Krave knew he could handle him. "I see him, Nyx."

"You are being given one chance to depart . . . our . . . world without any further mishaps," said the newcomer. "You must swear never to come back. And you must swear to return the female whom you stole."

At that, Krave laughed. "You have no business dictating terms to us. And I don't know what female you're talking about." Then his face darkened, and his antennae twitched in anticipation. "But what I do know is that you have made a very serious mistake. Very serious."

He reached for the newcomer's arm, with the intention of twisting it back and around, and possibly even wrenching it from the socket. For Krave knew that if the Litens were starting to put up resistance, the fun was going to be over.

And that's all they were looking for, really. Fun.

Because the university was just so damned *boring*.

No one could blame them, really, in their search for amusement. Granted, the Kondolf Academy was one of the foremost universities in the quadrant, capable of giving the best education to the best and brightest of the most influential and powerful families in the Federation. But the course work, the discipline, and the sheer crush of study that awaited students at that annoying satellite where they ate, slept, and worked . . . well, where was the fun? The excitement? The humor and drama of life? They were only going to be young once, after all. Shouldn't they be permitted to have their occasional amusements?

And Liten, and the residents thereupon, had provided that amusement.

Krave was no fool, though, nor was he completely amoral. He and his friends weren't out to cause any permanent damage. Just be entertained by the superstitious and fearful Litens, who knew nothing of the great plethora of sentient races out there. Oh, some of the faculty members knew about it, but they turned a blind eye to it. After all, the families from which Krave, Nyx, and Quiv came were among the most influential of all in the Federation, and no one at the school was going to want to gainsay them. Not over something as trivial as the sensitivities of a backward race like the Liten.

In a way, he was almost glad that one of them was offering some degree of resistance. Up to this point, it had been so easy that it was becoming just the tiniest bit dull.

So when he grabbed the newcomer's arm, he was actually looking forward to the challenge.

He stopped looking forward to it when the Liten's arm was abruptly not there.

The Liten had stepped aside, very quickly and smoothly, and the look on his face had been one of casual indifference, as if his mind was a million miles away. As if he was looking not toward what Krave had just done, but rather toward what he was going to do.

Krave, in reaching for the Liten's arm, stumbled as he missed, and before he could recover, the Liten had driven a knee squarely into Krave's midsection. Krave let out a startled gasp and staggered, and then a double-handed smash on the back of his neck sent him to the ground. The Widow Splean let out a joyous whoop as Krave tasted dirt.

He started to scramble to his feet, but his assailant moved with a studied lack of speed, as if he had all the time in the world. As if he knew precisely how long it was going to take Krave to get his breath back, and wasn't devoting a single minute more than was required to deal with the situation. Then his assailant swung a well-placed kick squarely at Krave's head and knocked the Andorian flat again.

By this point, Nyx and Quiv had realized that their companion was in trouble. With a yelp of alarm, they started toward him. They did not get very far at all, for the extremely large Liten had snagged them by the scruff of their necks and, in a stunning display of strength, lifted them off the ground. The two stunned Tellarites (for such they were) kicked furiously at the air, trying to wrestle themselves free and having no luck whatsoever. They emitted loud squeals of protest and hammered at the arms of the big Liten, but he didn't even seem to notice them.

"Kebron!" called the other Liten, as another well-placed kick sent Krave rolling. "Are you okay over there?"

"Of course," said Kebron. He drew his arms apart, holding the Tellarites to either side, and they had about a second to wonder what was about to happen. Then they realized it an instant before it actually occurred, and there was nothing they could do to stop it as Kebron slammed them together in midair. The impact was bone-jarring, and didn't appear to tax him at all, for he separated them and did it again. And again. Each time they crashed into each other, they would emit squeals of protest and howls of rage. But the quality and quantity of their protests started to change, as repeated threats very quickly changed into pleas for mercy.

Krave, in the meantime, had managed to roll far enough away from his opponent to get to his feet. He was not without resources of his own, and although he was in agony, he had enough strength left to still be a threat. He charged toward the Liten who had treated him so poorly, his focus on him and only him.

As a result, he didn't see the large club swinging into his face until it was too late. It completely blindsided him, and struck him so powerfully in the face that it shattered two of his teeth. Agony stabbed through his head and he hit the ground, rolling and moaning.

The Widow Splean, who had been wielding the club, came after him and hit him again and again. The Liten who had, until moments before, been so thoroughly manhandling Krave now seemed to have some degree of pity on the young Andorian. "All right, that's enough," he said to the Widow Splean, and he wrapped his arms around her from behind and hauled her off him. "We don't want to kill him."

"Oh yes we do! Then we can autopsy the remains!"

"No," he said firmly. "You've done your part. Leave them to us." And there was something in his voice that made it quite clear that he was not simply going to allow her to annihilate the Andorian, no matter how much she wanted to and no matter how much he deserved it.

With a frustrated sigh that acknowledged his obvious position on the matter, the Widow Splean backed off as the Liten walked over to the Andorian. "Go on inside, ma'am. We'll take it from here."

"All right," she said reluctantly, although she did take

the opportunity to spit at the fallen Andorian before going into her home.

"Who . . . are you?" gasped out the Andorian as the Liten hauled him to his feet.

"McHenry. Now . . . let's chat with your pals."

McHenry hauled the Andorian over to where the two Tellarites were lying on the ground, moaning and holding their sides. Kebron stood over them, his arms folded. "Now," McHenry said as he dropped Krave next to his associates, "this gentleman here is Adulux. Apologize to him."

"We're not going to—" began Krave defiantly.

Kebron glowered at them.

"We're sorry," Nyx said, and Quiv echoed the sentiment.

Krave quivered in frustration, but there was nothing he could do, for he certainly had no desire to deal with Kebron. The one called McHenry had already done enough damage, along with that awful old female. McHenry prodded him with his toe. "I'm sorry," said Krave.

"Now give Adulux back his wife. If you have to go get her from wherever you've got her hidden, I will accompany you while Kebron here stays with your associates, for safekeeping. Or is she on your vessel?"

"What wife? What are you talking about?" demanded Krave.

"My wife! My Zanka!" Adulux said with increasing agitation. "When you kidnapped her . . . took her in a flash of light . . . !"

"We never kidnapped anybody!" said Nyx with such a whine in his voice that the truth of what he was saying seemed impossible to doubt. "Never!"

"We just terrorized people, that's all! That's all!" Quiv added.

"No! It had to be them! It had to be!" Adulux said.

"Calm down, Adulux," said Kebron.

"Calm down! I can't calm down! If they don't return her—! But . . . but we can show them to the Elders," he began to say with excitement. "Show them that aliens exist! That might at least get them to believe me somewhat . . ."

"We're not going to show them to anyone," McHenry said firmly. "The people of this world don't need that sort of evidence. We just want them to return your wife and go away—"

"We don't have his damned wife!" shouted Krave, spitting out another tooth.

"Oh, really!" Adulux shot back. *"Then if you don't, who does?"*

That was when the light stabbed down at them from above.

It was blinding. All of them threw their arms in front of their faces to shield them from it. From overhead there was a deafening roar, mighty engines at work powering some gigantic vessel. They could only see the barest outlines of it owing to the intensity of the light that was pounding down upon them like a thing alive.

"It's them!" shouted Adulux. "It's the light! It's the ones who stole Zanka! Give her back! *Give her back!"*

The light increased in intensity all around them.

"This," Kebron said, "is ill-timed."

And that was the last thing any of them managed to say before they all blinked out of existence.

A moment later, all was silent, except for the placid sighing of the Furn, contentedly chewing its food in the middle of the field.

SOLETA

SHE DID NOT WANT to like him.

She was already accustomed to hating him, even dedicated to hating him.

She understood that the universe was not one of black-and-whites, but grays. She understood this, even though her scientific nature usually drove her to look for stark and straightforward answers with no shadings. Yet she had been certain that this aspect of her life was clear-cut. Rajari, the man who had brutalized her mother, was unrepentant slime.

Except . . .

He was repenting.

She sat in his apartment, wondering for the umpteenth time in the last two weeks what her mother would have made of the situation. If Rajari had come to T'Pas on bended knee, begging forgiveness, would she have granted it? Would she have found any logic in continuing to hate him for what he had done? Part of Soleta wanted to think that, yes, she would have continued to hate him. That was the aspect of Soleta that wanted that nice, tidy, black-and-white ethic.

But what if she had been willing to forgive him? What if T'Pas had considered continued antipathy to be an illogical waste of time and energy? What then?

Soleta's mind had been awhirl with the psychological and even philosophical ramifications that were part of any involvement she might have with Rajari. She had decided two things early on. The first was that under no circumstance would she tell him that she was his daughter. The second was that if he made any sort of aggressive move, if he gave her any reason whatsoever to think that he was about to hurt her, she would pull out her phaser and blast him into nonexistence. She knew, in her heart, that she was capable of doing it.

She had taken a lengthy meditation, had explored the innermost recesses of her resolve, and she was convinced that there was no mental block whatsoever. The fact that Rajari was her father was a biological happenstance only. The individual whom she truly thought of as father was back on Vulcan, and the fact that there was no genetic tie between them was purely incidental. So if Rajari became a threat, she knew that she would not hesitate to dispatch him. There would be no pause, no flash of guilt, no mental cry of *No, not my father!* She could, and would, do what had to be done.

With that in mind, she had met him several times at the bar. Remaining in one place had quickly become boring for both of them, and they had taken to walking around the city. Rajari was quite conversant in the ins and outs of Catalina City, and had even steeped himself in the history of the place. He seemed pleased to have someone to talk to about it. He would chat for hours on end about the original purpose for this building or that building, and how the city founders had taken meticulous care in laying the place out. Soleta herself had been unable to discern any pattern at all; despite all his explanations, the place still seemed like a confused hodgepodge. She saw no advantage to arguing it, however.

They would also talk about theology. And science. About philosophy and methodology. She could not believe how well read he was, how versed he was in such an amazing variety of topics. She remembered the evil, chortling creature that had sat in the brig those many years back in the *Aldrin* and tried to see something of that man in the Rajari she had now encountered. But there seemed to be nothing of him there. It was as if another being altogether had taken over his body and mind.

This alone was enough to make Soleta suspicious, to wonder if indeed someone or something else was impersonating him or had somehow seized control of his mind. During the time she was on Titan, she managed to get his medical records and matched his profile from the beginning of his stay to that which was assembled at the end of his stay. Allowing for some diminishment due to the passing years, it was indisputably the same individual.

Rajari had asked no more questions about Soleta's own background. It was as if he was afraid to find out, as if probing too closely to the circumstances that had brought her here might somehow drive her away. So instead he spoke mostly about himself, or those topics that were of interest to him. Soleta found it most disconcerting that many of those same topics were of interest to her as well.

She sent a message to her father, telling him that she had investigated the situation and was convinced that Rajari posed no threat. At the very least, she could alleviate whatever anxiety (controlled and hidden away, of course) Volak might be feeling. She did not, however, mention to him that she was remaining on Titan and spending an inordinate amount of time with Rajari.

She knew that it was insane to try and get to know him. Having ascertained that he posed no threat, the wise course would have been to leave. But the unwise course seemed to pose so many more interesting possibilities, and as a naturally curious creature, she found it impossible to pass them up.

She sat in his apartment, staring out the window thoughtfully, while he poured out a drink for himself. He had offered one to her, but she was not a huge fan of alcohol, and he appeared to have no synthehol in the small, cramped domicile that barely ranked as a room, much less an apartment. She also noted that what he was pouring out was Romulan ale.

The first time she had accepted his invitation to come up to his apartment, her heart had been in her throat. She had remained in a state of mental preparedness for the entire time that she had been there, wondering when and if he was going to strike. After a while there, she had discarded the "when" part and downgraded it to "if." As it turned out, he requested that she leave shortly after 2200 hours, claiming fatigue. Just before she had gone, he had extended the first two fingers of his right hand and chastely touched her on the side of her face. It had been the slightest brushing of finger against skin, but its meaning was standard in the unspoken Vulcan lexicon: it was a physical term of endearment. Soleta had flinched automatically. Rajari caught her reflexive reaction and immediately withdrew the gesture; he did not make any attempt after that to repeat it.

She kept telling herself that he was an experiment, a subject worthy of study. Even if she did not have the direct, undesirable tie to him that she had, he still would have merited an investigation.

"Rajari," she said as he sipped his Romulan ale behind her. "Do you believe in absolute evil?"

"How do you mean?" he replied, not quite understanding the question. He circled the Spartan apartment as he approached her. She noticed that he rarely went directly from one point to the other; he always seemed to adopt a circuitous route.

"The question is fairly self-explanatory. Do you believe that someone can be entirely evil."

"Are you thinking of anyone in particular?"

She tried to say "no." Instead she wasn't able to say anything.

"Ah, that damnable Vulcan penchant for honesty," chuckled Rajari. "But very well . . . let us pretend that we are speaking in abstracts instead of about me specifically. The question is not whether someone can be entirely evil. The question is, rather, does evil exist."

"Does it?"

"What is evil?" he asked. "That is the difficult proposition, you see. Because evil cannot be defined as itself."

"What do you mean?"

"I mean that evil can only be defined as the opposite of good. Evil is not a presence of one thing, it is the absence of something else. Evil is the absence of good, just as dark is the absence of light and a vacuum is the absence of air. So you are not truly asking whether pure evil, in and of itself, can exist. You are asking instead whether such a thing as a total absence of good can exist."

"And can it?"

"I don't think so." He pulled a chair up next to hers and joined her in gazing out the window. "Not if 'good' is defined as the impulse to try and do something on behalf of someone else. Anyone is capable, at any given moment, of performing an action that is selfless. The most brutal, most heartless individual in existence is still capable of—oh, I don't know—preventing a small child from being run over, for instance. Or doing a good deed to make life a little better, if even for a moment, for an elderly person."

"But a small act of the type you're describing can hardly mitigate a lifetime of evil deeds."

"True. That, however, was not what you were asking. You were questioning whether evil can be absolute. The answer is, I don't think so. Darkness can be absolute, for you can have a situation where there is no source of light and never will be, as in a black hole for example. But when you talk of matters of spirit, there are always possibilities for actions that will be of benefit. That's what hope is, after all. No one, and nothing, is truly hopeless. Look at me."

"Look at you," she said evenly. "Filled with light, are you?"

"That is it, yes. That is exactly it. I was evil. I was darkness. But then I was filled with light. It was a wonderful thing, Soleta."

"But if that is the case . . . then perhaps you are still evil."

He looked at her in curiosity. "How do you mean?"

"Well, the way in which you've described the circumstances of your luminous uplift, you appear to have been filled with this," and she gestured vaguely, "this spiritual comprehension. A gift to you from the gods, as you have said."

"That is true, yes. A fair summary, although I detect a hint of the famed Vulcan irony in your tone."

"I do not intend to be ironic, but consider: The light of your raised consciousness is not, in fact, coming from you. You are no more carrying the light of goodness within you than a moon is a source of light. It is simply reflecting the sunlight. So perhaps you yourself remain evil . . . and are simply deluding yourself into thinking that you are reformed. Without a true inner light, you may very well slide down into the spiritual abyss that you keep telling yourself you have climbed out of."

He was silent for a very long time, and when he spoke again there was clear anger in his voice. "Why are you saying these things to me? Why are you trying to wound me?"

"Wound you? I do not understan—"

"Oh, you understand perfectly," said Rajari, standing now and placing distance between himself and Soleta. "I have dealt with you in total honesty, Soleta. I have told you of my rebirth, of my having found myself. And you are unwilling to accept it."

"Why does my accepting it or not accepting it make any difference to you?"

"Because it does. I would like . . ." His voice caught and he visibly had to compose himself, "I would like one person to believe me. Just one. The Starfleet personnel who ran the camp, my fellow prisoners . . . everyone whom I would tell about my revelations would smile and look at me in a patronizing way. Not only was it clear that they did not believe me, but they obviously thought I believed them to be some sort of fools that I could easily deceive with a manufactured story about spiritual redemption. They thought it was a joke, or a charade. You want to know why I've seized on your companionship, Soleta? Because I thought that you might be that one hope, that one person who would believe me. I thought the gods had sent you to be the lone individual who would say, 'I'm happy for you, Rajari,' and actually mean it."

"Considering that the first thing you tried to do upon encountering me was crush my throat, that was hardly the sort of welcome designed to engender charitable thought or credulous acceptance on my part," she told him.

His anger had seemed to have been building, but now it began to disappear. Ire turned to that same, melancholic air of sadness that so often shrouded him. "That is a valid point," he admitted. "Tell me, Soleta, do you think it possible that, someday, you will believe all that I have said?"

"You have said it yourself, Rajari. Anything is possible." Suddenly feeling the need to turn the conversation in a different direction, she steered along the first path that occurred to her. "By the way, I am curious. That box is most attractive. What is in it?"

The box she was pointing to was an elaborately carved affair, a foot long and about eight inches wide. It had a series of symbols and patterns on it, none of which Soleta was capable of identifying for certain. But she was reasonably sure that at least some of them had to do with specific Romulan houses.

"In it?" he asked.

"Yes, in it. What are the contents?"

"Merely an heirloom," said Rajari vaguely. "Nothing you need concern yourself about."

"I am not concerned. I am merely . . ."

"It is none of your business, Soleta. I suggest you leave the matter at that."

The sudden turnaround in his mood, the harshness of his tone, all caught Soleta off guard. She hesitated a moment, then asked him about something else in the apartment. He was immediately forthcoming. The box, however, was obviously a sore subject. She knew that if she had any respect for his wishes or privacy, she would forget about the beautifully carved box and never make any sort of inquiry as to its contents ever again.

Naturally she set about determining just when she would sneak a look in it.

"I sense our time together is drawing to a close, Soleta."

It was several days later, and Soleta and Rajari were in the bar where she had first observed him. It seemed an appropriate place for Rajari to broach the subject that they both knew was inevitable.

It was evident to Soleta that Rajari was becoming weaker. Even in the few weeks that she had spent with him, the diminishment in his capabilities was getting evident. He was losing a few steps off his stride, and he seemed to be in pain more than he had been. He would try not to let on, but Soleta was trained as an observer. As a result, even when he thought she wasn't noticing and allowed the strains upon his body to cause him open discomfort, she saw it anyway. And she suspected that he knew that she saw it.

Nevertheless, out of respect for her carefully culti-vated obliviousness, she said, "Oh? And why do you think that is, Rajari?"

"Because you are a young and vital woman who must certainly have more interesting things to do than hang about in the presence of a dying man. Because our little chats have provided you very little of use aside from some passing thoughts and an oddity of a relationship. That is why."

"Do we have a relationship?" she asked, eyebrow cocked in curiosity.

"I believe we do, yes. I confess that I am not entirely certain what it is, but it is a relationship nevertheless." He was quiet for a time and then he turned to her. "I know why you came here. But why have you stayed?"

"I have considered—"

"No," he silenced her with a raised index finger. "Do not waste your time and mine telling me that I am some sort of . . . scientific experiment. A research project. A study of evil nature versus the capacity for good. Per-haps you have managed to convince yourself of that, but you have not convinced me. Look into your heart, Soleta, or whatever array of circuitry and hardwire passes for a heart within an emotionless race, and tell me . . . tell me truly . . . why you have stayed here."

She opened her mouth to respond in a brisk and straightforward manner, but nothing came out. Finally, she was forced to admit, "I do not know."

He seemed oddly satisfied with the response. "That is good to hear. The first step on the road to knowing everything is admitting that you know nothing."

"I had a philosophy teacher who said something much along the same lines," said Soleta.

"Indeed?"

"Yes. I found her to be equally annoying."

He laughed at that. "I suppose I should be flattered. Or should I?"

"I do not know that, either."

"Excellent. Do you know, Soleta, what the most common element in the universe is?"

"Hydrogen."

"No. Ignorance. Here is to ignorance, then, my scientist," and he raised a glass, "for without ignorance, you would be out of a job."

"That is very true," she concurred, and tapped her glass against his.

"So where will you go upon leaving this less-than-pleasant place? Will you return to your father, Volak . . . ?"

"Perhaps. I—"

She froze.

His eyes glittered with quiet triumph. "I knew it," he said.

Soleta felt like a complete fool. She had lowered her guard and suddenly she was paying for it. She had had no desire to let Rajari know of her blood relationship to T'Pas. She did not want to let him that . . . that close to her. "That is to say—" she tried to cover, even though she knew that the damage was done.

"I knew it," he repeated. "You are his daughter. And hers. 'Friend' indeed. I was certain of it from the moment I saw you."

"The moment you saw me, you tried to kill me," she reminded him.

He nodded in acknowledgment of that unfortunate fact. "True. Very well, some moments after that, then. But why did you not tell me? No . . . no, you do not have to answer. It is obvious. You thought me on some sort of vendetta. You said as much yourself. You thought I posed a threat to your mother, and because of that, I might be a threat to you as well." He shook his head. "That famed Vulcan logic. You have learned well."

"Thank you."

"But I am no threat. Do you believe that?"

She looked away from him. "I . . . would like to believe it. I would like to think that no one is beyond redemption. On the other hand, try as I might—and I have tried, believe it or not—it is impossible for me simply to forget what you have done. To erase the image from my mind of you brutalizing my mother. I think of her, helpless, the look on her face . . ."

"I was there," Rajari said harshly. He stared deep into his glass, and for a moment he reminded Soleta of the way he was when she had first spied him in the bar. "I run the moment in my mind, and I feel as if I am watching a total stranger. I am, in many ways, as repulsed as you. But I can never feel the sort of moral indignation that you must possess. She was your mother. She loved you . . . or at least what passes for love in the restricted environment that Vulcans allow. Perhaps it is best that you are taking your leave, Soleta. With the truth before us now, I would not blame you for not wanting to remain." He finished his drink, signaled for the check, and paid it without saying anything further.

"Rajari—"

"No. No need, Soleta. Anything you say at this point would be colored by what is before us. But I will say this," and he looked her in the eyes, "they say that if you desire to see what the daughter will be like, look to the mother. It follows that if one wishes to see the mother at a younger age, look to the daughter. If there is any element of your mother within you, any small flame or reflection of her *katra,* then I apologize to it now. I know that apologies oftentimes cannot be nearly enough . . . but in the end, it is all I have to give."

He rose then, and she did so as well. "I will see myself back home," he said.

"I will accompany you for the walk."

"That is not necessary."

"Actually," Soleta corrected him, "I believe it is."

He shrugged. "As you will."

They headed in the direction of his apartment in silence. He was walking slowly, and Soleta noticed that he was developing a slight limp. She wondered how much longer he truly had. Soleta knew that if she were dying, she would be doing everything she could to attend to "unfinished business," to put to rights anything that she had done wrong. What was it like, she wondered, for there to be things in one's past that could never, ever be truly put right? Sins that could be atoned for, but never actually repaired.

They passed the alley where they had first really "encountered" one another. The shadows were stretching, much as they had that first time.

And hands reached from the darkness, grabbed both Soleta and Rajari, and hauled them into the alley.

SI CWAN

"THIS IS RIDICULOUS. It must not be the right block," said Kalinda, and Si Cwan couldn't blame her for voicing her mounting frustration.

They had been walking up and down the same general area for half an hour, and had still been unable to find Jereme's school building, his training center. Even though the students to whom Si Cwan had spoken gave him an exact address, the actual building itself continued to elude them.

The journey to Pulva had not been a particularly comfortable one. The commercial transport had been crowded, and not especially plush. There was an elderly couple that had, astonishingly, never been in space before and they had panic attacks most of the way, and Si Cwan had also been subjected to a small child who insisted on kicking the back of his seat for the first few light-years of the journey. Cwan had si-

lenced him by turning in his seat and giving him a look
that would have intimidated a Klingon. "Little boy . . .
if you continue to kick this seat . . . I am going to obtain eight-inch spikes, and I will nail your feet to the
floor. And the blood. Will flow. Like milk," and he ca-
ressed the last seven words with sadistic enjoyment.
The child stared at him, goggle-eyed, and Si Cwan finished, "So stop it." The child immediately ceased his
activities and stayed absolutely paralyzed for the re-
mainder of the voyage. The child's mother scowled
fiercely at Si Cwan, but Si Cwan had looked into the
eyes of enough people who had genuinely been prepared to kill him that he found the glares of a miffed
mother to be of little consequence.

Upon arriving on Pulva, they had made their way to
the location that the students had provided, but were
having some degree of difficulty in reaching their destination.

"Why would they give us the wrong address?" demanded Si Cwan. He frowned suspiciously. "Could
they want to keep us away for a reason?"

"I don't know," said Kalinda in irritation. "I thought
you'd been here before."

"No. Never. And considering the difficulty in finding
the place, I'm amazed that anyone can—"

"Ambassador Cwan."

He and Kalinda turned. There was a young male
standing behind them, a Mook. He was slightly stoop-
shouldered, as were most of his race. His compound
eyes studied them up and down, and his mandibles
clicked when he spoke. He was dressed in loose black
robes, the style of which Si Cwan knew all too well.
Whenever he had lessons with Jereme, that had always
been the uniform he'd been required to wear.

"I am Ookla," said the Mook. "It is an honor to meet you. Jereme always speaks of y—" He stopped and had to correct himself with effort, the verbal hiccup of one who does not wish to deal with referring to someone in the past tense. "Always spoke of you most highly. He said your training and abilities were something that all of us should aspire to."

"Thank you, Ookla. This," and he indicated Kalinda, "is my sister, the princess Kalinda."

"Princess," said Ookla, and he bowed deeply.

"Did Jereme mention me as well?"

"Yes. Yes he did."

"Ah." She looked with a degree of satisfaction at Si Cwan. "And what did he say?"

"He said you were Ambassador Cwan's sister."

"And—?"

His mandibles clicked with faint apology. "There . . . is no 'and.' Does that present a problem?"

Had he been in anything other than the worst mood of his life, Si Cwan might actually have found the exchange, along with Kalinda's subsequent crestfallen expression, to be somewhat comical. "Ookla, I'm relieved that you showed up. Apparently we were given incorrect directions. The school is—"

"Right there," and he gestured directly across the street from where they were standing.

They turned and looked where he was pointing, and there was a small building front there that Si Cwan would absolutely have sworn, with his life on the line, had not been there before. He glanced at Kalinda and saw that she was equally slack-jawed, uncomprehending. "But . . . that wasn't . . . where did—?"

Si Cwan laughed softly. Considering his state of mind, it was an odd sound to be coming from him, and

Kalinda's expression made clear that she realized any amusement on his part was unusual.

"Jereme designed it, didn't he," said Si Cwan. It was not a question.

"Of course."

"Of course," Si Cwan echoed. "Look at it, Kalinda. The building itself is a testament to the art of camouflage, of disappearing. The lines, the structure . . . if you're not looking directly at it, your eye glides right off it. It's brilliant."

"It's annoying," Kalinda said.

"Brilliance oftentimes is. Lead the way, Ookla."

Within minutes they were inside the school, meeting and greeting the other students. There were only a handful of them, of various races. According to Ookla, a number of them had already departed. With the death of Jereme, they reasoned that there was no purpose for remaining.

"Of course there is reason," Si Cwan said impatiently. "Vengeance."

"Jereme taught us that vengeance is a hollow pursuit," said Ookla, and others of the students nodded.

"There were many things that I learned from Jereme. That I took to heart and sincerely believed," said Si Cwan. "But that was never one of them."

"Vengeance will not bring him back," said one of the other students.

"Unless you feel that it will enable him to rest more peacefully?" suggested Ookla.

"He's dead," Si Cwan said flatly. "What we do in this sphere will have no impact on the next. I will avenge him because honor will permit no other course of action. I will do it," and his voice grew in intensity, but not volume, making it all the more frightening. "I will do it because the one whose eyes looked upon Jereme's last moments has earned the privilege of also being able to look upon his own living heart being ripped from his chest and held up so that he can observe its final beats."

There was silence for a long moment.

"You'll have to excuse him," said Kalinda. "There was a child kicking the back of his seat on the trip over."

"Oh. Well . . . that's always irritating," said Ookla uncertainly, and there were brisk nods from the others.

SOLETA

It ALL HAPPENED SO QUICKLY that she barely had time to process what was happening.

One moment she had been walking down the street with Rajari, each of them silent in their private musings. The next, Rajari was suddenly yanked away from her. She looked around in momentary confusion, but only momentary. For she was still Vulcan, and she was able to grasp what was occurring with alacrity.

Someone was attacking Rajari. His concerns about assassins were apparently not unfounded.

Before she could react, however, someone was behind her and shoving her into the darkness as well.

Her sight was going to do her no good, thanks to the gloom that surrounded her. She glimpsed several forms, four or five at least. They were hooded to prevent any identification. "We have Rajari," she heard a rough voice say. "We don't need her. Kill her."

Keeping her eyes opened would force her to rely on them, so she closed her eyes in order to accomplish the opposite. Reacting completely on instinct, she twisted and managed to grab the arm of whoever was behind her. A quick bend, another twist, and the assailant from behind was sent flying.

She heard scuffling. She opened her eyes, her vision having adjusted slightly. She could see that Rajari was struggling as well. "Signal! Signal!" someone was shouting, and suddenly Rajari had torn free. One of them managed to trip him, though, and he fell against Soleta, his hands grabbing at her jacket.

"Get out!" he whispered. "Go! They don't care about you! Go!"

"Wait!"

Then they were upon Soleta and Rajari, pulling at them. Rajari let out a howl of fury that was utterly unexpected in its ferocity for someone of his poor health. Soleta actually heard one of his bones crack as he turned and slammed into them, driving them back, his fists smashing against whatever part of their bodies he could find.

She pulled out her phaser, swung and fired in one smooth motion, nailing one of the shapes that was coming at her in the dimness. The stun setting, to her surprise, simply knocked him off his feet. He landed hard on the ground of the alley with a grunt but otherwise seemed unharmed.

Even as the assailant scrambled to his feet, Rajari shouted once more, "Go!" For one more moment he shook them loose, and he charged at her and shoved her with such fury that Soleta stumbled back and out of the alley. Rajari turned to face his attackers and then they were upon him, piling on and driving him to the dirt-encrusted ground.

Soleta tried to take aim with her phaser, tried to find someplace safe to shoot . . . and suddenly she heard a telltale and very familiar humming noise. They were disappearing from the alley, a transporter working its peculiar brand of technological magic. Within moments the alleyway was empty.

The human thing would have been for Soleta to shout Rajari's name in frustration, but naturally such a pointless expenditure of time and energy never occurred to her. Instead she reached into her belt and pulled out a palm beacon to illuminate the alley.

Soleta had never been more glad that she had decided to take some of her Starfleet equipment with her than she was at that particular moment. It was not mandatory that Starfleet officers keep regulation equipment with them at all times, particularly when they were off duty. Opinions differed as to what was appropriate, and ultimately it was left to the individual's discretion. Some crewmen, when on shore leave, felt that leave meant leave. So they would leave behind anything having to do with their uniformed existence.

Soleta, however, was far more pragmatic. To her it was simply equipment, and although to sport the uniform might have made her too much of a target, equipment remained equipment. She played the flash over the ground, relieved that she had it with her, and almost momentarily checking to make sure that her tricorder and comm badge were also safely on her person.

The tricorder was there, just as it was supposed to be.

Her comm badge, however, was gone.

The first thing that occurred to her was that she had lost it in the scuffle. To that end, she studied the ground meticulously, looking for some sign of it. But it wasn't there. Within minutes she had combed every square inch of the alley and the comm badge was simply not to be found.

She ran the events of the previous few minutes through her mind, and immediately realized what had happened; Rajari must have snagged it when he had banged into her. But it made no sense. Why would he steal her comm badge . . . ?

That was when two possibilities hit her. One gave her hope. The other raised tremendous concern.

The first notion was that he had stumbled upon the comm badge when he had been thrown against her and immediately realized that it could provide his salvation. By snagging the badge, he had hoped that it would provide a means of her tracking him and rescuing him on something approaching her own terms. The element of surprise would be entirely on her side

The second notion was that this was all a set-up. That Rajari had arranged for the ambush in the alley. Although he did not know for certain that she was from Starfleet, he had as much as guessed that she was, and had hoped that he would be able to grab something off her that was traceable. He had lucked on to the comm badge and, the moment he had it, they were able to vanish on the assumption that she was going to come after them.

The latter theory certainly appealed to her sense of innate paranoia, and her suspicions about Rajari that she was not entirely able to lay to rest. On the other hand, it also didn't hold up terribly well under scrutiny. If the goal was to capture Soleta, they might very well have been able to do so without any sort of subterfuge. Why go to all the effort, to embark on some Byzantine plan? It made no sense. And nothing explained who his cohort might have been.

There seemed to be only one logical decision to make, particularly since time might very well be of the essence.

She pulled out her tricorder and keyed it to pick up on the frequency signal of her comm badge. It wasn't something that tricorders were customarily used for. One usually simply tapped one's own comm badge in order to locate a missing person, since that activated a conversational link. Either that or shipboard computers were more than capable of pinpointing the exact location of a badge. She, however, had access to neither, and so she was forced to make do. But it was not going to be easy, and it was also going to be limited. If Rajari had been beamed offworld, she'd never be able to—

The tricorder only took seconds to lock on to the comm badge's internal beacon.

She could scarcely believe her luck.

Unless it's not luck.

That same damnable internal voice was back, warning her not to take anything for granted. Rajari still was what he was, capable of great evil, of turning against her at any time.

Except that might not have been an accurate description at all. For all she knew, he was a perfectly decent individual who had found a higher power and internal peace. She hated not knowing for sure, she detested the uncertainty. But for all her frustration, there was one thing she did know for sure. She was going to have to try and find him, and quickly.

The tricorder at that point was simply telling her that it had managed to locate the comm badge, and gave her a fix on it that specified it along global lines. Looking for something a bit more accessible than longitude and latitude, she linked in with the file that gave her a street map of Catalina City. In an instant a small green dot appeared on the screen, pinpointing precisely where the signal was coming from.

It was only eight blocks away. That did not surprise her at all. They had been spirited away by a short-range portable individual transport device. SPITs (as one wag had dubbed them, much to the annoyance of the manufacturer) weren't especially powerful; they had been designed purely for the more affluent members of society to get around privately, rather than using a transport center as the "lower class" was obliged to do. Soleta had been reasonably sure, due to the sound and look of the effect, that a SPIT was being used. But she wasn't positive, and was relieved to see that her supposition was correct.

She could not delay, though. For all she knew, Rajari had been SPIT over to someplace where a shuttle had been readied, and was about to be removed from the planet. If that happened, then in the time that it took her to commandeer a private shuttle or rent one of her own, he would be long gone.

Even as she sprinted through the streets, she couldn't help but feel that she was out of her mind. No matter what he was now, she had to remember what he had once been. That would never, ever change. It really wasn't relevant that he wished he had acted in some other manner, because the fact was that he hadn't. One could ignore facts, but one could not change them. And ignoring this particular fact simply wasn't an option for her.

But another fact introduced into the mix was that Rajari had indeed tried to get her clear of danger. He had been willing to sacrifice himself in order to save her. Was she then supposed to turn away, to leave him to his own fate after he had saved her from a similar one? That was not acceptable.

You're trying to save the man who assaulted your mother. Don't tell me it's because of some misbegotten loyalty to the fact that he is your real father.

"He's not my father," Soleta practically snarled through gritted teeth as she ran. "Just because he biologically helped to create me, that means nothing. Nothing."

By that time she'd covered half the distance, and within minutes she had achieved her destination. It was hard to believe that she had managed to locate an even more depressing, more run-down section of Catalina City than she'd already been in, but that was indeed where she had wound up.

The tricorder told her that the comm badge—and, hopefully, Rajari—was inside a large building that was apparently one of the very first erected in Catalina City. It did not, however, have any sort of marker indicating that it was a historical site. Instead it was simply there, a structure that had been used to house machine parts and various mechanical supplies. It had fallen into disuse and disrepair. It was solid black, like a huge tomb. Soleta couldn't help but feel that it was a hideously appropriate comparison to make.

This time she was taking no chances. She had the phaser out and had thumbed it on. She was not the world's greatest marksman, but she was competent, and hefting the weapon certainly made her feel better. She glanced at the power grid and saw that the phaser was fully charged. Good. The last thing she needed was a surprise.

There was a door around one side that had obviously not been used for some time. As opposed to the sliding doors to which Soleta was accustomed, this was a primitive hinged door, sealed tight. There was a hand-grip and a thumbprint scanner built in, but the scanner was deactivated. Her phaser could easily blow a hole in it, but the noise involved would certainly have given her away. She would have been happy to just shoot the hinges off, but unfortunately they were on the inside.

Soleta took a deep breath and placed her hands flat against the door. She steadied herself, summoning her strength, focusing it. Then she began to push, making sure that her booted feet had enough traction so that she didn't sprawl on her face.

The door didn't even seem to notice that she was there. She continued the pressure, minute after minute, regulating her breathing, concentrating and not letting up for a second. After several minutes her strength began to flag, but then she felt the door bending under the pressure and that sent a surge of determination through her. Instead of letting up, she pulled from deep within her to find even more strength, and suddenly the door flew open.

She stumbled, lunged for it, tried to catch it, but it was too late. The door swung wide on its hinges and slammed against the wall before swinging partway back in the other direction. Soleta cursed the luck even as her training forced her not to let it bother her. She snagged the door, swung it closed, and prayed that the sound hadn't been heard.

"What was that?" she heard a rough voice call from somewhere within the building.

Yet another prayer that had been answered with a resounding "No" from whatever deity thought that mucking with Soleta's life would provide a nice day's entertainment.

Soleta shoved against the door from within as hard as she could, jamming it back into place. There were a few unclaimed crates scattered about, and she quickly took refuge behind one of them, crouching low while letting her eyes adjust to the dim lighting.

Two figures were approaching.

Her heart froze. One of them . . . no, both of them . . . were Romulan.

It is a trap! He did set this up! her increasingly annoying inner voice told her. She would have told it to shut up except then she would have been heard.

Just looking at the way they moved, she could tell that they were probably soldiers, or perhaps ex-soldiers. One of them had a vicious scar down one side of his face. Insanely, she felt a brief wave of nostalgia for the late Captain Calhoun.

They were wearing what appeared to be some type of heavy-duty armor that encased them the way an exoskeleton surrounded an insect. It was smooth with a metallic sheen to it, although she did take notice of the fact that the area directly at the base of the throat was exposed. There apparently was some sort of a latch-on area for a helmet, but they weren't wearing theirs.

That was how the assailant in the alley had managed to recover so quickly from a phaser blast. They were wearing what appeared to be some sort of Byrillium armor, capable of withstanding low-end phaser blasts by absorbing the intensity of the beam and redistributing it, diminishing its force. She did some rapid-fire mental calculations as to how much damage the armor could withstand and was not happy with the conclusions that she came to. Seeing no other choice, she thumbed up the intensity level on her phaser to maximum.

The scarred one looked the door up and down, then pulled on it experimentally. "Seems solid," he said.

"Shh!" said the other.

He was listening.

Soleta was positive of it. A Romulan's hearing was no less sharp than that of a Vulcan, and he was now taking an aural check of the immediate area to discern whether or not an uninvited guest had shown up.

She didn't budge. She didn't breathe. She felt her legs starting to cramp up and she willed herself to ignore it. Her heart sounded hideously loud as it thudded against her chest, and she was convinced that anyone could have heard it, so deafening to her was the thumping. She didn't even blink.

Now both the Romulans were listening, the minutes stretching to an eternity. Barely twenty feet away, Soleta had to sneeze. She dug her teeth into her lower lip so hard that small, green rivulets of blood trickled down her chin.

"Nothing," said the one with no scar.

Soleta almost reflexively let out a sigh of relief, which naturally would have been a less than brilliant move. Fortunately she caught herself at the last instant.

"Come. Let's get back to our guest," said scar face. "Adis has just arrived. This should be most interesting."

If Soleta had had any interest in moving at that point, the mention of the name "Adis" froze her in her place. She knew the name all too well. He was extremely high up in the Romulan hierarchy, said to be one of the Emperor's inner circle. A well-placed politician, rich and powerful. What in the world did he have to do with Rajari? The notion that all of this was some sort of elaborate scheme to ensnare her became less and less tenable. When one was dealing with individuals of the caliber and position of Adis, someone such as Soleta did not even register on his long-range sensors.

She was not at all concerned about losing them at this point in the confined area of the storage facility. She felt perfectly comfortable with letting them get completely out of sight. Even then she allowed another ten count before heading off after them. She did not follow them in any sort of straight line, but instead moved in the same general direction they had gone while, at the same time, staying close to the shadows of the perimeter. She continued to grip her phaser firmly, keeping all her senses extended in case anyone was lying in wait for her.

Just beyond one stack of crates, she heard voices. One of them was speaking in firm, commanding tones, and the others appeared to be responding with deference. It was not difficult for her to figure out who the one speaking in the commanding tones was. Keeping her back flat against the far side of the stack of crates, she slowly positioned herself so that she could peer around a corner without being observed.

Rajari was bound securely on the floor. They hadn't even been considerate enough to tie him to a chair. There were thick bands at his ankles, and his wrists were bound behind his back. From the way his right arm was jutting, she suspected that it was broken. If she had any remaining thought at all that this was some sort of vast, complicated conspiracy, seeing Rajari there, helpless, injured, put it right out of her mind.

On the far side of the warehouse she saw the transport equipment that had been used to kidnap Rajari from the alley. Stepping off of the pad set-up was a tall, aristocratic-looking Romulan whom Soleta could only assume was Adis. He wore his arrogance like a comfortable shoe. When he stared at Rajari on the floor, it was with the attitude of someone who clearly could not believe that he had ever considered the dying Romulan to be worth his time.

There were five men standing in a semicircle, including the two that Soleta had already spotted. Adis acknowledged them with a curt nod and then turned his focus to Rajari. "So," he said. "Rajari. How nice to see you."

"Oh, gods . . . fake pleasantries," moaned Rajari. "Is there any greater waste of time?"

"We are not brutes," Adis said archly. "We can follow protocols, certainly. So . . . it is my understanding that you are dying."

"Why are you doing this?"

"I shall consider that a response in the affirmative?"

Rajari moaned again. He seemed to be in too much pain to be paying attention to anything that Adis was saying.

Adis noticed that Rajari wasn't focusing on him. This was clearly an intolerable circumstance for him, and Adis took simple and direct steps to attend to it. He crouched next to Rajari, gripped his head firmly and turned it so that Rajari could not look anywhere except directly into Adis's eyes. Soleta winced when she saw the movement. If it was too violent, Rajari's weakened bones might very well snap just from the severity of the twist.

"You have inconvenienced me, Rajari," Adis informed him. Rajari whimpered slightly, but said nothing. "During your smuggling days, your activities infringed on my concerns."

"How was I to know . . . ?"

"You *should* have known." He sounded almost sad, as if gently scolding a frightened child. "Your problem is that you endeavored to play both sides. You smuggled weapons to races that were in opposition to one another. Did it never occur to you that I might be involved with one of them, and that it was therefore inevitable that you would interfere with my desires?"

"No."

"No," said Adis with that same air of mock tragedy. "No, apparently not. But that was not the worst of it, oh no. There were certain Cardassians with whom I also had some profitable and private dealings. And you aided the Federation in putting an end to those dealings when you helped terminate the conflict."

"But . . . but our government—"

"Our government," Adis told him, "has its concerns, and I have mine. Oftentimes the two overlap. Sometimes they do not, but I have been careful not to offend the wrong people or step on the wrong feet. You, on the other hand, have not taken those precautions. And that is why you are where you are, and I am where I am."

"Why . . . why can't you leave me . . . to . . . "

"To your fate? To die a slow, agonizing death?" When Rajari forced a nod, Adis continued, "I was sorely tempted to do so, I must admit. Granted, these men are in my service," and he gestured to those grouped around him. "They are faithful to my house, and have been for many years. Still, this little endeavor did cost me time, money, and energy. I could have let it, and you, pass."

Suddenly his foot swung sharply and cracked Rajari in the ribs. Soleta flinched inwardly as she heard one of the ribs snap.

With amazing casualness, as if he had not just viciously kicked his helpless captive, Adis went on, "But if I had done that, then that meant I would simply have tolerated your activities . . . except that your activities are, by definition, intolerable. Nature will always take its course, but what sort of Romulans would we be if we simply allowed our enemies to age out or die from illness, eh? I shall tell you. We would be Romulans who encourage others to become our enemies. That is not good or just or appropriate. And I would end up expending more time, money, and energy in defending myself against enemies who might otherwise not have come into existence. So if I take action now, I'm saving myself effort later on. Wise planning. That is the secret to a long and productive life. Perhaps you will have the opportunity to prove that in the next one."

He kicked Rajari once more. Rajari cried out and then lapsed into choked sobs.

Adis actually looked disappointed, even disgusted. "Is that the best you can do, smuggler? No profanity? No curses upon my name, my family, my ancestors? No vows of revenge? Do you know why I came here myself? Because it was my desire to kill you with my bare hands. But I see little to no point. You are not worthy to have your life slip away beneath my fingers. A shame, Rajari, for you at least. Here you could actually have died at the hands of one of the aristocracy, and you have failed even at that. A pointless life, a pointless death. Perhaps it's apt at that."

He stepped back and away from Rajari, turned to the scarred one, and said, "Krakis. Kill him."

McHENRY & KEBRON

ZAK KEBRON INSPECTED for perhaps the hundredth time the room that served as his prison. The fact that he had looked it over so many times really didn't mean anything, because he could continue to inspect the bare room another hundred times and still not be deterred in his course. Because he always felt that perhaps the next go-around might wind up presenting him with something that he had overlooked the previous times.

The room was completely circular, and did not have a stick of furniture in it. The lighting was not particularly bright, but neither was it too harsh on the eyes. Kebron continued to pace it, without letup. By moving about consistently, it helped to make him feel less of a target.

He hated his new body.

He was furious with himself that he had agreed to take on this idiotic assignment from Admiral Nechayev.

Not that his fury was displayed outwardly. When it came to commanding the ferocity of his emotions, Kebron could have made a Vulcan seem demonstrative in comparison. Kebron not only customarily looked like a large piece of statuary, but he oftentimes displayed the same emotional range.

Nechayev, who was reputed to have some involvement in some of the most secretive departments of Starfleet, had sought him out because she said she wanted exactly what he was capable of bringing into the picture: Someone who was sheer muscle. Someone who could shake some sense into those idiotic arrogant students. Someone who could so utterly terrify them just with his pure physical presence that they would never choose to target a harmless, helpless planet again and make it the subject of their juvenile pranks.

In point of fact, Kebron felt a bit foolish with the undertaking, but he did not see that ignoring a direct "request" from an admiral would be the brightest thing to do. He did feel, however, that he had made a smart move in having McHenry recruited as well. He might be an irritating presence, but he was a presence nevertheless. Their relationship—such as it was—went all the way back to their Academy days. As flighty and occasionally scatterbrained as McHenry could be, Kebron trusted him (at least as much as he trusted anyone). Furthermore, McHenry had a unique way of looking at a situation that prompted solutions no one else could conceive of. Kebron had felt that that might be a useful tool in dealing with the obnoxious students.

None of his forethought, however, had prepared him for this.

There was one door in the place, and it opened as Kebron happened to be on the far side of the room.

Something told him that it wasn't coincidence. And sure enough, there was his captor, or at least one of his captors.

The creature was from no race that Kebron had ever seen, or even heard of.

Like the Liten, it was green, but a much darker shade. It was remarkably tall, and so slender that it was a wonder its body did not break in half. If Kebron had half a chance, he would be more than happy to do the breaking. Its head was a perfect oval, its eyes deep-set and glistening like fiery jewels. It had yet to speak a single word.

The creature's long, tapered fingers were wrapped around the shoulder of a Liten female. It pushed the woman into the room toward Kebron with such casual force that she stumbled. Kebron's quick movement, belying his size, saved her from the fall as he caught her halfway down and righted her with an easy gesture. He allowed his momentum to carry him forward and made a quick move toward his captor.

The creature did not appear the least bit intimidated by Kebron's sudden charge. It raised a hand and suddenly Kebron couldn't move an inch. He struggled furiously and silently, trying to advance so much as a foot. But he was unable to do so, completely paralyzed.

In a sign of what could only be considered disdain, the creature then turned its back to Kebron and glided out without even a backward glance. Only once the door had slid shut securely did Kebron have control restored to his body. He strode quickly to the door and punched it with all his strength. It had no impact on the door at all. Once upon a time it wouldn't have hurt Kebron, either, but that was no longer the case. The genetic overhaul his body had been given had robbed him of some degree of his nigh-invulnerability. It had given him increased mobility, true, but he did not remotely consider it a worthwhile trade-off.

The Liten woman backpedaled away from him, clearly confused and uncertain of which way to look or whom to trust. She looked up at Kebron. "Who are you?" she asked, visibly making an effort to keep any stammer from her voice.

"Kebron," he said. He looked her up and down. "Zanka?"

"Yes!" she said, clearly astounded. "How did you know?"

"Your husband hired me. Hired us." Having ascertained her identity, he promptly lost interest in her and began to inspect the room yet again.

"Us? There's more than one of you?"

"Yes."

"And . . . and did you come here to rescue me?"

"Yes."

"How are you going to do it? Do you have a plan?" The words cascaded from her. "Yes, of course, you must have a plan. You're clearly experienced, and someone with experience would naturally have some sort of plan. Is it a cunning one? Only a cunning plan can get us out of this. Do you have a weapon? Or some sort of signal device? Or others coming to rescue you? Are you planning to—"

"Shut up," he said brusquely.

She seemed taken aback. "Adulux never spoke to me that way." But rather than appearing to be offended by his manner, her eyes glittered with a curiosity, even excitement.

Kebron was too preoccupied to notice. He was simply surveying the room. Then he turned to her after a few more minutes of futile inspection and said, "What have they done to you?"

"Since they captured me?"

"No, since the dawn of time." In whatever body he happened to be occupying, Zak Kebron did not suffer fools gladly. "Yes, since they captured you."

"They've subjected me to . . ."

She spoke in a low voice, and Kebron didn't quite catch it. "To what?"

"Tests," she admitted.

"Tests?"

"Yes."

He frowned. "What sort of tests?"

Krave, Nyx, and Quiv felt as if they were going to die. As their latest grueling test continued, Mark McHenry sat there and watched in silence.

This was not the first test that the three students had been put to by any means. McHenry had watched in quiet amazement as the Andorian and two Tellarites were subjected to what was quite possibly the most ludicrous series of physical demands that he'd ever seen. Quite against their will, they had been forced to shove eggs into their mouths and then expel them, with as much breath as they could muster, into pails set five feet away. They had been forced to run into walls repeatedly until they were nearly unconscious. A large board of wood had been set up in the middle of the room and they had been ordered to chop it in half using a dead fish. The board had been unyielding; the fish, on the other hand, had fared far less well. These, and other increasingly preposterous, endurance trials had been foisted upon them while McHenry witnessed it all, trying to determine what rhyme or reason there could be to it.

And their very strange host was overseeing all of it.

At this point, the three students had their arms folded, hopping up and down in place on one foot. They had been engaged in the rather ludicrous activity for the better part of an hour, but every time they tried to put one of their feet down, an electric shock from the floor would jolt them back into ongoing hop.

McHenry was seated on a small folding chair, which had been provided by his odd "host." The tall green creature had made clear to the students exactly what was expected of them when he had entered the room, pointed at the three of them, and demonstrated the hopping motion that he wanted them to adapt. The three of them had not moved, but instead simply glared at him. They didn't want to do it, and held on to some last shred of hope that if they mutinied then perhaps these absurd tests would come to an end.

They were overly optimistic. Instead their captor had simply gestured, and suddenly they were on their feet and hopping as instructed.

They had tried to stop the moment their captor had left the room, but the jolting floor had dissuaded them. So they hopped, and hopped, and hopped, until they were crying out in agony and begging for McHenry to do something, even just shoot them. Anything that would put an end to this insane endurance test. McHenry, for his part, had nothing to say or do in the matter. He simply sat there in the provided chair and watched them.

It was Quiv who ran out of energy first. Unable to sustain it any longer, he didn't put his foot down; instead he simply fell over, like a great tree. McHenry braced himself, waiting to see a massive jolt of electricity pumped through the fallen Tellarite. None, however, was forthcoming. He simply lay there, beached.

Thrilled that their ordeal was over, the other two put their feet down, and were promptly jolted for their impertinence. They started hopping once more. Nyx, suddenly seeing a way out, flopped over, expecting that to be the end of it. Instead electricity danced around him, his limbs quivering, and with a startled and frustrated howl he got back to his foot and started hopping again. A few minutes later, however, he truly did run out of steam, and when he collapsed, there was no further punishment.

For Krave the Andorian, his greater endurance proved to be something of a curse. He was able to keep going for longer than the others were, and somehow whatever seemed to be controlling the circumstances of the test seemed to be aware of it. If he tried to stop voluntarily, he was immediately jolted. He sobbed in frustration, he let out a string of profanities, he begged, he threatened, he did everything, and nothing seemed to help.

"Why aren't you doing anything?" he cried out to McHenry at one point.

"I am," said McHenry. "I'm watching."

"Do something beside that!"

"All right," said McHenry. He closed his eyes and turned away. And that was how he remained until Krave tumbled over, practically unconscious. The floor did nothing to him at that point.

A door slid open at the far end of the room and the mysterious green alien stepped in, looking at them with apparent curiosity. Its eyes flared slightly, as if it had come to some sort of conclusion.

McHenry got to his feet. "Who are you?" he demanded. "What race are you? What do you want? And how do you do that sparkling thing with your eyes, because really, that's pretty interesting."

The alien turned away from him and headed out the door.

From the floor nearby, Quiv growled, "That sparkling thing? What kind of stupid question was that?"

McHenry shrugged. "Just trying to make conversation."

"Conversation?" The strength was now surging back into Quiv, and he was getting to his feet, his hands flexing, and he shouted, *"Conversation?"* He lunged toward McHenry, who was too surprised by the sudden charge to do anything to get out of the way.

Quiv left his feet, hurtling forward, and he crashed into the chair that McHenry was sitting in.

Except that McHenry was no longer in it.

McHenry felt the air rushing up at him, and the sun was searing against his eyes. He raised an arm to shield himself from the glare, and tried to figure out just how he had wound up outside. For that matter he couldn't quite understand just where outside he was.

He started to take a step back and immediately fell.

The fact that he did not plunge to his death was miraculous. Displaying a truly impressive degree of quick reaction, to say nothing of considerable upper body strength, McHenry twisted around as he fell and slammed into the upper section of the small platform he'd been standing on. The platform was floating in midair with no apparent means of support, but that wasn't what concerned McHenry at the moment. Instead, his only priority was climbing back up onto it.

His legs pumped in midair under the platform, reflexively looking for support that simply wasn't there. Below him was a yawning, cavernous drop so deep that he couldn't even begin to figure out how far it was.

Yet even as he fought for his life, even as he felt his fingers losing their grip, part of his mind was elsewhere, analyzing the engineering structure of the small round platform to which he was clinging. He could not detect any sort of hum of a power source, nor did it seem to come equipped with any type of antigravity technology with which he was familiar. This platform was just . . . there. It appeared to be right in the middle of some sort of vast canyon. He saw the edges of the canyon, but they had to be at least a hundred yards away on either side.

The platform began to tilt in response to the shifting of McHenry's weight, but with Herculean effort he managed to straighten it and then slowly, carefully, climb upon it. His breath came in ragged gasps before finally steadying. Then he dusted himself off and looked around once more, as if to see whether his immediate situation had changed in any way that might be more favorable. Unfortunately, things hadn't altered one bit.

No.

No, that wasn't quite true.

The platform that he was on was sinking.

It wasn't by a lot, but it was enough to get his attention. It was only a few millimeters over the course of several minutes, but it was enough to indicate to him that things were not going to get better for him anytime soon.

He looked up at the sun. It was sinking toward the horizon.

He sat down to watch it. If it was going to be his last sunset, he wanted to appreciate it.

KALINDA

THE MOMENT THAT KALINDA walked into the room, she wanted to run screaming from it.

That, however, was not appropriate behavior for a princess of the Thallonian Empire . . . even the fallen Thallonian Empire. One of her breeding and background simply did not bolt from that which she found unpleasant or daunting, no matter how tempting that impulse might be.

The room that had been the last one that Jereme had ever spent time in was exactly as she had seen it in her dream. It had no furniture in it at all. It was some sort of practice room in which Jereme honed his skills and continued to train, even though he was ostensibly re-tired. The walls were sparkling white, or had been, which had made cleaning it that much more problem-atic. The blood had been cleansed, or at least the best effort possible had been put into cleaning it up. There were, however, still dark stains on the wall that she could see because she knew precisely where to look for them. Her gaze was drawn, however, to the center of the room where Jereme had been standing. For a brief moment the hyperreality of the dream overlapped with the reality of the world in which she was standing, and she thought that she could actually see Jereme standing there, only a few feet from her.

"Are you all right, Kally?" It took Kalinda a few moments to realize that not only was Si Cwan speaking to her, but also he had said the same thing several times. Each time he spoke, it was with growing concern.

"Yes. Yes, I am fine, Cwan," she replied. However, she looked anything but fine. Every aspect of her body language signaled that what she truly desired to do, more than anything else, was turn and leave. Si Cwan very likely knew that, but he was not about to make matters that much more difficult for her by inquiring about it. "I just . . . need a few moments to prepare . . ."

Ookla was standing next to Si Cwan, and in unison they both said "Prepare?" in obvious confusion.

"Yes. Prepare. I know what needs to be done here. And I'm reasonably sure I can do it."

"Kalinda." Si Cwan drew nearer to her, and there was deep concern on his face. He had addressed her by her full name rather than the diminutive, and the stern tone of voice made him sound vaguely like a teacher about to issue a scolding. "Kalinda, what 'it' are you referring to? What are you playing at?"

"I'm not playing, Si Cwan. This is no game to me. It's just . . . something I am certain I can do. Ever since I returned from the Quiet Place, my connection with those who have departed is . . . strong."

"That is absurd . . ."

"You were at the Quiet Place, Si Cwan. You heard the silent screams, you saw with your own eyes the anger that the departed can emit. Who are you to tell me that their cries from beyond are inaudible to me just because you cannot hear. Cannot, or will not."

"Kalinda," he said with a carefully even voice, "you are beginning to concern me."

"I am concerned as well, Si Cwan. Concerned that whoever did this terrible thing may get away with it, unless I do something about it. But before I do, I must ask you to leave. You and Ookla." She thought that her voice was starting to crack, betraying the concern that she was feeling and trying desperately to rein in. "I think it better if I am in this room alone."

"What are you planning to do?" he demanded.

"Whatever I can. That is all any of us can do." She pointed the way out. "Please, go now."

"Kalinda, I am not—"

"*Go.*" There was a force and anger to her that was of such controlled ferocity that Si Cwan was taken aback. At first it seemed as if he was not only going to ignore her request, but pick her up bodily, sling her over his shoulder, and cart her out of there himself. But then he bowed slightly, turned, and headed out. Ookla lingered a moment, not saying anything, but simply clicking his mandibles, and then he shuffled off as well.

Kalinda had had a strong feeling of what she was going to do—what she had to do—since she had first resolved to come. To that end, she had done everything she could to stay awake as much as possible on the journey to Pulva. While Si Cwan had dozed next to her (after scaring the hell out of the child behind him) Kalinda had struggled, and succeeded, in staying awake and wide-eyed. She was hoping that it was going to pay off now.

She was not in the Quiet Place itself, of course. The Quiet Place was a place of power, *her* place of power. The connections between those who had gone ahead and those who remained behind was much tighter, the walls of separation far more thin. But the separations here were also quite feeble, primarily because of the violence that had been committed here, and the strength of personality of the departed.

Kalinda went straight to the place in the room where her mind's eye had told her that Jereme had bled the last of his life's blood. There was no visual sign of it, but her instincts, her sight, told her all she needed to know. Slowly Kalinda sank to her knees, the first tell-tale signs of exhaustion beginning to appear. She yawned widely several times in a futile effort to remain awake. Staying awake, however, was not her plan, or at least not fully wide-awake.

She ran her palms across the floor. Some parts of it felt warmer to her than others. She thought it might be her imagination, but suspected that it was not. "Yes," she murmured, and again, "Yes." She thought she heard something at that point, but if it was indeed a voice it was not one that she could yet fully comprehend.

She lay back upon the floor. Visualization was especially helpful at these kinds of moments. She closed her eyes and called to her mind, as best as she could remember, the images that had torn across her slumber. It was not an easy thing for her to do; in fact, it was exceedingly painful. But she did it nonetheless, assembling it piece by piece. It was as if she were producing a painting, bit by bit. She sketched in the general shape of the face as she had seen it, and then came the details, the eyes, filled with betrayal, the mouth which was not twisted in fear, but rather was locked in a sneer of near contempt. And the blood, everywhere the blood, tinting the entire image red.

All of this she crafted in her mind, as if constructing a still-life.

And then the blood began to flow.

She had been pulled into a sort of waking dream before she was even aware of it.

The emanations that had been left behind in the room by the violent death which had occurred there had been completely absorbed into her. They had permeated her being, had suffused her very essence. There was no way for her to turn away from them.

But she realized that she was not seeing the events in the room as they necessarily were, but rather the way that Jereme had perceived them himself.

Jereme was not yet dead. He was getting to his feet, facing someone whom Kalinda could not see. She strained to look around, to see the source of the attack, but she was not in control of the vision. She did not yet have enough craft, enough honing of her abilities, to take charge of the situation in that manner. Instead she felt disoriented, ill at ease. If she'd been able to, she would have clawed her way out of there, but she was in too deep. There were voices in her head, low and angry, shouting, except that Jereme was not shouting. He was speaking calmly, albeit firmly. And it was the other . . . the other . . .

The other . . .

She saw him.

She had conjured up her own thoughts as to what the murderer would look like. But she had never envisioned him as being so . . . so handsome.

That, however, was what he was. If evil had a face, this was most certainly not it. He had a glorious smile, and even though it was being worn because he was about to inflict terminal mayhem upon somebody, it was a resplendent smile just the same. He was young, somewhere in his mid-twenties at most. His hair was blond and combed tightly back, a widow's peak coming to a perfect point. Indeed, everything about him was perfect. Kalinda, much to her revulsion, actually felt drawn to him. It was something about his eyes, a virtual magnet of attraction that she felt all but helpless before.

And his hands . . .

Those were the next things she noticed, because they were moving with incredible speed, so fast that she could not even track them. Jereme, for all his arts of defense, was not able to defend himself in the slightest. Oh, he tried. The blond man advanced on him, and the first ten times that he struck at Jereme, Jereme was not there. But the eleventh time, he connected, and suddenly there was a huge gash across Jereme's chest. Then came another six attempts, all futile, but the seventh struck home, and a crisscross of deep gashes was on Jereme's torso. He staggered, grim but smiling, and he laughed and he was unafraid. Kalinda couldn't tell whether he had truly been overcome, or whether he was bored with life and simply was taking the opportunity to end it, or perhaps he was truly so chagrined that he was being defeated by this young sadist that he was burying his anger deep, deep down, displaying an insouciant attitude to his murderer while knowing that his fury would rise from beyond the end of his life to be used against him who had ended it.

There was a pull at Jereme's chest, and a thrust, and

then came the fountain of blood. And he heard Jereme shout a name, and she wasn't sure, but it sounded something like "Olivan." She couldn't be sure. The name was completely strange to her.

And then Olivan—if that was who it had been—was gone. Kalinda was in his place, and the blood was all over her, splattered in her face, soaking her clothes. She let out a silent shriek, trying to tear away the blood-drenched clothes, but it did no good, for the blood had soaked right through and was all over her body.

She began to sob uncontrollably, at once mortified by her weakness and simultaneously not caring whether she seemed weak or not. The grim determination that she had displayed earlier when it came to doing her job was gone. Instead all she wanted to do was get out of there, before she herself was dragged down somehow into the pits of despair where the shade of Jereme now resided, waiting for someone to avenge him.

"Si Cwan!" she screamed, clutching at air, seeking reprieve, finding nothing except terror. Suddenly she was sinking. The blood had so completely softened the ground that she was literally sinking right into it, even though she was standing on a previously solid floor. She had forgotten that she was in a vision. It was all too real, and now she was sunk to her knees. The floor was still pulling her in, and she unwisely but instinctively shoved her hands down to try and find something solid to push against. This was an extremely bad move, for her hands sank in as well, and now there was nothing to stop her as the floor sucked her down, the blood bubbling up all around her, and she cried out as the blood oozed around her, up her nostrils, down her mouth, and she was choking on it, unable to breathe . . .

"Kalinda!"

She snapped back to consciousness and coughed up a huge clot of mucus.

It spattered all over Si Cwan's boot, and he looked down at it with distaste. But he only let it distract him momentarily as he focused back on his sister. "Kalinda . . . do you know where you are?" He was holding her firmly by the shoulders, trying to make eye contact. Her head was flopping about so much that it seemed affixed to her shoulders by means of a string. "Kalinda, do you know where you are?"

"Yes . . ." she managed to say. "I am . . . I am . . ."

"Where are you?"

"Here."

He shook his head and sighed. "Yes. That's right. You're here. Do you know where here is?"

"Yes . . . with you . . ."

"That's right . . ."

"And . . ." Words, names, images, were still tumbling through her brain, fighting for dominance. "And . . . with Jereme . . . and Olivan . . ."

The mention of the last name immediately sparked a reaction from Si Cwan. He turned and looked at Ookla, whose mandibles clicked even more animatedly than they had before. "Was Olivan here?" demanded Si Cwan.

"No. Absolutely not. It never even occurred to us that . . . I mean, it was so long . . ."

"Not long enough, apparently," Si Cwan said tightly. "It would seem that Olivan had a long memory."

"Happened so quickly," Kalinda was saying. "So fast . . . how long was I out . . . two minutes? Three?"

"Five hours."

"Oh." She saw that it was true; the shadows were becoming longer in the room. "Not especially time-efficient method. Sorry."

"No apologies necessary. It appears you got results. Let's get something to drink into you. You're shivering."

"Did my saying . . . what was it . . . Olivan . . . mean anything?"

"Yes, it does," Si Cwan said grimly. "It means that the bastard who owns that name is not going to be needing it much longer."

SOLETA

THE ROMULAN GUARDSMAN called Krakis was the only one who was wearing the helmet attachment to the armor, making him damned near impervious. He pulled a long, curved, and vicious-looking blade from its scabbard on his belt and took a step toward Rajari. The blade, however, was of less concern to Soleta than the disruptor that hung on the other side of his hip. Of the Romulans there, he appeared to be the only one wearing any sort of heavier armament than a blade. She wasn't entirely surprised; the local authorities took a dim view of energy weapons. They had given her some problems when she'd first arrived with her phaser, and only her Starfleet status had gotten them to back off. So they were very likely being discreet with the amount of weaponry they were carrying on them. She didn't recognize him from the alley; perhaps this Krakis had remained behind during the initial raid, and was considered to be some sort of enforcer, a second-in-command to Adis. All well and good, but it meant that disabling him in any sort of simple way was not going to be . . . well . . . simple.

Having just been ordered by his liege lord to dispose of Rajari, Krakis seemed all too happy to accommodate. Before he took a second step toward Rajari, however, he was frozen in his place by the steely voice of Soleta as she said, "Stop."

Slowly all eyes turned toward Soleta. Adis looked the most annoyed. "Who is this?"

"She was in the alley," said one of the other guardsmen. "She was with Rajari."

"I see. Are you his whore?" inquired Adis. "Perhaps you could service me."

"If you consider having your head blown off as being serviced, I shall be most happy to oblige you. You," and she gestured with the phaser to Krakis. "Use that blade to cut him loose. If you do not do so immediately, or if you endeavor to injure him or me," and she took a deep breath, "I shall kill you."

Krakis studied her very carefully, very thoroughly. Then his face twisted into a sneer. "Pacifist fool, just as all your misbegotten and genetically inferior race. You're bluffing," he said, and made a quick move toward his disruptor.

Soleta blew a precisely placed hole through his chest. Krakis was dead before he hit the ground. From the reactions of the other Romulans, it was clear that the seriousness of the threat that she presented had suddenly gone up several notches.

"We may be pacifists . . . but our reputation for our inability to bluff has apparently not preceded us," Soleta informed them. Her face was inscrutable. Never had her training been of greater use to her. She gestured to another Romulan and said, "You. Pick up the knife. Sever the bonds."

"Or you'll kill him, too," inquired Adis. "And me as well?"

"If necessary."

He looked at her thoughtfully. "You wear the shell of the Vulcan sheep . . . but there is more the wolf in you than appears at first glance. I wonder as to the purity of your blood, woman, for I see something of us in you. Perhaps more than you would like to admit there being. Who are you?"

Soleta was less than ecstatic about the direction of this conversation, and was rather anxious to terminate it. "The person holding the phaser. That is the only aspect of my identity that need concern you at the moment. I am waiting for you," she said to the Romulan guardsman, "for you to obey my orders."

"No," said the guardsman defiantly, looking to Adis for approval. Adis nodded, indicating that he'd given the right answer.

An instant later he was writhing on the ground, a chunk of his leg charred beneath his melted armor.

"I appear to be doing all the work here," Soleta said to Adis. "I know. You select the next victim. Unless you wish to volunteer."

There was no longer the slightest trace of amusement in Adis's hard eyes. "You are making a grave mistake."

"Perhaps. But at this point in time, I have a wider margin for error than you do. I am waiting for your decision."

Adis hesitated a long moment, and then he knelt next to the man who was clutching his ruined leg and picked up the long blade. He turned the cutting edge of the blade around so that it was facing him, thereby presenting no possible threat to Rajari. Then he slid it behind Rajari's bonds and severed them with one quick stroke.

"Get up, Rajari," Soleta said.

"I'm . . . not sure I can."

"Then I will leave you here."

"You . . . wouldn't . . ."

Soleta's face was unreadable. "One man is dead and another is crippled because they assumed that I was not as good as my word. I would hope you would not make that same miscalculation."

That was all the incentive that Rajari needed. He rose on unsteady and fragile legs, wobbling slightly. He took a few steps toward Soleta and was actually smiling slightly, clearly pleased with himself that he was able to move at all.

And then, abruptly, the smile evaporated, to be placed by a look of total horror.

Soleta had no idea what was happening, and before she could fully register the change in his attitude, Rajari was shouting "Move!" and with all the strength in his weakened legs, he lunged forward and shoved her to one side. It was at that moment that she heard the shrill, discordant howl of a disruptor and then Rajari staggered, a huge splotch of green blood covering his chest.

The only thing that prevented him from hitting the floor was Soleta's powerful arm which caught him.

And then, realizing that the move was a complete mistake, Soleta allowed the momentum of Rajari's fall to take them both down. It was a move that saved their lives as another disruptor blast cut through the air right where they'd been standing. The blast missed them clean. It did, however, happen to nail the Romulan who was standing right next to Adis. It burned away the back of his head and he went down, clutching at air spasmodically, the body not yet acknowledging that the life was over.

But Soleta landed hard and badly, and her elbow slammed into the floor, a jolt of pain washing down and causing the phaser to clatter from her hand.

For a moment, the three remaining Romulan guards, plus Adis, froze, as if unable to believe their good fortune. And then Adis shouted, *"Get her!"*

The shout unfroze them, and they charged.

Soleta shoved the unmoving Rajari aside and back-rolled, trying to get at the phaser. Just as she almost got to it, the foot of one of the Romulans kicked it just beyond her reach, sliding in between two stacks of crates. The move, however, brought his ankle close enough to her, and Soleta grabbed it with everything she had. She shoved upward, sending him stumbling back and crashing into Adis, who was waving his blade with the clear intention of using it. They both went down and suddenly there were Romulans on either side of her, grabbing her arms, slamming her against a stack of crates. But they didn't have a solid enough grip on her, and one of her hands managed to spear forward and clamp firmly onto his shoulder, her anger-driven strength crushing his armor, allowing her to reach through to the vulnerable area. His head snapped around, his eyes went wide, and his body slackened as the Vulcan nerve pinch did its job.

The other Romulan, however, had a firm grip on Soleta's wrist and was keeping her hand away from his shoulder. They struggled, and then Soleta spotted a sheathed blade in the belt of the Romulan she had just rendered unconscious. He was sagging to the floor, but her hand moved quickly enough to yank the blade free. She did not hesitate. The short blade flashed in her hand, slicing across his face, and the Romulan howled as he released her, reflexively grabbing for where she had carved him. His momentary lapse of focus was all Soleta needed as she grabbed him by the neck and sent him to sleep.

Then, instinctively, she grabbed him and held him in front of her, even as she turned to face Adis. She was jolted by a sudden thud, and there was a loud curse from Adis. She looked down and saw that Adis's blade was still quivering from where it had thudded into her makeshift shield's forehead.

The remaining guardsman and Adis came at her. She shoved the dead Romulan she was holding in front of her, and he careened into the oncoming assailants. Turning and moving as fast as she could, she clambered up one of the stacks of cartons nearby. Adis lunged at her and the stack swayed beneath her feet, tipped precariously, and then toppled forward. Soleta fell off backward. The guardsman, who was closer, let out a howl of protest, but it did him no good as the boxes toppled down upon him and he disappeared beneath them.

Soleta was down amid the fallen cartons, wedged in between, and suddenly she heard someone other than Adis shout, "Freeze." She looked up and saw another guardsman approaching, with a disruptor leveled right at her. It was obviously the shooter who had taken down Rajari moments before. He was coming toward her with the careful respect that one would display for someone who had proven herself to be a lethal force. Soleta was partly obscured by the cartons all around her, but he still had a clear shot at her.

"Shall I kill her, sir?" he inquired of Adis.

"No, Mekari," Adis said slowly. "She is too great a curiosity. We will take her prisoner and return with her to the homeworld. There we can run tests on her and see just what, precisely, she is, although I have my suspicions. Suspicions that I suspect are fairly close to the truth, eh, half-breed?"

Soleta was too self-controlled to allow the taunting epithet to register any sort of emotion on her face. She did, however, say, "I would not come any closer if I were you."

Mekari, the guardsman with the disruptor, laughed and came closer, seeing only a helpless female before him.

What he did not see was that she had managed to retrieve the phaser that had fallen in between the crates. It was nestled securely in her hand, and now Soleta fired. The beam evaporated both hand and disruptor. The guardsman stared at the smoking stump in stunned silence, the immensity of what had just occurred not fully registered upon him yet. In a way it was almost comical, if one were inclined toward truly morbid humor. It was at that point that Mekari let out an agonized shriek of dismay and he sank to his knees, unable to tear his gaze away from the charred remains of his limb.

Adis at this point appeared only mildly surprised by the turn of events. "Impressive marksmanship," he said.

"Not really," said Soleta evenly. "I was aiming for his heart." She managed to stand, shoving the remaining cartons aside, and she spied Rajari on the floor. Remarkably he was still alive, but his breathing was a rattling in his chest and his face was ashen. Keeping the phaser leveled at Adis, she went quickly to Rajari and hauled him to his feet. He was little more than dead weight, but he made some token effort to support himself.

"You have made this a far more costly endeavor than it needed to be," Adis advised her, but he did not sound particular worked up about it. "Particularly when you consider that the outcome was exactly the same. You have a dead man leaning on you."

"And I will have a dead man conversing with me if you are not quiet," Soleta warned him.

He contemplated her, as if considering her to be a problem only in the abstract. "Would you do that, I wonder? Could you? If I make no threatening move toward you whatsoever, would you be capable of cutting me down simply out of a sense of vengeance? Have you that much of the wolf in you, I wonder?"

"It seems to me," Soleta said, "that you are seeking an excuse not to attack me, so that you need not find out."

"Perhaps. Perhaps not. I suppose we will never know. Take him, for all the good or ill that he will do you. I will not try and stop you. Indeed," and he laughed softly in a rather unpleasant way, "I would prefer that you live a long life, carrying with you the knowledge that you risked your life to save this creature and, ultimately, failed to do so. Tell me this, though. You seem reasonably intelligent and resourceful. What possible interest can you have in this . . . thing?"

She made no reply, for none seemed necessary . . . and also because she was not entirely sure what she could say.

There were still moans coming from the Romulan with the injured leg and the one with the ruined hand. The latter, Mekari, looked at her with pure hatred and snarled, "I will kill you for this."

"Perhaps. But not today."

She was surprised by how little weight Rajari actually seemed to have. Perhaps it was the effects of the illness that racked his body. Still, for someone who had loomed so large in her nightmares for so many years, he had remarkably little substance when it came down to it.

She never allowed her gaze to waver from Adis, who had lapsed into contemplative silence, even as she hauled Rajari away. Rajari was eerily silent, and only the faintest strains of his labored breathing allowed her to determine that he was still alive. She said nothing but simply kept pulling him grimly toward the nearest exit, which was, unfortunately, a hideous distance away. "Help me, Rajari, if you're at all able," she whispered to him. She wasn't really expecting any response, but to her surprise, some reserves of energy seemed to flicker in him still. He supported a reserves of his own weight to aid her as they made their way to the door through which she had first entered the facility. She knew there were likely others about, but she didn't want to take the time to try and locate them.

With no need for stealth, she aimed her phaser and disintegrated the door. The cool night air beckoned to them and, repositioning her burden once more, she half-walked, half-stumbled out the door with him.

"Listen . . ." It was Rajari, and the rattling in his chest was not only awful, but also telltale. She had bare minutes left at most, and the force of will that was keeping him alive at this point was nothing short of amazing.

"We have to get clear . . ."

"No time . . . listen . . . in apartment . . . in box . . ."

The strain of supporting him was beginning to weigh

on her. Reluctantly, she eased him to the ground, cradling his upper body in her arms as she knelt next to him. Blood was fountaining from his ruined chest, his lifeblood literally pouring into the street around them.

She heard a rumble of thunder from overhead. The atmosphere processors on Titan were still working to their functional norm, apparently, and their timing could not have been worse. Unfortunately, no one was asking Soleta whether precipitation would be convenient to her. Within moments of the overhead warning, rain began to pour in thick, wet drops. "Perfect," muttered Soleta.

All the strength was gone from Rajari's body, and for half a heartbeat she thought he was gone as well. His eyes were glazed over. Suddenly it was as if he was physically hauling his half-departed spirit back into his body as he convulsed a moment and then focused directly on her. "In apartment . . . box," he whispered.

"The box, yes. What about it?"

"Inside . . ." He steadied himself and took a long, deep breath into the remains of his chest that, she sensed, was the last he was going to be able to draw. "Inside . . . family heirloom . . . I stole long ago . . . stole from my own family . . . if you can believe that . . ."

"I can believe it," she muttered, and then mentally chided herself for her ill-timed display of cynicism.

He did not appear to have heard her. "House of Melkor . . . that is my family name . . . hoped to return it . . . with my own hand . . . stealing it . . . unpardonable sin . . . if not returned . . . I will never go to afterlife . . ." His body was shaking, his hand clasping spasmodically on her shoulder. The rain was coming down harder now, plastering her hair and clothes to her.

But even though it was spattering full in his face, his eyes weren't reacting to it. She wondered how much he was even aware of his surroundings, or aware of anything save for this great transgression that he was unburdening to her. "Must be returned . . . promise me . . . you will . . . promise . . . please . . ."

Leave him. Leave him and never look back.

The inner voice made such eminent, perfect sense, and the action it recommended would have been wholly appropriate for her, were she still dealing with the monster that she had carried in her darkest memories for all these years.

Except the stark, irrefutable truth that she had to admit, even to herself, was that she wasn't seeing him that way. From the monster that he had been, he had been reduced in her eyes to a tragic figure that had carried within him an innate spark of nobility. For whatever reasons, the spark had never been fanned until it was too late, and all she could see before her now was a creature of infinitely wasted potential. Who knew how much he would have been able to accomplish if the circumstances had been different.

And she heard her own voice saying, "I promise."

"Swear. Swear on the memory of your mother . . ."

"I swear by the memory of T'Pas, I will do this thing for you."

He actually forced a smile. He let out the last, remaining bit of his breath as he managed to say, "If I'd ever had a daughter . . . I would have wanted her . . . to be like you."

And then he was gone.

She stood then, the rain cascading about her, and watched as the remains of his blood swirled away into the gutter. She felt the thudding of her own heart even as she set the phaser for wide beam, took aim, and fired. The beam enveloped his corpse, scattering his molecules to the wind as Rajari vanished in a haze. She made a slight choking noise as she turned away from the spot where her father had died and headed back to his apartment to make good on a promise she had regretted the instant she had made it.

KEBRON

KEBRON AWOKE BY DEGREES, wondering why he was
feeling a pressure on his arm. Since Kebron was not really accustomed to feeling much of anything, thanks to
the toughness of his normal epidermis, any sensation—
however gentle or innocuous it might be—was enough
to catch his attention.

He also heard a gentle snoring.

Zak Kebron had fallen asleep leaning against a wall
of the fairly boring room that he had been thrust into.
Zanka, at his specific instruction, had kept the hell
away from him. The woman had gotten on his nerves
extraordinarily quickly, and he was wondering why in
the world this Adulux fellow had any interest in staying
with her in the first place. His reason for wanting her
back was obvious; if he could manage to find her and
produce her for the authorities, then he would be off the
hook. It would be extremely difficult for anyone to

make any sort of convincing murder case against him if the alleged victim was standing there hale and hearty. But why in the world had he desired to reconstruct their relationship? She seemed little more than a bundle of neuroses. She was clingy, and annoying, and . . .

. . . and her head was, at that moment, leaning against Kebron's forearm.

Clearly she had disobeyed his specific instructions to keep her distance. Sometime during the night (night? was it night? time had lost its meaning) she had moved over to the sleeping, disguised Brikar and sought some measure of solace. Or security. Or whatever it was she thought she was getting from resting her head on his arm.

He looked down at her with vague disinterest. Still, he couldn't help but notice that in repose, she seemed somehow a bit less obnoxious. Indeed, while slumbering her face had actually settled into something that was not too unpleasant to look upon. She even had a small smile on her lips, which was a pleasing contrast to the look of overwhelming concern that she'd been wearing since they'd first put her in there with him.

What Kebron actually found slightly disconcerting was that her head felt oddly comforting resting where it was.

It was a bizarre feeling for Kebron. As one of the very few Brikar in Starfleet, he had grown accustomed to being alone. Solitude was not the same as loneliness. By his build, by the physical requirements of his mass, by the impervious skin that cloaked his mammoth frame, they had helped to carve a separate niche for Kebron that he had very comfortably inhabited. He had never sought any way out of the box that circumstances had created for him, because truthfully . . . where was there to go?

Zanka's head on his arm, though, filled him with a vague sort of warmth. He adjusted his position slightly and now Zanka—still asleep—insinuated her body against his.

And then he saw that tears were running down her face. Even in her sleep, she was so upset that she was not able to rest comfortably.

Kebron reached over and, with a tenderness that he once would not have been capable of, wiped some of the tears away. The moisture felt hot on his fingertips. Curious, he brought his fingers up to his mouth and tasted it gingerly. Salty.

Her arms waved about aimlessly and then wrapped themselves in a grip around his. She was no longer simply leaning against him; now she was actually clinging to him, as if he were some sort of life preserver in a sea of uncertainty. He wanted to pry her off, to move away from her, but something within him stopped him. And he wasn't sure whether he was pleased about that or not. He was so accustomed to people counting on him, needing him, but not in any sort of emotional manner. If people required physical protection, then naturally it was within his purview as head of security to provide it. He went about his job with brisk and ruthless efficiency.

Some even claimed too ruthless; when attacked with deadly force, Kebron had not hesitated to return it in kind. There had been some raised eyebrows and noises made by Starfleet, but the comments had never gone anywhere. Kebron had always suspected that Mackenzie Calhoun was responsible for running some sort of interference between critics and Kebron. Not that he was ever going to have the opportunity to ask Calhoun about it.

The thought saddened him. And in being saddened, he actually drew Zanka slightly closer to himself. He did so unconsciously, totally unaware that he had done it. Zanka, however, was more than aware enough for the both of them, for the small movement brought her to full wakefulness. She put a hand up against Kebron's chest and seemed to draw solace from it. It just made Kebron feel uncomfortable . . . but uncomfortable in a way that he couldn't really express.

"Are we going to get out of here?" she asked.

"Yes," he said firmly.

"How do you know?"

"I do."

"How?"

"Because I said so."

The bravado seemed to impress her, bring her some measure of comfort. Then her face clouded. "But . . . but do you think you can protect me from that . . ." Her hand wavered in the direction of the door. ". . . from that creature?"

"Yes."

"But how are you going to . . . ?" Then, despite the seriousness of the situation, she actually managed to laugh ever so slightly. "Of course. Because you said so."

He nodded.

"Believe it or not, that's actually good enough for me. You know, Kebron . . . you're so unlike any other man I've ever met. You seem so much . . . bigger. Powerful. Confident."

He said nothing.

"How do you do it?" she asked. "How do you maintain such boundless confidence? It's remarkably attractive, you know."

Kebron definitely did not like the direction the conversation was going. "No. It's not."

"Yes. It is."

And then, before he could once again tell her that it wasn't, she kissed him.

It was something that he was familiar with by having observed it, or similar gestures, in other races. The Brikar had no such tradition. Their rocklike hides made such gentle and subtle sensations utterly futile. Which was why Zanka's sudden movement caught him completely by surprise.

His reaction was swift and immediate. He reached up and clamped a hand on her shoulder, but he found that he was holding it far more gently than he would have thought. Nor was he pushing her away. He wasn't drawing her toward him, either. It was as if he was assessing what was happening to him.

Naturally the door to the room chose that moment to slide open, and in stumbled Adulux.

Adulux looked utterly disoriented, but his attention focused very quickly on Kebron and Zanka, and, more important, on what they were doing. He gaped in shock, as if his brain was having trouble processing what his eyes were telling him. All the emotions of the moment tumbled about within him, warring, trying to chart a course to guide him. But there was nothing simple and immediate, and he looked like someone cast adrift, unsure of what to think or whom to trust.

He did not see the kiss, for they had parted by that point, but their proximity and Zanka's body language were unmistakable. As stunned and confounded as Adulux was to see her, Kebron saw that Zanka's reaction to seeing Adulux was about as far from confusion as a person could be. There was no confusion in her mind, oh no. She was clearly afraid, even terrified. Of everything that she had experienced up until that point, it was the presence of Adulux that seemed to fill her with the most consternation.

"What are you doing," demanded Adulux, sounding much less like a relieved husband than an infuriated one, "with him? What's going on here?"

"Smile. You've found her," Kebron said. He was careful to physically distance himself from her, even though his instincts were quite different. What he really wanted to do was draw her close, hold her tight in powerful arms that did not have to be concerned about breaking her in half accidentally. He knew that there was no reason for him to feel that way. That it was a purely visceral reaction in response to sensations foisted upon him by the genetic surgery. Inside he was still the same. But on the outside, he was being fed all sorts of stimuli that were playing havoc with the Zak Kebron that he had always been. He made a conscious effort to push it aside as he said, "Aren't you pleased?"

He looked as if he had to remind himself to say so. "Of course I am, Zanka," and he took a step toward her, his arms outstretched.

She scuttled around so that she was behind Kebron, keeping him between herself and her husband. "Keep him away from me!" she said. "Don't let him hurt me again!"

"Again?" Kebron's voice was suddenly low and deadly. "What do you mean, 'again.'"

"She's upset. Distraught," Adulux said quickly. "They've done something to her while they had her up here ..."

"He hurt me, Kebron. He always did! Beat me up, smacked me. It's why I wanted quit of him. You have no idea," and she was clutching at him again, "no idea what it took for me to leave him. He spent years breaking down whatever sense of self-respect I had. I kept thinking it was my fault. But it wasn't. It was his! His!" and she pointed an accusing finger at Adulux.

"Zanka," Adulux said very quietly, with supernatural control, "you don't know what you're talking about. The Sentries . . . they believe I killed you . . ."

"You would have! Given the chance, you would have. You'd have done anything to stop me from leaving you!"

"That's ridiculous. Kebron," and he looked imploringly to Zak, "speak to her. Make her listen to reason. They did something to her."

"When we get out of here," Kebron told him firmly, "she lets the authorities know she's alive. You're clear. And then . . . that's it."

"What do you mean, 'That's it'?" There was something in Adulux's face that seemed most unpleasant.

"I mean you leave her alone, from that point on."

Adulux bristled openly. "Who do you think you are? You have no business telling me that. No right telling me that. You work for me. You're supposed to be on my side."

"Am I?" Kebron was not especially impressed by Adulux's spiraling temper tantrum. Then again, when it came to anger, bellicose displays, or most methods of attack, Kebron was tough to intimidate.

"Yes!" Adulux was looking back and forth between Kebron and Zanka with increasing agitation. Yet to Kebron, it also seemed that there was a cold, quiet cunning that served up a stark contrast to that outward frenzy. "Yes, you're supposed to be on my side! You're supposed to be helping me! But I can see what's going on here! It couldn't be more obvious. You're falling in love with her!"

"No," Kebron said firmly, and he knew beyond question that his denial was candid. Whatever curious sensations he might be experiencing at the moment, there was not a shred of love in his heart for her. On the outside he might look like something else, but in his heart he remained Brikar. As a Brikar, this female simply held no interest for him.

At least, he believed that to be true.

Immediately, his mind recoiled at the passing thought. This wasn't a matter of "believe." This simply was.

So why was he holding her tighter against him? Doubtless it was from a desire to protect her. It came naturally to one whose main profession was to provide protection.

"Yes! You are! And you think I'm afraid to do something about it!"

"He knows you are!" Zanka said challengingly.

"You're not helping," he informed Zanka.

Pushed beyond all endurance, motivated by fear, lack of sleep, anger, and whatever else might be tumbling about in his head, Adulux made the spectacularly bad decision of coming at Kebron.

Kebron angled Zanka around himself so that she was standing behind him, out of harm's way. The threat of an infuriated Adulux was not especially daunting to him. He might not have been what he was, but he still outweighed Adulux by a considerable margin, and also had been in more than a few fights.

He was not, however, prepared for the ferocity of

Adulux's charge. Under ordinary circumstances, Kebron could have knocked Adulux on his rump in less than a second. But the Liten had going for him unbounded fury, adrenaline (or at the very least the appropriate parallel chemical) pumping through his body, and a berserker fury at seeing Zanka so quickly and easily transferring all her adoration and ardor over to Kebron.

With all that taken into consideration, that was why Kebron actually required three seconds to knock Adulux on his rump.

It would not have been all that difficult even if Adulux had not come wading right into it. But he was paying no attention at all to style or finesse or intelligent pugilism. He simply wanted to get within range of Kebron so that he could start pounding on him. Although he did get within a few feet, that was as close as he was able to make it before Kebron's fist swung in a very leisurely manner, catching Adulux squarely on the point of the chin. Adulux spun in place, then staggered for a moment as the world whirled around him. "You!" he bellowed in indignation, pointing in fury to a spot about two feet to Kebron's left. "How dare you—I—you." Then he fell back and hit the ground hard.

Zanka came from around Kebron's back and hugged him tightly. "You were so brave!" she cried.

"No," said Kebron. "Bravery requires a . . . threat . . ."

His voice trailed off as he saw the unexpected development that matters had undergone.

When Adulux had fallen, he had landed on something. That much was easy to see, because he was arching his back and moaning in annoyance, twisting about to try and pull whatever-it-was out from under his back. Then his eyes widened as he saw that it was some sort of heavy-duty blaster. It was not a design that Kebron recognized, but he had absolutely no reason to doubt that it did not present a threat.

Adulux's eyes glistened in silent joy as he scrambled back to provide a bit of distance between himself and Kebron. Kebron took a step forward, but now Adulux had the blaster up and pointed squarely at Kebron's chest.

"Get away from her," said Adulux.

"No," said Kebron.

"Do you love her?"

"No."

"Are you that anxious to die for her anyway?"

"Not especially," Kebron admitted.

Zanka let out an alarmed squeal. "Kebron! Don't you care whether I live or die?"

He looked down at her, and the words *Not really* came to mind. But there was something in her face, something in her utter lack of guile, which stirred something within him. He had no idea what that something might be, but it was there no matter how much he would have liked to ignore it.

Kebron's hesitation was all Adulux needed to see. With a howled curse that damned Kebron and all his ancestors going back several generations, Adulux squeezed the trigger. The Brikar had no idea at all what it was that blasted out of the gun's muzzle at that point. All he knew was that it was energy, it was considerable, it was crackling and black, and it knocked him flat. He lay there, paralyzed, his body twitching, his mind numb, and Adulux approached him and placed the barrel of the gun squarely against his temple.

"I don't like you," he said, and pulled the trigger.

SOLETA

IN THE YEARS THAT SHE HAD SPENT on her own journeying around the Federation—and outside the Federation—Soleta had picked up more than a few tricks, made quite a few contacts.

In the past, her greatest achievement had been managing to make it into the heart of Thallonian space in a privately owned shuttle that had been a gift from her parents. However, the shuttle had been lost shortly before her assignment to the *Excalibur* during an unfortunate crash-landing incident on Risa. That world's guidance computers had misfired and sent her on a collision course with a runabout that nearly shredded her. She'd been lucky to come away from it in one piece. They had made restitution, but she had not yet taken the time to obtain a replacement personal shuttle.

Besides, an individual shuttle might draw attention she didn't want. Adis, a powerful and well-placed individual, had had more than enough time to see her and familiarize himself with her. It might very well have been that some of Rajari's paranoia had rubbed off on her, but she could not help herself: She was concerned that Adis might have people watching the ports of Romulus. Or maybe he had circulated a picture of her, composed from memory or perhaps a hidden camera that she had not known about. Granted, relations with Romulus were cordial at the moment, but she was still a Starfleet officer and a Vulcan, and would be subject to intense scrutiny. She could, of course, try to sneak onto Romulus in a solo shuttle, but she doubted she would be able to elude the planetary detectors.

Her sneaking into Thallonian space had been quite an achievement. Getting onto Romulus on her own was doable, but carried with it a number of hazards.

So she had required help. Very special help.

After some casting about, she had wound up coming to a fairly experienced smuggler nicknamed "Sharky," with whom she'd had some dealings during her wandering days. (It was a nickname that she absolutely abhorred, but he had chosen it himself and seemed rather enamored of it, so there wasn't all that much she could do.) She had bailed him out of a rather sticky situation and consequently earned a debt from him that she now decided to cash in. Sharky, unfortunately, was not terribly interested in being cooperative. He was a heavyset, dyspeptic human with hair that was matched in thinness only by his temper.

It had taken Soleta many weeks, but she had managed to catch up with him at a spaceport, holding court in his freighter. Sharky never emerged from the ship if he could help it. He was paranoid that someone would steal it, having formed an attachment to the vessel that could be described charitably as "interesting" and uncharitably as "obsessive." He had a habit of addressing it occasionally, as if it were sentient. Others might have been concerned that it was evidence he was unstable. Soleta simply chose to find it peculiar.

"You can't be serious, girl," he had said. He always addressed her as "girl." After the first dozen times that she had informed him that she didn't wish to be addressed that way, she gave up. Obviously he was saying it just to get a rise out of her. If she did not respond, he would stop saying it. It was a nice theory. She'd stopped responding, and he'd gone right on saying it. She took some measure of consolation in feeling that at least she wasn't wasting time trying to prevent him from saying it. "You want me to sneak you on to Romulus to run an 'errand,' wait for you to run it, and then take you off Romulus? It's insane."

"I am perfectly serious, Sharky. Thanks to me, you are still breathing."

"And if I do this thing, then perhaps I won't be still breathing, also thanks to you."

"You owe me."

"And that is supposed to be your most persuasive argument?"

"Sharky," she said coolly, "I will be back on a starship before too long. A starship has tremendous communicative range. And I will assure you that, whatever port we go to, whatever planetary heads we may deal with, I will be certain to let them all know that you cannot be trusted in any transactions of any sort. Having a Starfleet officer badmouthing you throughout the quadrant cannot be good for business."

He gave her an appraising stare, as if trying to figure out the likelihood that she did not mean every word she said. But the Vulcan reputation for veracity served her extremely well, and the dismissive scowl was replaced by obvious consideration as he gave thought to just how likely it would be that he could pull this off. "All right," he said slowly, "let us put forward a hypothetical . . . since I have to remember that I am speaking with a Starfleet officer and wouldn't wish to admit to activities that are frowned upon by your superiors."

"You are being overcautious."

"I'd rather be overcautious than under arrest."

"Point taken. Hypothesize as you desire."

"Let us suppose," he said, fingering a few stray wisps of hair on his chin, "that I had a contact on Romulus who provided me, on occasion, with fine cargo of Romulan ale for certain customers of that rare substance."

"Go on," Soleta prompted.

"Let us further suppose that, although it would take some effort, an ale run could be scheduled in, say, a week's time. All the appropriate clearances have been made, palms have been greased, latinum secured, and so on."

"And there would be room in your cargo bay for a stowaway who would be able to attend to certain errands while you attended to yours."

"A stowaway!" His ample chin now quivered with suitable indignation. "I am shocked . . . shocked and . . . and . . ."

"Appalled?" she offered.

"Yes, thank you. Shocked and appalled at the notion of someone successfully stowing away on my vessel! I would hate to hear of such criminal activities carried out under my very nose!"

"Far be it from me," she said politely, "to cause you such angst and agitation. We will speak no more of it."

"I should hope not," he told her, straightening his jacket and recovering from the brief flurry of distress he so convincingly exhibited. "My vigilance in such matters is undisputed. Why, I would hate to think that if a would-be stowaway showed up here in precisely one week's time at precisely 0800 hours, she would be able to sneak in while my back was turned. It would be almost as outrageous as thinking that there would be space for her in my cargo bay already set up, including sleeping and sanitary accommodations."

"Unthinkable," Soleta said. "I cannot even hazard a guess as to what had entered my mind."

"See that it doesn't happen again," said Sharky.

The ship took off without incident, but then again, Soleta hadn't been expecting any sort of trouble in that regard. The problems, if there were any, would most certainly occur once they were making their approach to Romulus. She couldn't help but wonder just how many "palms" had been "greased" to make certain that passing through the Romulan Neutral Zone did not result in instant assault by several Romulan vessels. She reasoned that the patrol ships on the Zone border ran in some sort of scheduled pattern. It was the only reasonable assumption; the border was too wide, space too vast. Ships couldn't be everywhere, it just wasn't possible. So in order to pass through unmolested, all one had to do was be familiar with whatever the scheduled routes of the patrol ships were. The proper information from the right people on the inside could be obtained . . . for a sufficiently greasy palm, she surmised.

All of these, however, were details that Sharky had already attended to. That was, after all, what he was good at. Soleta had other considerations. As she crouched in the makeshift area that had been cleared for her in the hidden cargo bay in the ship's bowels (Sharky being a smuggler, after all, so naturally the cargo bay would be concealed and shielded from scans), she once again opened the box that she had secured from Rajari's apartment.

It was a remarkable heirloom inside. She picked it up and marveled at the weight and coolness of it. It was an ornately carved disk, with an odd pattern of rods crisscrossing its middle. It was solid silver and glistened even in the dim lighting of the cargo bay.

Not for the first time, she wondered once more why she was doing this. She had promised, yes, but she did not have to promise. And having made the promise, was she really obligated to keep it? Considering what this man was, what he had done . . .

And yet . . .

Soleta let out an uneasy sigh. She had thought about it, pondered it, meditated on it, and was reasonably sure she knew why she was doing it.

It wasn't for him. It was for her.

Ever since her chance encounter with Rajari back on the *Aldrin,* Soleta had carried with her the knowledge and awareness of the circumstances of her conception. As unreasonable as it seemed, it had made her feel tainted. Unclean. She was not spawned from a moment of joy or desire, or even from a simple biological drive that had perpetuated her species for centuries. No, she was the product of a brutal, barbaric act. And because of that, because of the beast who had lain upon her mother and conceived a child, Soleta had felt as if she were a lesser being. She knew intellectually that what she was feeling was illogical. She had never felt any lack of self-worth earlier in her life. She had always serenely been certain of herself, of her capabilities, of her Vulcan heritage. That serenity had dissolved beneath the acid rain of Rajari's chortling nostalgia for his savagery.

But Rajari had changed. He had found some higher power, he had wanted to redeem himself. His sacrifice to save Soleta had been part of that redemption, and the returning of the amulet in the box was the final step. Rajari was now purely a being of the past, a memory, and Soleta had been handed a means of purifying that memory. Well . . . perhaps not purifying it. That was taking it too far, certainly. She would, however, be able to lessen the sting of the memory somewhat. She was helping to set right something that Rajari had done wrong, and in doing that, she was reclaiming a bit of her own sense of inner peace. For if Rajari was not fundamentally and irredeemably evil, then that gave Soleta some hope for herself.

"You're not evil. You never were," Soleta reminded herself, and she knew that to be true . . . up to a point. Who knew, though, what she was capable of becoming? After all, she had Romulan blood within her, and blood had a habit of betraying one at the oddest times.

She thought about one of her earliest classes in training in the Vulcan Way, when a rough voice interrupted her and said, "You look thoughtful."

She glanced up at Sharky, looking at her with a mildly amused smile. "I was under the impression you did not know I was here."

"I have extensive short term-memory problems," he replied. "As soon as I walk out, I'll forget I saw you. What's on your mind?"

"I was recalling," she said, "the First Three Rules of Vulcan Discipline."

"And they would be . . . ?"

"The First Rule is: Know yourself completely. The Second Rule is: Rule One is Impossible."

"That makes no sense. It's totally illogical," he said.

"That is basically Rule Three," she said. "Rule Three is: To Know Oneself completely is to know that the Impossible is Illogical."

"I'm completely lost."

"Do not be concerned," Soleta consoled him. "It is but a joke common at Starfleet Academy. Very common. And yet I believe there may be some truth to it."

"You do?" he asked.

"After a fashion."

He snorted derisively. "Y'ask me, there should be a fourth rule that says, 'Ignore previous three rules.'"

"That's the fifth rule, actually."

Sharky stared at her for a moment, trying to see through the wall of inscrutability that she had thrown up around herself. And then he laughed once, very loudly and very coarsely, and slapped her affectionately on the shoulder. "You're quite a piece of work, Soleta, you know that?"

"So I have been told," she said.

And with that said, Sharky clambered out of the hidden cargo bay, leaving Soleta to her musings.

ROMULUS

NOT A SINGLE ROMULAN in the streets was giving her a second look, which suited Soleta just fine.

She was dressed rather unassumingly, sporting the typical garb of a Romulan street merchant. In addition to the loose-fitting grays she wore, she also had the traditional bandanna wrapped around her head. On a practical basis, it helped keep her long hair from dropping in her eyebrows. Even more usefully, with the bandanna pulled down low it obscured her less-than-Romulan brow, although she kept it tucked under her ears so that the distinctive points would show. That way she was able to pass for Romulan from any casual glance, and hopefully no one would be inclined to afford her anything more than that.

There was brisk activity going on all around her, and she moved through it quietly and efficiently. Even as she went about her business, Sharky was attending to his. She had made her way from the spaceport where Sharky's vessel had landed. (And from which, naturally, Sharky wasn't budging. Sharky's contact or contacts were coming to him, and that was perfectly fine with Soleta. This errand was something she wanted to attend to entirely on her own.)

It was her first time on Romulus, and it was all that she could do not to come across exactly like someone who was a newcomer. She wanted to take in every aspect of the city, stare at everything, and ask a thousand questions. She had always been ashamed, even mortified over her Romulan heritage. It was her great shame, and her great secret. Indeed, in some respects she couldn't believe that she had confessed her background to Shelby. She had been trying to prove something to Shelby, and using herself as a guinea pig had been a foolishly rash and impetuous thing to do. She could only hope that she would not live to regret the decision.

In any event, this was the first time that she ever felt some measure of pride in her less-desirable ancestry. The buildings, the architecture, were dazzling and impressive, with much hand-carved statuary that indicated an eye for art, for detail. The statues depicted great Romulans of the past, and they were either carved directly into the buildings themselves as reliefs, or were freestanding in places ranging from squares to street corners.

There was one sight that struck her in particular, catching her attention so thoroughly that she stopped in her tracks and just observed it for several minutes. It was the sight of several Romulan children, laughing and playing, clambering up the base of one particularly impressive statue of some Romulan hero or another. He was pointing toward the sky in a very heroic fashion, the face carved with such intricacy that she felt convinced that the eyes were going to turn from their resolute gaze upward and instead fix on her. In contrast to the regal air of the statue itself, the children's laughter and activities were the height of innocence. There were three of them, two boys and a girl, none of them over the age of eight. They carried on for some minutes, garnering amused glances or comments from passersby, until their mother (or at least the mother of one of them) showed up to rein them in and hustle them off.

For some reason, it was not how she had envisioned the Romulans. She was accustomed to thinking of them as a race filled purely with deceit and treachery. Skulking about the galaxy in their cloaked ships, seeking to cause destruction and sabotage wherever and whenever they could. That was not what she was seeing here, however. She saw people, no more and no less, going about their business or living ordinary, unremarkable lives. She had gotten used to thinking purely as a Starfleet officer, for to such an individual, the Romulans were simply an enemy race who deserved exactly the amount of attention that was required to keep them at bay. Beyond that, they weren't worth much thought. At least, that was how she was accustomed to feeling. Now she had no idea what to think.

"Are you lost?"

She turned and saw the mother who had just collected the children from the statue. She was holding one with either hand, and the third—the girl—had wrapped herself around the woman's leg. The Romulan woman stared at Soleta inquisitively, but not in any sort of threatening manner. She was simply trying to be polite. A polite Romulan! Up until that moment, Soleta's definition of a polite Romulan was one who, before he reached into your mouth to rip your tongue out, would wash his hands first.

"I am . . . looking for the Rikolet," she said.

"What's that, Mother?" inquired the little girl from her position on the leg.

She glanced down at her child and said, "The City of the Dead." Then she looked back to Soleta. "Mourning one who has gone on?"

"Paying respects," Soleta said judiciously.

"As you wish. It is," and she pointed, "three blocks in that direction, and then to the left. It is impossible to miss."

"My thanks," said Soleta. She bowed slightly to show her appreciation and then headed off in the direction the woman had indicated. Within minutes, thanks to her brisk stride, she was passing through the gated entrance of the Rikolet.

The Rikolet was not actually a city per se. It was simply called that. It was a sort of city within the city, surrounded by high walls and filled with crypts as far as the eye could see. Soleta let out a very, very low whistle of amazement as she saw the paved streets of the Rikolet extending practically to the horizon line. She had never seen anything quite like it.

The Rikolet was reserved for the rich families, for the nobility, for the senators and praetors. In short, for those people who could both afford it and were worth it from a societal standpoint. Even from where she was standing, Soleta could see that the stone and masonry work throughout the Rikolet put the rest of the already formidable city to shame.

There was a holo guide at the front of the Rikolet, and she consulted it. The tomb for the House of Melkor was down and to the left. Soleta started on her way. As she walked, she passed others walking around, either individually or in groups. The place was not simply filled with mourners. Most of the people there were taking in the scenery, openly admiring the effort that had been expended in creating this amazing place. Soleta couldn't blame them. It was indeed quite an accomplishment. Even though she had come there with a special purpose and she had her own deadlines to attend to, Soleta took her time.

At one point she stopped to take in a particularly striking piece of scenery. Far beyond the boundaries of the walls, some distance to the north, several very impressive towers stretched toward the sky, seemingly only falling short by a small margin. The domes gleamed gold in the sunlight, and great winged creatures of prey were poised atop them, looking ready to leap from their posts at a moment's notice and charge into battle against all enemies of the empire. She knew immediately that it was the Noble House: a popular and ancient gathering place for some of the richest and most powerful in the Romulan Empire. Some said that the Noble House was an even more important place in Romulus than the Senate . . . although, for that reason alone, senators did not even like to admit that the Noble House existed. It was seen as something of a challenge to the power of the Senate. But no one wished to make a move against it, and so the enmity had simply smoldered for many years.

Still, it was a most impressive structure, and once again she felt a stirring of pride.

And once more, for the first time in a while, her inner voice spoke to her. *Do not become carried away with this. You are Vulcan. You were raised as Vulcan, your mother is Vulcan, and the only man whom you have ever truly called Father is Vulcan. That is where your roots are, not here. Not here. You are simply over-compensating for these years of uncertainty and self-disgust.*

She knew, in her heart, that that was true to some degree. Nevertheless, it brought her some measure of comfort. The years when she felt that she had lost herself were still a very stinging reality to her. Anything that she could do to regain some of that was fine with her.

Some minutes later, she had located the crypt belonging to the House of Melkor. What she found interesting were the plaques on either side of the entrance. On the left was a list of those members of the Melkor house who were "in residence," as it were, their bodies lying entombed within. On the other side, however, was a plaque with far more names. Upon closer inspection, she saw that the latter contained all the names of those who had been born into the august House of Melkor. Furthermore, each name was mounted on a tab that was removable. Immediately she understood why; upon their demise and entombment, each of their names could be switched from one side to the other. It was a symbolic way of noting their passing from this sphere to the next.

She did not see Rajari's name there.

This puzzled her somewhat, and she felt a brief moment of suspicion. She glanced over at the side of the dead, just to see if someone had already moved his name over there. It was certainly possible, since he had in fact died. The fact that he was forever forbidden from returning to Romulus would preclude the need for waiting for his body. Such banishment, Soleta knew, stretched even unto death. But his name was not on the side of the deceased either.

Then she noticed that, on the living side, one of the tabs was blank. Curious, she reached for it and slid it out of its small receptacle. She turned it around, and sure enough, there was Rajari's name on it. There was no telling how long it had been that way, but whoever had made the gesture had sent an unmistakable message. The irony was that they had done so even though it had been reasonably assumed that he would never know of it.

It reminded her of just how spiteful and vicious the Romulans could be. A pity, considering she was just starting to develop the smallest iota of respect for them.

She turned the tab around and put it in its proper place. She wondered how soon it would take someone to notice it, and if they would then return it to its position of dishonor. Well, there was only so much she could do about any situation at any particular moment.

Slowly she entered the crypt, descending the gleaming stairs one tentative step at a time. Unlike the relatively warm stone surfaces of the City of the Dead above her, the actual crypt area was gleaming and modern. The walls were shining metal, although a thin film of dust dulled the reflection that Soleta saw against them. There were slots in the wall, "drawers," where the dead lay, each sealed out of respect. That, and because Romulans still told their children of the day that would eventually come, the *Mra'he'nod,* when the skies would blacken forever and the dead would rise and rampage through the cities, taking all that lived with them into the abyss for the rest of eternity. It was reasoned that, if the dead were sealed in, they could not emerge. This made no particular sense to Soleta, who could only assume that if all sanity and reason were tossed out and all the dead were able to arise, certainly they'd be able to get around something as mundane as sealant. She, however, had not created the legends, nor did she set much store by them, so she didn't dwell on it.

She withdrew the amulet, which had been sitting in her small shoulder pack. The walls around her were utterly smooth. She had no idea where or how she was supposed to leave the thing. She could simply deposit it on the floor and walk away, but that seemed so . . . pedestrian somehow. Plus she suspected that the amulet had some degree of intrinsic value or worth. This crypt, like most others, was not sealed. Romulans were always invited, at all times, to visit with and commune with any dead at any time (presumably to try and stay on their good side in the event that *Mra'he'nod* should actually occur).

For long minutes, nothing seemed to suggest itself as a proper resting place, and she was almost resolved to place it on the floor and be done with it, when something caught her eye. At the far end of the crypt, positioned in a corner just above the gleaming floor, was what could only be described as a receptacle. There was a hollowed-out section that matched, exactly, the curves of the amulet in her hand. No wonder Rajari had not been concerned about her figuring out where the amulet should go; it was impossible that it could go anywhere else.

She held the amulet up to it, tilting it experimentally, marveling at the perfect way in which it fit. He must have taken it out of there as some sort of a souvenir, a memento, and the guilt for absconding with it had been too much. In returning it now, she was going to be able to undo that unfortunate act and fulfill her promise at the same time.

"This is for you, Rajari. Rest in peace," she said, and she inserted the amulet carefully into its place.

At the very last second, she suddenly realized that the reason she had noticed the place to insert the amulet was because it was clean. There was no dust there at all. And there were infinitesimally small metal shavings, as if someone had just carved the receptacle into the wall very recently.

Except Rajari had not been on Romulus for some time.

Which meant that someone else had carved it there into the wall.

Recently.

Which meant it hadn't been stolen, but rather created for specifically that purpose.

Faced with a sudden unknown, Soleta tried to pull the amulet out. But the instant that she had put it into its place, it had clicked in there with a terrifying finality that seemed to reverberate throughout the tomb.

She heard a whining, like energy starting to build up, heading toward some sort of detonation.

Soleta pulled at the amulet, not comprehending what was happening, but certain that if she could just pull the damned thing out again, it would halt whatever process had been set into motion. But it didn't work. Nothing worked. The amulet resisted all the effort she put into it.

The amulet started to turn. That was impossible, she thought, and then she realized that the amulet was actually set into a disk in the wall, about eighteen inches in diameter. She could see the lines of it now that it was turning, the seams showing, and she cursed herself for not having spotted it earlier. She had been so pleased, so relieved, to have come this far to accomplish this idiotic quest, and so busy questioning herself, that she had neglected to question or challenge the circumstances of the situation.

She shoved against it, trying with all her strength to push it counterclockwise to the way it was turning. It didn't help, didn't slow it in the least. The disk was turning slowly but inexorably, and it suddenly occurred to her that if the crypt was about to blow up—as now seemed likely—it would be an extremely good idea to be anywhere else but there.

She spun and bolted for the exit. She was certain she could feel gears and levers shifting under her, preparing to push a door into place that would slam shut and seal her in, guaranteeing that she would pay the ultimate price for her foolishness. The distance to the door was not that far, but it seemed to spiral off into infinity. Twenty paces, then ten, and Soleta leaped, arms extended. She tumbled through the door, hit the stairs, banged her elbows and knees and pushed away the pain for another day. She scrambled to her feet, stumbling up the stairs, leaving the rumbling behind her but determined that she had to put as much distance between herself and the family crypt as possible.

She had no idea what sort of deranged sense of vengeance would prompt Rajari to destroy the crypt of his family, but she was in no position to second-guess the efforts of a dying (and now dead) man. Her legs pistoned beneath her as she sprinted away from the crypt. She had gotten all of thirty feet when suddenly the rumbling in the crypt behind her ceased.

She slowed, stopped, and turned, looking behind her in a very puzzled fashion . . .

. . . and that was when the explosion hit.

Soleta hit the ground reflexively, hoping to dodge any debris that might go flying over her head, trying to present as minimal a target as possible. But even as she dropped, she realized that she was in no danger. The crypt had not detonated at all. Instead the explosion had come from some distance away.

And then debris began to rain down around her. She covered her head as small, flaming bits of rock hit the ground, bouncing away, and the air was filled with smoke and distant screams. And something else struck the ground nearby her. It was small and leathery and she realized belatedly that it was a foot shod in what had once been fine leather, but was now little more than a smoking husk.

She risked a glance toward the north.

The golden spires of the Noble House were gone. In their place were plumes of black smoke, reaching all the way to the sky that the towers had only tried to touch.

McHENRY

McHenry was lightly dozing, but when he woke up he came to the realization that the platform on which he was perched had stopped sinking. That was the good news. On the other hand, the bad news came quickly thereafter, namely that the platform was now getting smaller.

He had completely lost track of time while he'd been stuck up there. The sun had gone down and come up again. The platform remained stable and he stuck a tentative foot off the edge. The fall yawned beneath him.

At least, he thought it did. Then again, he thought that the sun had set and risen, but he was not the least bit hungry, nor had he developed any beard stubble. It made him wonder how much of time was an illusion. Then again, pondering that question was nothing new for him. However, in this instance it went beyond a simple matter of time. There was all of reality itself, or at least the reality as it was being presented to him. It was not a reality that he was terribly satisfied with, and he wondered if there might be some tweaking of it possible.

He knew that there was one way to find out, but it certainly would have its own share of hazards.

"Oh well. No one lives forever," he said, and then added as an afterthought, "except for immortals."

McHenry promptly started to think about something else. There was no great trick to that; in point of fact, it's what he was rather good at. Indeed, it was a trait that any number of his superior officers had found to be extremely disconcerting. McHenry was renowned for sitting at his station and looking for all the world as if he were dozing. But in truth, he was simply devoting as much of his brainpower as was required to handle the situation at hand. Which was what he was intending to do now.

What McHenry had to do was get to the far edge of the canyon. A fall of some considerable distance awaited him if he stepped off the platform, but the platform was shrinking anyway. He had no reason to think that it was going to shrink into nonexistence. On the other hand, he had no reason to think it wasn't going to. On that basis, it would probably be best just to proceed as if the latter were the case and not wait around.

But if he were dealing with the real world, and real world rules, then there was no way that he could simply step off the platform without plummeting to his death. The fact, though, that time was unquestionably passing, and yet his body was not showing any signs of that passing, made him question the reality of the world. If he was dealing with an unreal world, then unreal rules should apply.

At least, that's what his study of ancient animation seemed to tell him.

And if that were the case . . .

. . . then he could step off the platform and not fall. Because gravity would not apply if he paid it no mind. It would cause him to plunge only if he acknowledged it. It was a scenario he'd seen played out any number of times in the animations that Janos had shown him. A cartoon character would dash off a cliff and keep going a considerable distance, until such time as he realized that he was in jeopardy. At that point, one of two things would happen: Either gravity would, after much delay, seize him. Or else, he would actually be able to pivot in midair and make a desperate dash back to safety. On one or two occasions characters had actually made it (although some further contrivance would then serve to send them plummeting anyway).

If it was good enough for them in their unreal world, reasoned McHenry, it was good enough for him in his.

Walking was no big deal. All McHenry had to do was start walking and then ignore the fact that he was doing so. The other elements might be trickier, though.

He took a deep breath and cleared his mind.

The moment his mind was clear, it was like a vacuum. And since nature tended to abhor such things, then naturally everything and anything was sucked right into his head.

Numbers, images, concepts, and assorted situations tumbled about in his skull. The many wonders and possibilities of the universe, all suggesting themselves to him at once, all vying for his attention. There were so many options that he literally did not know where to look first. And so, as he usually did in such circumstances, he proceeded to look everywhere.

A particular conundrum regarding an obscure contradiction in a series of novels he'd read three years back suggested itself. He started to work on that. While he did so, he went back to working out "pi," which was one of his favorite pastimes, and he also tried to determine how many instances there were wherein a straight line was, in fact, the longest distance between two points. He also gave passing thought as to whether, in fact, the duck-billed platypus was a simple outgrowth of nature or a demented joke on the part of a higher power, and if that were the case, then just who might that higher power be and what did that imply about the structure of the universe. In relation to nothing at all, he also started to wonder whether life actually imitated art, or whether art was simply an intuitive prediction of where life was going. As a result of this, an old song lyric flitted into his mind and he devoted approximately six percent of his brain toward trying to determine just why fools *did* fall in love. He also came to the realization that four hundred years hence, every computer in the Federation was likely going to shut down and total anarchy would range through the length and breadth of all known space . . . or maybe not. Maybe nothing would happen at all.

He pondered all of this and more, and as he kept thinking about it and thinking about it, he suddenly tripped slightly. He caught himself, but the slight stumble was enough to attract his attention and make him wonder what he had just tripped over.

He looked down, without giving any consideration to the notion that looking down might not be the brightest move in the world. As it turned out, though, it didn't make any difference, because he was standing on solid ground.

It took him a few moments to remember why that should be an extraordinary thing, and when he did recall, he turned and looked back the way he had come. In the distance was the still-dwindling platform that he'd been standing on. The infinitely deep fall still yawned all around it. But he was safe on the far side.

It had worked. The experiment had worked. The laws of physics of an unreal world had applied to him in this unreal situation. With his mind elsewhere, occupied with so many other things, he had begun walking in a straight line without paying attention to the fact that he was, indeed, moving. So when his feet had trod air, he had not noticed. Because he hadn't noticed, gravity had been helpless against him.

"That was easy," he said.

At which point he suddenly heard a loud whistling sound right above him. He stepped back quickly, just in time to avoid an anvil slamming to the ground directly in front of him. This immediately caused a massive crack in the ground directly in front of him, and instantly the previously solid ground upon which he was standing crumbled away, sending him falling back and down into the darkness.

SOLETA

ALL AROUND SOLETA WAS CHAOS as people in the city, who only minutes before had been going peacefully about their business, were running this way and that, shrieking, crying, shouting questions, getting a hundred different answers. Of the Noble House, there was almost nothing left except half of one wall. The explosives had been most thorough in their task.

Different answers rang out everywhere. It was the Klingons. No, it was the Cardassians, no, the Federation, the cursed Federation had struck in this cowardly fashion. No one knew how many were dead yet, but the odds were spectacular that anyone who had been inside the building when it had gone up was now residing with the gods.

The distant stench of smoke and charred meat mixed with the stink of fear in the air. And through it all, Soleta passed like the angel of death at a holiday feast.

She was part of the crowd, but apart from it at the same time. Her mind was numb, the logic circuits had shut down. It was as if all the blood was gone from her entire body. She couldn't feel anything, not the slightest sensation.

He'd used her.

The son of a bitch had used her.

She walked to the spaceport like one in a trance. People would run into her, bump up against her, even slam into her, and she reacted to none of it. They might as well have run into a walking corpse. In a hurricane of activity, she was a distant and icy eye of the storm.

He'd said it. If only she has listened, he had said it. He had spoken of allies, of friends. He had spoken of the terrible vengeance the government had taken against them, talked bitterly of how they had exiled him. All that time she had been so suspicious of him, but the suspicions had wilted when she had learned of his illness, and had finally died when he had died. His impending death had prompted her to believe that he had nothing to gain. She knew now that she'd been wrong. His impending death had simply left him with nothing to lose.

Those allies he had spoken of, those hidden allies, had rigged the explosives. And they had put the triggering device in the tomb. It had been Rajari's intent to sneak back to Romulus somehow and insert the amulet, which would set the explosives into motion. But he had waited too long, his illness progressing faster than he had anticipated. Even then he might have made the endeavor himself, but two things happened that changed that. The first, obviously, was the assassin squad of Adis. The second was the arrival of Soleta herself.

He had obviously seen within her a potential

cats-paw, and he had batted her around with feline expertise. It was incredible, phenomenal. On the one hand a young woman, burning with anger, had come to him. On the other hand a vengeful Romulan noble, with guardsmen at his side, had also come to him. He had played one against the other masterfully, the only cost to him being his own life, which was forfeit anyway.

And she . . . Soleta . . .

She looked at her hand as if it belonged to someone else. It was the hand that had turned the amulet, and she could only think that if she had a knife or large blade handy, she would hack it off at the wrist.

All the ruckus, all the chaos around her, had happened because of her. Yet she felt disconnected from it all. Her mind simply could not wrap itself around the immensity of what had happened. She kept waiting to wake up and find that she was still back on Vulcan, visiting with her father and finding amusement in a worst-case scenario that was simply too insane to have any credibility.

She was following the signs to the spaceport almost as if she were a sleepwalker, but as she approached one of the entrances, a massively built guard was suddenly in her way. She looked up at him impassively.

"Identification," he said.

"What?"

"No one is going into or out of this port without proper identification and reason for . . ." Then his eyes narrowed. He stared at her, really stared. "Wait a minute . . ." he began to say.

Soleta did not need to wait for the rest of the sentence. She knew that he had looked too closely and saw that he was not dealing with a fellow Romulan. As an offworlder, she would be arrested immediately, questioned in that unique and wonderful way that Romulans had. There would be nothing left of her by the time they were done. Her mind would be in smoldering ruins. Part of her almost welcomed the notion. Another part of her, however, acted on instinct, and before he had even completed the sentence, her right hand speared toward his shoulder.

But the guard was quick and he caught her hand before it could clamp down. He twisted his other shoulder away from her, his height and angle taking it from her reach, even as with his free hand, he went for his weapon.

Soleta's left hand lashed up and clamped onto his face.

"Our minds are merging," she whispered.

The Vulcan mind-meld was always intended to be used as a bonding. A mutual joining of thoughts that would allow two Vulcans to have a better understanding, not only of each other, but also of themselves. It was never intended to be used as any sort of weapon, and doing so went against not only Vulcan philosophy and teachings, but against decency itself. When Ambassador Spock had written his memoirs, he had stated that of all the things in his life that had brought him pain, it had been the forcible mind-meld with the traitorous female, Valeris. He had described it as a "mind rape," and had needed to embark on several months of meditation and spiritual cleansing in order to try and distance himself from that distasteful moment. Even with that "cleansing," he had never been able to leave it behind.

For Soleta, a woman born of violence and rape, to engage in such an activity would bring her closer to the very roots that she found so appalling.

She did it without hesitation.

The guard's eyes widened as he realized what was happening, but he could offer no resistance at all. Another Vulcan might have been able to fight her off, or at least delay the actions enough to mount a defense. But the Romulans, for the most part, had left behind such spiritual niceties as telepathy in exchange for the sheer, cunning ferocity that was their trademark. So the guard had no abilities at all that would allow him to combat Soleta's assault.

He tried to pull his weapon from his belt. Had he done so, he would have had her cold, because she was right up against him and could offer no physical defense at all. He could have blown a hole in her the size of a cantaloupe. He was unable to do so, however. No matter how much he tried, he could not force his hand to move the additional few inches required to produce his weapon, for his hand was no longer his hand, it was their hand. Soleta had as much command over it as he did . . . more, in fact. She had driven her mind deep into his with wolfish abandon, as if some aspect of her had been unleashed for the first time in her life.

"We are putting our hands down," she said, and his hand dropped to his side. "We are offering no resistance. Our minds are merging . . . merging . . . you cannot kill me . . . you would be killing yourself . . ."

He trembled, but it was nothing more than the last-ditch effort to provide some minimal resistance. Her eyes were locked into his, but whereas her gaze was filled with cold, channeled ferocity, his was empty.

Had she chosen to, Soleta could have driven her thoughts into his like a spike through tissue paper. She was almost tempted, for a heartbeat, to do it. But then she dismissed the notion as the guard, unable to do anything to prevent it, sagged under the Vulcan nerve pinch that was now applied with no difficulty. His mind spiraled away into unconsciousness and Soleta pulled herself free from him before the meld rendered her insensate as well.

She eased him to the ground, glancing around to see if anyone was paying attention. No one was. They were still busy looking to one another, asking who knew what, and whether there were any survivors. So many questions, with no answers forthcoming.

She pulled out his weapon from its holster and tucked it into the folds of her garment. Then she made her way into the spaceport.

She crossed the field unmolested. The place was a hive of industry, and now that she was inside, no one was making any further efforts to impede her. For a moment she considered the unfortunate possibility that Sharky might have already departed the planet. That had always been something that had worried her; she'd had no real way of ensuring that he would stay put. Fortunately, he had. She could see his vessel from halfway across the field, and she sprinted the remaining distance, anxious to get off the accursed planet before anything else went wrong (although it was hard for her to imagine that anything could go more wrong than it already had).

She dashed up the gangway to the main control room, calling, "Sharky! I think it would be best to depart expeditiously!"

She stepped through the control room's entrance and froze.

Sharky was rising, a look of grim concern on his face. "Have you heard what happened?" he asked. But that wasn't what had caused Soleta's blood to ice up. It was the other individual who was there, turning to face her.

It was a Romulan, in the distinctive uniform of a private guardsman. What immediately caught Soleta's attention was his right hand, which was made of gleaming metal. It was there to replace the one that Soleta had blown off back on Titan.

Sharky saw the flash of recognition between the two of them, but misread it. "Do you two know each other?"

Mekari raised his weapon. Soleta pulled the stolen disruptor from concealment. In half an instant, both of them were pointing their disruptors at each other's respective heads, the barrels trained unflinchingly. They were no more than two feet away from one another.

Nobody budged.

"I'll take that as a yes," Sharky said mildly, breaking the sudden silence that had fallen upon the control room. He clapped his hands together briskly, as if this sort of occurrence in his vessel was fairly routine. "On Earth, this is what we call a Mexican standoff. Whoever fires first will also very likely die as well, because when one person is hit, his or her finger will reflexively tighten on the weapon and cause it to discharge."

"Thank you for that history lesson, Sharky," Soleta said.

"You said that perhaps I would kill you on another day, Vulcan bitch," said Mekari. "Is this a better day for you?" His disruptor didn't waver.

"To be blunt," Soleta replied, who was keeping her own weapon equally trained on him, "this has not been a terribly good day for me, no. Dying would not improve it. Although, upon further consideration, it might actually be the high point. What is he doing here, Sharky?" she said, her gaze never straying from Mekari.

"Mekari is my supplier for Romulan ale."

"Wonderful."

"I suggest you leave this room, Sharky," Mekari warned him. "This could be unpleasant."

"This isn't really necessary," Sharky began, "because you could—"

Soleta saw the look in Mekari's eyes. "Do as he says."

"Soleta, if—"

"Now." Her voice was flat and unyielding and clearly not allowing for any dissent.

Sharky very carefully moved his heft around the edge of the control room, stepping through and out with no further comment.

They remained frozen for a time.

"Is there no other way than trying to kill each other?" Soleta finally said. "Does your service to Adis require—"

"Adis," he told her, "is dead. He was in the Noble House when it was blown up. You were responsible for that, I take it?"

Vulcans never lie.

"No," she said flatly.

"So your presence here is simply coincidence."

"Coincidence happens," she reminded him. "Were that not the case, you would not be standing here holding a disruptor on me. And I on you."

"You cost me a hand. You must pay for that."

"I have paid greater prices in my life than you can possibly know."

"I do not care about those. I care about now."

"And do you wish to die in endeavoring to kill me? How will you savor your vengeance if you are not alive?"

"Vulcan logic. Dazzling as always."

"Lower your weapon. I will lower mine. And you will have an opportunity to dispose of me without risk to yourself."

He arched an eyebrow. "An interesting proposal."

"Thank you."

"A pity I must kill you. You would be an interesting individual to mate with."

"I am told that by most individuals who desire to kill me."

It was everything that Soleta could do to sound like her old self. It was a façade, a reconstruction of who she was. She was saying things that sounded like Soleta, gave the impression that it was Soleta talking to him. But deep within herself, she felt as if the real, true Soleta had crawled away somewhere to hide and die.

Slowly, and with the slightest bit of hesitation, Mekari started to lower his weapon.

She did likewise.

It was nerve-splitting. Each passing second, lower and lower went the weapons.

Mekari was watching Soleta's disruptor.

Soleta was watching Mekari's eyes.

She saw it in his eyes before he saw it in her disruptor. The sudden gathering of nerve, the quick flash of, *Now* in his mind which signaled his intent a half-instant before he actually did it.

Soleta dropped to the ground just as he swung his weapon back up and fired where she had been. Soleta fired off a shot and the disruptor struck him squarely in the chest, knocking him off his feet and sending him crashing back against a wall. His own weapon clattered from his hand as he sagged to the ground.

Soleta, holding her own weapon firmly, not letting

down her guard for an instant, crossed over and knelt next to him. He was staring fixedly into the air at nothing. There seemed to be no sign of life in him. She turned to call to Sharky.

Mekari snapped upright, howling in fury. Whatever he was wearing under his guardsman armor had absorbed the blast from the disruptor, or at least had diminished the damage enough to leave him alive and kicking. His head had had no such protection, which was obviously why he hadn't made his move earlier and taken his chances with her shooting at him.

His move was so abrupt, so unexpected, that it caught Soleta completely unawares. Before she knew it, a wide sweep of his hand had knocked her disruptor away. She tried to reach for his shoulder, to render him unconscious, but her position was bad. Given a few moments to reposition herself, she might have been able to accomplish it, but he didn't present her with them. The much larger Romulan grabbed both of her hands in his, shoved them back and her down. Her arms pinned under her, Mekari was atop her, driving his knee into her stomach. She gasped, the air knocked out of her, and he kept her flat on her back, one hand planted firmly on her chest, the other at her throat. He had her completely helpless.

"You are a feisty one," he snarled, and there seemed to be a primitive form of appreciation in his eyes. And there was something else in there, too, a desire dark and primeval, building up with a fearful life all its own.

He brought his mouth savagely down upon hers, and his breath stank, and horror rampaged through Soleta's mind as his hands began to do things and she realized what was about to happen. And there was the voice once more in her head, but it was not her own voice but her mother's, screaming, *No, not again, not again, not again* . . .

Soleta snapped.

With a strength that Mekari could not have known that she had . . . with a strength even she did not know she had . . . Soleta swung her legs up and around his midsection. She clamped them together like pincers and began to squeeze. She had positioned them directly under the joint of the armor's torso section, where there was no protection, and Mekari suddenly felt his lower ribs bending under the strain. Soleta's expression was not remotely Vulcan. It was barely that of a sentient creature, but rather the infuriated expression of a feral beast.

Mekari was shoved partway back, and that was all Soleta needed to pull her arms out from under her. She twisted, drew one leg out and under him, relieving the pressure on him for a moment but giving her better leverage, and she thrust out with the leg, sending him toppling back. Before he had even hit the floor she was upon him, quick as a cat, and Vulcan training was gone from her, the nerve pinch was gone from her. Now it was her Romulan blood hammering through her, and she utterly gave herself to the savage call of it as she brought both her fists together down on his head. The blow stunned him momentarily, and then he tried to fight back, but Soleta did not provide him the opportunity. She started pounding on him, without letup, and in her head she could hear the screams of her mother, just as she had imagined them all these years, but they were screams of triumph and retribution, of getting back a piece of that which she had lost.

Soleta lost awareness of where she was or what she was, the world turning to a black haze around her. She knew she was doing something with her fists, but she could no longer remember what.

And then firm hands were grabbing her from behind, hauling her into the air, shouting, "Enough! Enough!" She whirled, ready to lay into whoever had interfered, and through the cloud of fury that permeated the air around her, she saw Sharky looking at her with a mixture of concern and fear. She raised her hands and he flinched automatically, even as he called, "Soleta! Enough, I said! He can't hurt you! Look! Look!" And there was such force in his voice that Soleta was able to force herself to turn and look down at Mekari.

His face was covered with blood, all his own. His nose was broken, his right eye pounded shut, the left in the process of closing. His lips were going to be the size of balloons by the time they were done swelling. She wasn't sure, but she thought his jaw might be broken.

Her breath rasped in her chest as she fought to bring her adrenaline levels back to something approaching the norm. Sharky looked with blasé fascination at Mekari's ruined face, and he commented, "I could be wrong about this, but I think I've just lost my contact for Romulan ale. I don't think he's going to be especially cooperative in the future."

She tried to speak, but nothing would come to her. It was as if her vocal cords were paralyzed.

"All right . . . here's what we do. We take off and just dump him into space."

She couldn't quite believe she'd heard him properly. She looked at Sharky, who was staring back at her with impassive, dead eyes, not unlike the Earth creature for which he was named. "You mean . . . kill him?"

"Ah, she's found her voice. Don't sound so appalled,

girl. If it hadn't been for me, he'd probably be dead already, at your hand."

"That was . . . in a battle."

"That was no battle. That was a slaughter. Leaving him alive could lead to complications, as could discovering his corpse. Unless you have your phaser with you. We could just incinerate—"

"No. We push him out of the ship and just go."

"That, girl, would not be the wisest—"

"It's what we're doing, Sharky," and there was something in her tone, something in her look, that made it very clear that any other option was not going to be an acceptable one.

Sharky clearly was weighing the possibilities of what he would likely encounter from Soleta, in terms of resistance, if he followed the course that he had proposed. Obviously he thought better of it, because he finally said, "You grab the head, I'll take the legs. We toss him and get the hell off this planet, while we're still able to." All Soleta was able to manage was a nod.

Together they picked up the unconscious Mekari and dragged him to the gangway. They glanced around, saw no one in the immediate vicinity, and then pitched him off. Mekari rolled down the length of the gangway and onto the ground with a thud. Sharky didn't even give so much as a backward glance as he headed to the control room to fire up the ship and depart Romulus. Soleta, for her part, didn't move from the spot. Instead she simply looked at his unmoving body until the gangway cycled shut, cutting him off from view.

McHENRY & KEBRON

"I DON'T LIKE YOU," said Adulux, and he pulled the trigger of the gun that was right up against Kebron.

They always say that at the moment of your death your life flashes before your eyes. Kebron had heard that any number of times, but had never believed it. Yet now, much to his astonishment, he found it to be true.

He saw stretched before him, or behind him as the case may be, a life of isolation. He had separated himself not only from his fellow crew members, but from his fellow Brikar. He tried to determine why that was the case. What was it that had driven himself to his solitary state? And the profession that he had chosen! He was a security chief, someone who was conditioned and accustomed to suspecting everyone of being a threat.

He had never had a serious relationship with anyone, Brikar or otherwise, in his life. As he had so succinctly put it at one point, he did not desire romance. He had goldfish instead, and they were more than enough for him.

Had he taken advantage of his massive build, his invulnerability and separateness, to construct a life for himself where no one and nothing could touch him in any way? Why? Perhaps here, at the end of his life, he should use what microseconds were left to him to take a long, hard, piercing look at himself and determine, once and for all, where the truth of the being known as Zak Kebron truly was.

He considered that for perhaps half a microsecond before deciding that it was a stupendously bad idea and he should be content with dying as he had lived: in blissful lack of self-awareness. Self-awareness was useful if you were then going to use that knowledge to change. He had no intention of doing so. So forget it.

At that moment, Mark McHenry fell on Adulux.

No one in the room had any idea where in hell McHenry had come from. One moment he wasn't there, the next, he was. He crashed down on Adulux, sending the shot wild, and it chewed up a section of the floor but otherwise did no damage.

Adulux, however, did manage to hold on to the blaster even as he and McHenry went down in a tumble of arms and legs. Adulux tried to disentangle himself and bring the blaster around to fire on Kebron once more. But McHenry, quickly discerning what was happening, knocked the blaster from Adulux's grip. It skittered across the floor and came to a rest some feet away.

Credit Adulux with refusing to accept turnabouts in his fortune. He tried to make it to the blaster, but McHenry wasn't letting him go. Instead he had wrapped himself around Adulux's middle and was holding him firmly. Adulux let out a howl of fury and tried to shove McHenry off him, and suddenly two large feet were planted directly in Adulux's path. He looked up, and then up even further.

Kebron stood over him, looking extremely displeased. "One side, McHenry," he said, and without waiting for Mark to comply, he grabbed Adulux by the front of his shirt and hauled him to his feet.

"You," he said sharply, "have been a good deal of trouble."

He pivoted and threw Adulux halfway across the room. Cautiously and correctly, he sent him tumbling away from the blaster, so that he couldn't snag it and start more trouble. Adulux crashed to a halt against the far wall, but he was still not done. He tried to haul himself up . . .

. . . and then Zanka was upon him. For she had picked up the blaster and she was now holding it by the business end. She swung it fast, sending the butt crashing against Adulux's skull. Adulux let out a moan and sank to the floor.

"This is all your fault!" she shouted, obviously far from done. "You tried to kill Kebron! That's all you ever do, is try and hurt people! Well, I'm tired of it! I'm tired of you, and all the things you've done!" She reversed the blaster and aimed the business end at him. It was quivering slightly, reflecting the fact that her hands were trembling, but her face looked determined. "And now I'm going to . . . to . . ."

"You're not going to do anything," Kebron informed her. He had gotten to his feet and now was walking across the room, looking quite calm and in control.

"He tried to kill you!"

"Zanka, if I killed everyone who tried to kill me . . ." Then he paused, giving the matter some thought. "Actually, I suppose I *do* tend to kill everyone who tries to kill me. But that's usually in combat situations. This is a helpless person . . ."

"He might not stay helpless! If I leave him alone, he might try to come after me and . . . and . . ."

"He won't," Kebron said firmly, his gaze never wavering from Adulux. "For he knows that if he does, I will come after him. You would not want that . . . would you, Adulux."

Adulux, thoroughly intimidated, managed to shake his head.

Zanka did not appear entirely convinced. But she appeared to lack the resolve to fire the weapon and put an end to Adulux. After long moments of indecision, she lowered the weapon and handed it over to Kebron. Kebron took it and gave a brisk nod of approval.

"And . . . what about you? And me?" asked Zanka.

"There is not," Kebron said firmly, "a you and me. Your attentions are flattering. But that is all they are. I do not reciprocate."

"Why not?" There was a tinge of desperation to her voice.

It actually stirred something within him. The fact that it did so annoyed the hell out of Kebron, who definitely did not need any sort of entanglements fouling up his life. "The simple fact, Zanka, is that I am not who, or even what, you think I am."

She stared at him uncomprehendingly, and then understanding seemed to shine within her. "I . . . think I understand. You are saying . . . you do not like women."

"What?" It took him a moment to comprehend. "Oh. No, I'm not saying that."

"You do like women, then!"

"No. I don't like anyone. People annoy me. That's why I do what I do. So I can shoot people while earning a living."

"That seems very . . . sad."

He shrugged. He liked shrugging. It was eloquent in its silence.

McHenry, in the meantime, had not gotten up. Instead he was simply sitting on the floor, staring toward nothing. It was an attitude that Kebron had seen him display on any number of occasions. It had always annoyed him. It still did. "McHenry," he started to say.

And to his surprise, the response he got was a curt "Shhh!"

It was understandable that Kebron was startled. McHenry was rarely forceful or vehement about anything. But this time, he actually seemed to have something very specific on his mind. Kebron couldn't begin to guess what it was. The thing was, McHenry's thought process—by his own admission—tended to be all over the map. If McHenry was actually focusing on just one thing, that was a very daunting prospect. It made it seem as if practically anything was possible.

"What's he doing?" asked Zanka.

"Shhh!" was Kebron's reply.

Zanka shrugged because she'd seen Kebron do it, then turned her attention back to Adulux. Her face darkened as she saw him there, crouched in a corner, looking not at all threatening. He was rubbing his head where she had struck him. "If I hadn't disappeared, you would have killed me, wouldn't you," she demanded.

"No," he said softly. "I know that's what you'd like to believe . . . because it makes it that much easier to demonize me in your own mind." He looked up at her and said sadly, "I've made mistakes. I know I have. I guess the biggest mistake I made was thinking that it's always possible to make up for mistakes. And it's not. So . . . so if we get out of this, I just . . . I want you to know that you really, truly, don't have to live in fear of me. Sometimes it just takes getting some sense knocked into you."

"All right, well . . . well, good," she said uncertainly.

He turned his back to her then and just sat there, looking very small and not particularly threatening.

"Platypus," said McHenry.

Of all the things that Kebron had expected him to say, somehow that wasn't very high up on the list. "What?" he asked.

"None of this makes any sense," McHenry said slowly. "The tests that we and the others were subjected to, wildly random, like they were drawn from a hat or something. The haphazard nature of it all. There has been any number of instances where superior races . . . or, at least, so-called superior races . . . subjected captives to a series of tests. If you believe the autobiography of James Kirk, it frequently happened to his people during their mission. But they always seemed to be designed around learning something about us . . . or even teaching us something as well. This, though . . . this has all just been idiocy."

Zanka and Adulux were looking at each other in confusion. "What is he talking about?" said Zanka to Kebron. "He's talking as if . . . as if there's other beings, or races, or some sort of . . ."

"Quiet," Kebron said.

"Don't you tell her to be quiet!" bristled Adulux.

Kebron fired a glance at him. "You, too."

There was something in the way Kebron looked at

him that made Adulux realize that saying anything further might be counterproductive to his health.

But even if they had been inclined to try and keep chatting, the booming voice that filled the room at that moment would certainly have silenced them.

"Idiocy! How DARE you!"

The almost sepulchral voice filled the room, and Adulux and Zanka both let out high-pitched screams of horror. Even Kebron was taken aback by the intensity of it.

McHenry didn't seem at all fazed. His expression was carefully neutral, his manner unruffled. "That's right. Idiocy. If you ask me, you're losing your touch."

"And who asked you!" More than anything, the owner of the strident voice sounded irked that McHenry was not the least bit intimidated, or even startled. *"You little nothing! You no one! You—"*

"Master of chaos and confusion," McHenry said, folding his arms and looking more amused than anything. "Gamester. Trickster. I was thinking of all manner of things, and along what I like to refer to as the tortured paths of my mind, I thought of the duck-billed platypus. And that, in turn, for no reason I can really put my finger on, made me think of you."

Kebron was completely lost. He had no idea whatsoever what McHenry was talking about. Nor was he accustomed to seeing the erstwhile helmsman in this manner. Usually McHenry spoke as if he were preoccupied with something else—anything else—beside whatever they happened to be working on at any given moment. It was as if he was in his own time zone somewhere. But now, McHenry was so focused that he seemed to be one big targeter. He even seemed a little taller somehow.

What struck Kebron the most, though, was that the booming voice had stopped talking. It almost seemed to be thinking about what McHenry had said.

And then it spoke again, and the voice had lost a bit of its ostentation. In fact, it sounded almost . . .

. . . flattered.

"Did you really like it? The platypus, I mean."

"It had you written all over it. Anyone with twenty-twenty hindsight could see that," said McHenry.

There was a sudden flash of light, and Kebron automatically took a step back. The green, long-limbed alien was there . . . and then another burst of light, and the alien vanished. He was replaced by what appeared to be a human male of somewhat moderate size, black hair combed back, and a look of barely restrained contempt in his eyes that was intertwined with an almost blasé amusement.

"Hello, Q," said McHenry.

SOLETA

VOLAK STARED AT THE SILENT statue of a young woman whom he had always called daughter, gazing out the window for yet another day, just as she had been doing every day for the last week since she had returned to Vulcan.

"Burgoyne. And Selar. They are shipmates of yours, are they not?"

Soleta had barely said ten words since coming back. It was as if she was in a sort of mental fugue state. Upon hearing those names, however, she turned and looked at her father as if noticing for the first time that he was there. "Yes. They are."

"They were here, on Vulcan. Caused quite a bit of commotion. Some very spirited debate over . . ."

He had lost her attention again. She was staring outside once more. "It is an impressive view, is it not."

No reply.

"I find it . . . oddly reassuring."

No reply.

"There is much in life that is uncertain. To wake up each morning and be able to look out upon Vulcan and see it much as I left it the previous evening brings with it a certain degree of reassurance. It is the same as it ever was and, logically, will remain that way."

"No," Soleta said. "Nothing remains the same. Everything changes."

"Soleta . . . do you wish to discuss what happened?"

"I see no logical reason to do so, Father. Discussing it will not alter what has passed. And since I doubt that such circumstances will arise once more, they have no bearing on the future."

There was a long pause, and Volak took a deep breath, as if steadying himself. "What was he like? The Romulan."

Soleta did not bother to ask how Volak had figured out that was where she was going. Instead she simply said, "He is dead and poses no further threat to you or to anyone."

"Dead." Volak raised an eyebrow. "How did he die?"

She looked up at Volak. "Saving my life."

It was not the answer that he had expected, but one could not have told by the barely discernible flicker of surprise on his face. "I see. So he reformed. He was not totally an irredeemable individual."

"Actually . . . he was. Irredeemable, and manipulative, and scheming. Just like all Romulans."

"All?"

She thought for a moment about the children she had seen frolicking on the statue. She thought about how normal everyone around her had seemed. How she had even felt brief embers of pride flickering within her.

Then she remembered Mekari's foul breath, his mouth upon hers, his body pressed up against her. And worse, she could hear the distant but distinct laughter of Rajari in her imagination. Laughing at her foolishness, at her gullibility. She had allowed herself to trust someone against all logic, and she had paid for it. She, and all the other Romulans who had died in the explosion. Whatever those children would grow up to be, it would be something just like their sires. Whatever their architectural accomplishments, it was just a façade of nobility to hide hearts full of bile and betrayal.

"All," she said flatly.

Volak clearly considered her words for a time. Then he said, "It must be most difficult for you. You know of your Romulan blood . . ."

"Father, I do not wish to—"

Ignoring her preferences in the matter, Volak continued, ". . . and you feel that it diminishes you. Taints you. Makes you that which repulses you. Fosters a degree of self-hatred and loathing."

"All right, Father," she suddenly said with barely restrained exasperation. "Let us say that you are right. That I feel exactly the way you describe. What am I supposed to do now? What would logic dictate? What would Vulcan philosophies of rational thought and discourse propose? When I feel unclean down to my very DNA, when the circumstances of my own creation fill me with nausea, what answer could there possibly be? What solution would you propose?"

Volak looked her straight in the eyes.

"Get over it," he said.

She stared at him. "Get over it? That's it?"

"You will find, Soleta, that the answer to most of life's difficulties can be boiled down to that essence.

There are many trappings to aid you in doing so. You can embrace those trappings for what they are, pick and choose those that suit your immediate needs, and prolong the process. Or, as would be the logical thing to do, you could simply envision in your mind the desired outcome—"

"That outcome being my getting over it."

"Correct. Then embrace that outcome, accept what you are since you cannot change what you are, and move on."

"It is not that easy, Father."

"Not for a human," he agreed. "Nor for a Romulan. For a Vulcan . . . yes . . . it is."

She thought about that for a bit. "Get over it."

"Yes."

She let out a low, steady sigh. "When will I know that I have gotten over it?"

"When you no longer need ask if you have."

"I see."

Volak went away then and said nothing more to her that day, or the next.

Two days later, she rose from her chair, the motion catching Volak's attention, drawing him away from the text he was reading. He looked at her with a cocked eyebrow.

"Are you over it?" he inquired.

"I believe so."

"Then you are not."

A day and a half later, he was preparing dinner in the kitchen when Soleta walked in. She stared at him with reserve.

"Are you over it?" he asked. It was the first words he'd said to her since the last time.

"Yes."

"Good. Then let us go out to dinner and leave behind this repast that I am in the process of botching."

"A most logical course of action," said Soleta.

And they went out to dinner, with Soleta carrying a carefully maintained expression of contemplative serenity on her face, and Rajari's laughter still ringing in her mind.

McHENRY & KEBRON

Q, THE MASTER COMPLICATOR, the terror of worlds, the
occasional redeemer of the universe, stared at McHenry
with both ill-concealed contempt and also morbid fascination. "How did you know it was me?"

"I didn't," McHenry said reasonably. "I guessed. I
didn't know for sure until you appeared just now."

"That's not the question and you know it." He looked
at him askance. "What sort of odd appearance is that?
That's not what you're supposed to look like." He
snapped his fingers and both McHenry and Kebron
were enveloped in flashes of light. When the glare
faded, the genetic surgery that had created their exteri-
ors was gone. McHenry was back to his human appearance, while the enormous Kebron had been restored to
his Brikar status.

Zanka let out a shriek. "Kebron!" And then her brain
simply overloaded from sensory input. She sagged and

then passed out. Adulux could have caught her and prevented her from hitting the floor, but he made no motion to do so since he himself was transfixed by what he was seeing in front of him. So Zanka fell with no impediment from her husband.

"What . . . are you?" Adulux managed to gasp out. He pointed at Q. "And who is he? And . . . and . . ."

"Oh, be quiet," Q said in irritation. Immediately a large tube appeared around Adulux, completely enveloping him. He called out, pounding on the tube, but his voice couldn't be heard and even the thudding of his fists was undetectable audibly.

As if Adulux had simply vanished from the face of existence, Q promptly lost interest in him and looked back to McHenry. "A human and a Brikar, operating side by side in disguise to help some groundworms on a backward world. You *must* be from Starfleet. Only they would go to such involved lengths to aid a bunch of lesser beings who are simply not worth it. But how do you know of me?" he asked.

"You're not serious," said McHenry. "How could I not? Pictures of you have been circulated to every officer in Starfleet. Entire treatises have been written as to your methods of operation. There's a paper called 'The Q Scenario' which analyzes all your previous activities and everything you can be expected to do in any given situation."

Q's eyes widened and he started to laugh. It was not an especially pleasant sound. The laughter grew and grew until it was echoing back upon itself, building in volume until Kebron's head was ringing. McHenry, however, didn't react at all. He just stood there, his gaze never wavering from Q.

"Everything I can be expected to do?" Q finally

managed to get out. "Do you mean to say that some Starfleet drones actually endeavored to second-guess everything that I, an omniscient, omnipotent being who walked creation when the first light was aborning, and will be there to shut the light out at creation's end, might do? The nerve! The presumption! What imbeciles thought that they could know me so well, that they would have the slightest scintilla of hope in even beginning to scratch the surface of me!"

"Jean-Luc Picard, and Commanders Data and Riker."

Q paused a second when he heard that. Then he shrugged. "Oh. Well . . . they might have a shot. A very small shot, to be sure, but a shot." Then he shook off the momentary doubt. "In any event, that's not the point."

"No, Q. The point is that this sort of petty indulgence is beneath you. Showing up on a backwater world and playing with the minds of people who can't even begin to comprehend you for what you are?" He shook his head and actually looked a bit sad. "It's a little beneath you, don't you think?"

"I suppose," Q sighed, and to Kebron's surprise he actually had a touch of melancholy about him. "But that was why I did it, really. I mean, I have so many responsibilities now. A wife, a son, the future of the Q Continuum to think about. And I found that I missed my old self. The sadistic torturing of lesser beings, the sense of accomplishment in reducing uncomprehending inferior species to gibbering idiocy for no reason other than to see them gibber . . ." He sighed. "Those were the good old days."

"You're insane," said Kebron.

Q looked at him in irritation and snapped his fingers. Kebron vanished. In his place was a small, red block.

"From Brikar to brick," Q said, eminently pleased with himself.

"Change him back, Q," said McHenry.

"Oh, as if you have anything to say in the matter," Q shot back. "You, who come along and spoil my fun. Are you that upset about the state of your friend? Perhaps you'd like to join him for a bit."

He snapped his fingers once more. He didn't have to. It was really more for dramatic flair than anything else, a slightly showboat tendency that he had undoubtedly picked up from hanging about humans too much.

A brief flash of light enveloped McHenry. And when it faded . . .

. . . McHenry was still there. He simply stood with his arms folded, watching Q with an almost distant boredom.

"Change him back, Q."

Q looked at the fingers he'd snapped as if they'd betrayed him. Then he looked back at McHenry, then his fingers once more. "I don't understand," he said. "I had no trouble transforming you from that ridiculous appearance to your true self. But why couldn't I change you now to—?"

"Q . . . please." There was no begging in McHenry's voice. It sounded more as if he was simply making an endeavor to be polite.

Clearly befuddled, almost as an afterthought, Q gestured and Kebron snapped back to his normal state.

"You can do anything, Q. We both know that," McHenry said. "Please put things back the way they were. Take these two people," and he gestured toward Adulux and Zanka, "and put them back with no memory of what happened here. You can do that, I'm sure."

"Of course I can," Q said with obvious impatience. "But how did—?"

"And as for the three students, put them back but let them keep their memories, so they can remember what it feels like to suffer at the hands of a power greater than their own. That way they'll be disinclined to toy with the lives of others."

Q was nodding absently, but he was still staring at McHenry. Kebron, who was still trying to figure out what had just happened to him moments before, and why time seemed to have jumped for him, was looking from one to the other with the sense that something was occurring here that he wasn't totally following.

"What is it about you?" demanded Q finally. "There's something about you . . . you're not what you appear to be."

"Which of us is?" said McHenry mildly.

He frowned, and it seemed to Kebron as if Q were somehow mentally X-raying McHenry, using his infinite senses to analyze in great detail every aspect of McHenry's being. McHenry took a step back, and it seemed to Kebron as if, for the first time, he was actually uncomfortable.

Then Q's face cleared. "Of course." There was something akin to amusement in his voice. "Oh, of course. I should have realized. How very embarrassing," he said, and he did indeed sound a bit chagrined, which was—to put it mildly—rather unusual for Q. "I didn't recognize you for who and what you were before."

And now McHenry appeared disconcerted. "Drop it, Q. Now," he said sharply.

But Q didn't seem the least bit perturbed by McHenry's controlled distress. "With all that you know . . . with all that you are . . . why in the universe are you hanging around with these Starfleet types?"

"Because I am a Starfleet type," McHenry said tightly. It was the closest to looking upset that Kebron had ever seen McHenry. "Now let's drop this, all right?"

"Oh, but I don't want to."

"I do."

There was something in the way McHenry said it that Kebron actually found chilling. He was going to brook no further discussion of the matter . . . and there was an implicit warning to Q that there might be dire consequences if he endeavored to push the subject.

At first Q looked obviously amused that anyone would so much as entertain the notion that they could take some sort of forceful bottom line with him. Then he saw that McHenry looked deadly serious. It was a surprising thing to see. In all the years that Kebron had known McHenry, going all the way back to the Academy, the most extreme reaction he'd ever seen out of McHenry was vague confusion.

McHenry didn't take his eyes off Q. He seemed to be concentrating rather fiercely. Q, for his part, had a poker face.

Finally, he said, "I do believe that this experiment has been something of a success. But the entire secret of any game is knowing when it's time to put it away."

He gestured, and there was a blinding flash of light . . .

Three students—one Andorian, and two Tellarites—who had never known inconvenience, or personal worry, or any sort of discomfort at all, found themselves back in their small shuttle vessel in the middle of space. Their university, situated in its gleaming satellite home, hovered not far away.

The three of them looked at each other, and then without another word, angled their ship toward the satellite. Once docked and aboard, they never set foot out of the university again during the rest of their tenure. And every so often, they would wake up screaming, or be known to jump for no reason whenever extremely bright lights happened to be shone in their direction.

Zanka and Adulux found themselves on the surface of Liten.

They had no idea what had happened. They had no clue as to how they had come to be standing in a field at night.

All they knew was that they were utterly terrified for no reason that they could begin to articulate. And in their mutual terror, they threw their arms around each other, held each other close. In their panic, their lips came together, and they began to do things to each other, greedily, desperately, anxious to find some aspect of normality even though they did not fully understand the abnormality that they had just been through.

They sank to the ground of the field. And when they arose some hours later, Adulux never raised a hand to her or to any other being again. He was peaceful, benign, the most unviolent individual that anyone on Liten had ever laid eyes on.

Six months later, Zanka left him anyway for an extremely well built Liten with rippling muscles and an air of calm self-confidence. She never quite knew what attracted her to him. Adulux, for his part, was too at peace to care.

"Oh. You're back. And what do you gentlemen want?"

Kebron and McHenry looked at each other in confusion, and then at their surroundings.

They were in the Strange New Worlds, the pub on Earth in which they had last seen their fellow crewmates.

Kebron had absolutely no idea what to say.

McHenry didn't hesitate. He held up two fingers and said, "Two synthehols."

"You certainly know how to live dangerously," said the waitress, as she turned on her heel and went to fetch their drinks.

"Why are we here?" said Kebron.

"That's a good question," McHenry replied thoughtfully. "Philosophers have been debating that for many a—"

"Not in this world. Here. In this pub."

"Oh." McHenry shrugged. "Q sent us here. Maybe he thought we needed a drink. So I guess you'd call our mission a success. Here's to us. And you, Kebron. How did it feel to be out of that superhard skin of yours for once?"

Kebron thought of Zanka pressing herself up against him, of the lips on his. Of the warmth.

"Boring," he said quickly. Then he looked suspiciously at McHenry. "You. Q."

"That's two. Twenty-four more, you'll have the whole alphabet."

But Kebron was not to be distracted. "The way he reacted to you . . ."

"He was just trying to mess with your mind, Kebron," McHenry said dismissively. "You know that. He likes to confuse people, make them wonder about each other, second-guess each other. It was all just some big game to him. Don't dwell on it. If you do, you'll be playing right into his hands."

The two synthehols were placed in front of them.

Kebron looked McHenry straight in the eye, and there was a coldness in that gaze as he said, "Are you one of his people? From his continuum?"

McHenry openly laughed at that. "One of his? Oh, come on, Zak! You've known me since we were practically kids! Do I act like a Q?"

"You don't act like any other human I know."

"That just makes me unusual. Not omniscient or all-powerful or . . ." He shook his head. "If I were all-powerful, don't you think I'd have stopped the ship from blowing up? Don't you think I would have saved the captain? You should never look for simple answers, Zak."

"You're right."

"Of course I'm right," said McHenry, and he drank his synthehol.

Kebron didn't touch his. "But I'll still look for answers," he said, continuing to scrutinize McHenry.

Slowly McHenry lowered his glass. And he smiled in that same old McHenry manner.

But there was something else there as well.

And Kebron suddenly knew that he wasn't going to rest until he figured out just what that was.

SI CWAN

"I WILL NEVER FORGET the first time I saw him."

Si Cwan, Kalinda, and the students were seated around the simple table in the central dining room. Food had been prepared, but much of it had gone untouched.

"Calling Olivan a student, as you and I were, would be to understate it," continued Si Cwan. "He was more of a disciple than anything else. Jereme would bring Olivan with him to help demonstrate his techniques. It helped to make the lessons more accessible, for Jereme was, of course, Jereme. He was in a class of his own. But Olivan was as near his level as anyone had ever been, and to see him in action gave the rest of us hope. It was as if they were saying to us, See? It can be done. You can learn. You can accomplish these things, because Olivan did it."

"Where did he come from?" asked Kalinda.

"He was a Terran," said Si Cwan. "Our understanding is that he was an orphan, his parents having died when he was quite young. He was sent to relatives to care for him . . . but apparently they did not. So he ran away. How he heard of Jereme, I have no idea. But he came, entirely on his own. Made his way through a series of freighters and the like, working his way across until he got to this very facility. By all accounts, he was quite a sight when he arrived. Thin, haggard, bedraggled. He stood in the doorway, shivering, ill with fever, barely able to stand up. Jereme took him in. For the first week that he was here, the fever raged, and Jereme thought for a time that he was going to lose him. Eventually, however, the fever broke, and Olivan recovered, for the most part."

"For the most part?" asked Kalinda.

"He had a slight physical tic or two as a result. Nothing noticeable. In any event, he stayed with Jereme in full-time residence. Why not? He had nowhere else to go. Jereme always said that he saw something in the young man . . . seeds of greatness. There was one time where Jereme and Olivan came to the palace. A number of young nobles, including me, were given a simple assignment: Find them."

"Anywhere in the palace? Si Cwan, that place was huge. You could hide a spaceship in there. Where's the challenge in that?"

He smiled and shook his head. "No, it was a rather confined area. A three-room radius, that was all. We spread out and we thought we would be able to round them up in no time. We were wrong. We wasted an entire hour, didn't even so much as catch sight of them. Finally, we became convinced that we had been victims of a hoax. While we were scurrying around, we reasoned, the two of them had left entirely. We figured they were out having a nice meal somewhere while we ran about in an exercise in futility. And I swear to you, the gods are my witnesses . . . the moment, the *moment* we gave voice to that belief, they were there. Right there, in the room. Jereme even began quoting things we'd been saying to each other during the previous hour, things we were muttering to each other. He practically would have had to be at our shoulders in order to hear it, but we never saw Jereme or Olivan."

"He would do that sort of thing to us as well," Ookla said softly, and there was pleasant, reminiscing laughter from around the table. For a moment it helped to break the somber mood.

"And once," continued Si Cwan, "I actually fought Olivan, face-to-face, head-to-head. I was not yet even a teen, and by that point he had gone from being the trembling teen who first appeared on Jereme's doorstep to Jereme's full-grown assistant. More than that; he was the heir apparent. Even at that point, Jereme was already not a young man, and he was grooming Olivan for taking over the school someday. Me, I was an arrogant young man back then . . ."

"As opposed to the arrogant older man you are now," Kalinda said playfully.

He afforded her a brief, slightly annoyed, smile. "Very amusing. Very droll," he said. "Anyway, I took an instant dislike to Olivan. He seemed condescending, insufferably pleased with himself. During the course of one of our lessons, I made the incredible mistake of challenging him. He accepted the challenge. It was the only time I ever saw Jereme openly express anything along the lines of annoyance with him, but he did nothing to interfere. I faced off against Olivan, convinced that I could take him."

"What an honor that must have been," said another

student, "that he agreed to engage in single combat with you."

Si Cwan chuckled. "It didn't feel like an honor at the time, I can tell you. He destroyed me. I didn't have a prayer against him. As you know, Jereme's main discipline was to teach defense, rather than offense. I was standing about as far from Olivan as I am sitting now from you, and no matter how many times I would swing—arm thrust, kicks, what have you—I could not come in contact with him. He was as lightning. He could strike at will, and remain untouched by me. I was infuriated. I felt that this was certainly no way to treat a prince, a noble of Thallon. And he laughed. That was all he did: laugh. He thought I was quite the spectacle.

"I came at him faster, more intent with every passing moment to flatten him, show him that his attitude and arrogance were misplaced. I came right at him with a series of kicks and punches that—by all subsequent accounts—was quite impressive. Didn't land a one. Wherever I was, he wasn't. He completely wore me out, which naturally was his intention all along. And when I was sufficiently exhausted, without having injured him in the slightest, he knocked me flat. Jereme used that as a way of driving home a lesson. The wise thing to do, whenever possible, is to cause an opponent to use his strength against himself. Wear himself out, do the work for you. Useful in face-to-face combat. Also useful in Jereme's amazing ability to conceal himself. At first I saw little point to it. It seemed almost cowardly to me, hiding while an enemy is running around trying to find you. My reasoning was, if someone wishes to engage in combat with you, the honorable thing is to meet him head-on. Hiding was cowardice. Jereme, however, taught me that the art of concealment was just that: an art. Simply another weapon to be used, no more or less than that. Let an enemy expend all his resources trying to find you, while you watch him from hiding. Build up his level of frustration until, when you finally do make your appearance, he is so frustrated that he makes stupid mistakes."

The others were nodding, recalling similar words that had been spoken directly to them by Jereme.

Ookla's mandibles clicked worriedly. "But there is something I do not understand, Ambassador Cwan."

"What would that be?"

"Well, if he was that great a student . . . why have we never heard of him." He looked around at the others for confirmation, and they all nodded. "Jereme never spoke to us of him. We have not seen him in the time that we were in residence here. There are no pictures of him, nothing . . ."

"They had . . . a falling-out," Si Cwan said slowly. "I heard about it secondhand, from another student. You see . . . Olivan developed what can only be termed a streak of genuine cruelty. He became self-obsessed, over-confident. He felt that he had learned everything that Jereme could possibly teach him, and who knows? Perhaps he had. But his further sentiment was that there was much that he could turn around and teach Jereme, and that the master was not interested in learning. He felt that Jereme's techniques could be refined further, not just to frustrate or defeat an opponent, but to humiliate him entirely."

"What would be the purpose of such humiliation?" asked Kalinda.

"That was the point, you see. Olivan felt that such humiliation was necessary in order to crush one's opponent. Jereme did not share that belief. He felt that the best enemy was one who could eventually be turned into a friend, and utterly demolishing an opponent's spirit—humiliating him, dragging him through the mud, as it were—would preclude any sort of future alliance. After all, who would ever wish to ally themselves with someone who rejoiced in their mortification."

"And that wasn't something that Olivan agreed with."

"No, Ookla, he didn't. He felt that an enemy is an enemy is an enemy. That defeat was not sufficient; they had to be crushed entirely, and even that wasn't necessarily enough. The ideal, as far as he was concerned, was to use them as an example for anyone else who might be foolish enough to try and combat you.

"Olivan wanted Jereme to change his methods. To teach students to be more ruthless, more aggressive. Jereme, unsurprisingly, was not interested in altering his way of doing things just to accommodate anyone else . . . even someone who had been with him for as long as Olivan had.

"So it came down to a confrontation between Olivan and Jereme. It started out verbally . . ."

"And escalated into something physical?" asked Kalinda.

But Si Cwan shook his head. "No. Everyone who bore witness to it was certain that it was going in that direction. Jereme, however, simply said, 'Would you raise your hand against one to whom you owe so much?' Olivan seemed daunted by this question, and considered it, and then finally said, 'No. No, I would not. But there are . . . other ways. And you will regret the decisions you have made this day.' Then he left, and that was that. It was many years ago, though."

"What happened to Olivan?" asked Ookla.

"I've been doing some checking on that," said Si Cwan. "I admit, I have not been keeping track of him all these years. But it appears that, after departing, he developed quite a power base. My surmise is that he traded upon alliances he made while he was here. Used the skills he had developed and honed through the years, not for self-defense, but to accomplish questionable deeds of even more questionable nature. He built up wealth, power . . . became quite the industrialist. And then he died."

There was a stony silence from around the room.

"I'm sorry . . . what?" said Kalinda.

"He died. That's what my research has told me."

"How?"

"All right . . . I missed something," admitted Ookla. "I admit, Ambassador, that my culture is somewhat different from yours. However, in mine, when someone dies . . . that precludes their returning and causing more problems."

"Well and delicately phrased, Ookla," Si Cwan said with quiet sarcasm. "I appreciate your concern over my tender sensibilities. In my culture as well, the deceased generally do not pose much of a difficulty."

"Generally," Kalinda softly chided him.

"The thing is, I have not been able to determine precisely how he died. He was simply 'reported' dead, by supposedly reliable witnesses. Witnesses, however, can be bought off, 'facts' altered to suit the needs of whoever is doing the altering. I wouldn't consider it satisfactorily conclusive."

"This person you saw in your vision," Ookla said, turning to Kalinda. "What did he look like?"

She proceeded to describe him. It was not difficult. Clearly every aspect of his face was permanently embedded in her mind.

"That," Si Cwan said thoughtfully, when she had finished, "presents a bit of a problem. Alive or dead, the man you've described is considerably younger than Olivan would be."

"But Jereme called him Olivan. I didn't pull that name out of thin air."

"I know you didn't," he told her. "The thing is, your description of him does match the man that I recall from many, many years ago. The resemblance may be ascribed to any number of things. Still . . . I mislike it. A simple resemblance would not fool Jereme. If he called him Olivan . . . then he was. There is simply no other explanation possible."

"So . . . what happens now?" asked Ookla. "What do we do?"

"We?" echoed Si Cwan. "We . . . ," and he looked around at them sadly, "have a ceremony that needs to be performed. I look forward to it no more than do you. But it must be done. I have spoken with the authorities. All has been prepared." He rose from the table, and the others did as well. "Come, gentlemen. As with all things in life . . . we must do what needs to be done."

It was a simple ceremony. Jereme's body lay upon the pyre that had been built, with reverence, in a great open field. It was an ancient, traditional means of disposal that had not been practiced on Pulva in over a hundred years, but Jereme's will had requested it specifically. The will had very minimal provisions. The building he had left to his students, to do with as they willed. And his body . . . his body he desired to be returned to the nothingness from which it had come.

They stood around the pyre, watching the smoke curl to the skies. Si Cwan, Kalinda, and the students stood in a semicircle around it, looking as if they had lost a piece of themselves.

And then Ookla said, in much the same tone as he had earlier, "Now . . . what do we do?"

Si Cwan actually laughed softly at that. "Again, 'we.' " He rested a large red hand on Ookla's shoulder and said, "We do nothing. You, young men, go on with your lives. You have homes, yes?" They nodded as one. "Then you return to them. You carry with you the lessons that you have learned here. As for me . . ."

"Us," Kalinda quickly corrected.

"Us," he amended agreeably. "As for us . . . I have some ideas, some plans. I have managed to compile a list of known associates of Olivan. When one carves a career as an industrialist, there are many—friends and foes alike—that one encounters in that career. One of these people knows what happened. One of them knows the truth," and his voice became graver, more intense. "And we will go to all of them, and to everyone they know, and we will do whatever is necessary, and we will track down Olivan, whatever he may be calling himself. For he has slain our teacher . . . and he will pay."

To Be Continued in

**Star Trek
New Frontier**

**Book Ten:
Renaissance**

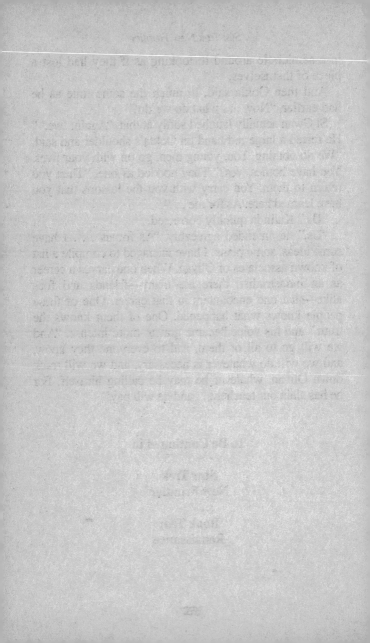

Look for STAR TREK fiction from Pocket Books

Star Trek®: The Original Series

Star Trek: Deep Space Nine®

Star Trek: Voyager®

Star Trek®: The Captain's Table

#1 • *War Dragons* • L.A. Graf
#2 • *Dujonian's Hoard* • Michael Jan Friedman
#3 • *The Mist* • Dean Wesley Smith & Kristine Kathryn Rusch
#4 • *Fire Ship* • Diane Carey
#5 • *Once Burned* • Peter David
#6 • *Where Sea Meets Sky* • Jerry Oltion
The Captain's Table Omnibus • various

Star Trek®: The Dominion War

#1 • *Behind Enemy Lines* • John Vornholt
#2 • *Call to Arms...* • Diane Carey
#3 • *Tunnel Through the Stars* • John Vornholt
#4 • *...Sacrifice of Angels* • Diane Carey

Star Trek®: The Badlands

#1 • Susan Wright
#2 • Susan Wright

Star Trek® Books available in Trade Paperback

Omnibus Editions
    Invasion! Omnibus • various
    Day of Honor Omnibus • various
    The Captain's Table Omnibus • various
    Star Trek: Odyssey • William Shatner with Judith and Garfield
      Reeves-Stevens
Other Books
    Legends of the Ferengi • Ira Steven Behr & Robert Hewitt Wolfe
    Strange New Worlds, vols. I and II • Dean Wesley Smith, ed.
    Adventures in Time and Space • Mary Taylor
    Captain Proton! • Dean Wesley Smith
    The Lives of Dax • Marco Palmieri, ed.
    The Klingon Hamlet • Wil'yam Shex'pir
    New Worlds, New Civilizations • Michael Jan Friedman
    Enterprise Logs • Carol Greenburg, ed.

STAR TREK
DEEP SPACE NINE®
CD-ROM GAMES

ℑHE FALLEN

A dazzling 3rd person action/adventure game

Energized by an enhanced version of the revolutionary Unreal™ Tournament engine, The Fallen places the player at the heart of an exhilarating 3-D adventure.

"A stunning accomplishment...establishing the standard for the next generation of games."—Adrenaline Vault

www.ds9thefallen.com

DOMINION WARS

A cinematic real-time tactical strategy game

Join this epic struggle as you take command of Federation, Klingon, and Dominion Alliance fleets. With unprecedented control over all facets of space combat, Dominion Wars asks YOU to decide who lives or dies. Strategize! Maneuver! Anticipate! And when you have your enemy where you want him—STRIKE!

Bonus Feature: Import ships from Star Trek: Creator Warp II and use them in multiplayer battles!

www.dominionwars.com
To Order, Call 1 888-793-9972
AVAILABLE FALL 2000!!

SSI1

ANALOG

SCIENCE FICTION AND FACT

Hours of thought-provoking fiction in every issue!

Explore the frontiers of scientific research and imagination. *Analog Science Fiction and Fact* magazine delivers an intellectual blend of stimulating stories, provocative editorials, and fascinating scientific fact articles from today's top writers.

Kristine Kathryn Rusch • Jerry Oltion
Vonda N. McIntyre • Catherine Asaro • Kevin J. Anderson

CALL TOLL-FREE TO SUBSCRIBE
1-800-333-4561

Outside the USA: 303-678-8747

Mail to: Analog • P.O. Box 54027 • Boulder, CO 80322-4027

☑ **YES!** Send me a free trial issue of *Analog* and bill me. If I'm not completely delighted, I'll write "Cancel" on the invoice and return it with no further obligation. Either way, the first issue is mine to keep. **(9 issues, just $19.97)**

Name _____

Address _____

City _____

State _____ ZIP _____

❑ Payment enclosed   ❑ Bill me

Send for your FREE trial issue of Analog today!

We publish a double issue in July/August, which counts as two issues towards your subscription. Please allow 6-8 weeks for delivery of first issue. For delivery outside U.S.A., pay $27.97 (U.S. funds) for 9 issues. Includes GST. Foreign orders must be prepaid or charged to VISA/MasterCard. Please include account number, card type, expiration date and signature. Billing option not available outside U.S.A.   5T91

STAR TREK
COMMUNICATOR

3 ISSUES FREE!

FOR A LIMITED TIME you can get 9 issues of *STAR TREK COMMUNICATOR* magazine for $19.95 – that's 3 FREE ISSUES!

STAR TREK COMMUNICATOR is your source for the inside scoop on all incarnations of *Star Trek*!

HURRY AND TAKE ADVANTAGE of this offer – simply call **1-888-303-1813** to subscribe!

Or send your name, address, phone number and payment to
STAR TREK COMMUNICATOR
P.O. Box 111000,
Aurora, CO 80042

We accept checks, money orders, Visa, Mastercard, AMEX and Discover Cards.

Please reference code **TBOOK** when ordering.

Canadian 1 year subscription
$22.95, Foreign 1 year
subscription $34.95.
(U.S. funds only)

Offer expires 3/1/01

STCK

STAR TREK
THE EXPERIENCE
LAS VEGAS HILTON

Be a part of the most exciting deep space adventure in the galaxy as you beam aboard the U.S.S. Enterprise. Explore the evolution of Star Trek® from television to movies in the "History of the Future Museum," the planet's largest collection of authentic Star Trek memorabilia. Then, visit distant galaxies on the "Voyage Through Space." This 22-minute action packed adventure will capture your senses with the latest in motion simulator technology. After your mission, shop in the Deep Space Nine Promenade and enjoy 24th Century cuisine in Quark's Bar & Restaurant.

Save up to $30

Present this coupon at the STAR TREK: The Experience ticket office at the Las Vegas Hilton and save $6 off each attraction admission (limit 5).

Not valid in conjunction with any other offer or promotional discount. Management reserves all rights. No cash value.
For more information, call 1-888-GOBOLDLY
or visit www.startrekexp.com.
Private Parties Available.

CODE:1007a

EXPIRES 12/31/00

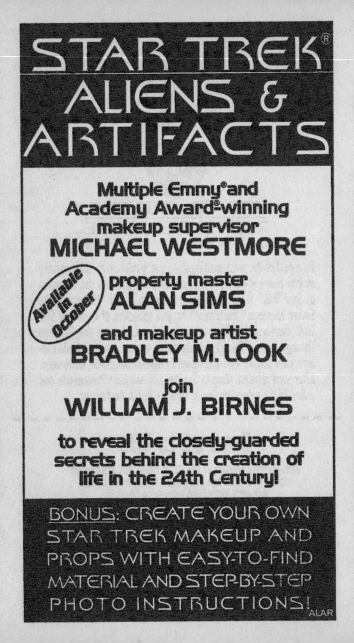

STAR TREK®
ALIENS &
ARTIFACTS

Multiple Emmy® and
Academy Award®-winning
makeup supervisor
MICHAEL WESTMORE

Available in October

property master
ALAN SIMS

and makeup artist
BRADLEY M. LOOK

join
WILLIAM J. BIRNES

to reveal the closely-guarded
secrets behind the creation of
life in the 24th Century!

<u>BONUS</u>: CREATE YOUR OWN
STAR TREK MAKEUP AND
PROPS WITH EASY-TO-FIND
MATERIAL AND STEP-BY-STEP
PHOTO INSTRUCTIONS!

ALAR

POCKET BOOKS IS PROUD TO PRESENT
SIX CLASSIC *STAR TREK*® NOVELS
REISSUED THIS AUGUST AT A CLASSIC PRICE!

SAREK
A.C. Crispin

SPOCK'S WORLD
Diane Duane

CORONA
Greg Bear

UHURA'S SONG
Janet Kagan

Including the first books in Diane
Duane's ongoing Rihannsu series

MY ENEMY, MY ALLY
Diane Duane

THE ROMULAN WAY
Diane Duane and Peter Morwood

The saga continues this October!

CLRI.07

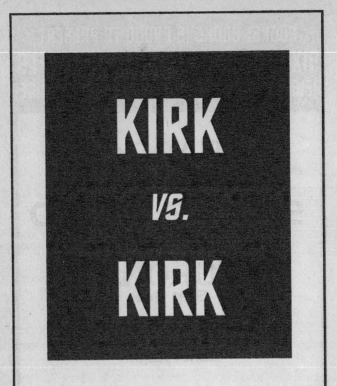

KIRK

vs.

KIRK

STAR TREK®
PRESERVER

A novel by William Shatner
Available now from Pocket Books

PRES